SIX MURDERS TOO MANY

ALSO BY DALLAS GORHAM

The Carlos McCrary PI Mystery Thriller Series

Six Murders Too Many

Double Fake

Quarterback Trap

Dangerous Friends

Day of the Tiger

McCrary's Justice

Yesterday's Trouble

Four Years Gone

Debt of Honor

Sometimes You Lose

SIX MURDERS TOO MANY

CARLOS MCCRARY PI, BOOK 1

DALLAS GORHAM

ePublishingWorks!
love what you read.

Cover and eBook design by eBook Prep
www.ebookprep.com

December 2021

ISBN: 978-1-64457-207-8

ePublishing Works!
644 Shrewsbury Commons Ave
Ste 249
Shrewsbury PA 17361
United States of America

www.epublishingworks.com
Phone: 866-846-5123

ACKNOWLEDGMENTS

My thanks to my editor Marsha Butler who can be reached via email (swmpwriter@gmail) or by phone (303-931-4698). She makes me a better writer.

PROLOGUE

The trespasser picked his way through the night along the rocky beach. The city lights of downtown Cleveland reflected off the cloud cover, but they barely relieved the darkness. He stumbled again. *Damn rocks. Why can't they have a nice, sandy beach like we have at the Gulf.*

He dared not use his flashlight app. He made do with an occasional glimpse from the dimmed light of his cellphone screen. It had been more difficult to find his footing the previous two nights, but he had managed with a skinned knee and torn pants, a small price to pay for invisibility.

The back fences of the lakefront mansions ran down to the water's edge, forcing the intruder to wade around each of them. The six o'clock news had said the water in Lake Erie was sixty-five degrees, but the north wind whipped across the lake and made it feel colder. *Goddamn cold water.* He had been here four days and still couldn't believe how cold it felt. He was used to warmer water and gentler breezes where he came from.

The intruder waded around the last fence, shivering. He examined the slope above by the light of his cellphone and stepped carefully into the footprints he had left the night before and the night before that. He climbed to his hiding place in the azaleas at the edge of the lawn, resigned to wait in his cold, wet shoes until dawn.

The north wind blustered against his wet pants. He shuddered, stuck his hands further into his pockets. *God, I wish I had a cigarette. Or a joint. Yeah, as long as I'm wishing for something I can't have, why not wish for a toke? My parole officer hasn't made me pee in a cup in months.*

From his outpost, the stranger watched the glow of the TV in the living room of the old, stone house. He thought about what a great chimney those stone walls would make for the bonfire of dry, weathered joists and floorboards inside. *When will this damned weather get cold enough for the friggin' furnace?*

Soon, he reminded himself. *Soon.*

Inside the stone house, a mother and her two grown daughters were watching the eleven o'clock news and weather. "Current temperature is fifty-two degrees," the meteorologist said, "with lows expected in the lower forties inland and the upper forties near the lake."

"Sounds like it'll be chilly by morning," the mother said. "I'm going to turn on the furnace and throw a blanket on my bed. Do either of you want one?"

"Not me, Mom," replied the older daughter. "The furnace heats this place too hot as it is."

"I wish you wouldn't set the thermostat so high," said her sister. "The furnace sucks the moisture right out of the air and I wake up with a headache every morning. I would rather have an extra blanket. Let's keep the heat off."

"God, no! I nearly froze to death growing up in this old house. My mother—your grandmother, God rest her soul—refused to turn the furnace on unless the temperature was down in the thirties."

"If you hate this house so much, why didn't you sell it after Grandma died?"

"I don't hate the house, honey; I love this house. When I thought about this old place sitting here empty, I knew Mama would roll over in her grave if I sold it."

"Well, you could have updated the heating system—maybe put in a humidifier."

"I know, sweetie, but I kept thinking I would move to an apartment in town when you girls went off to college."

"But, Mom, we love this old house, and it's easy to commute to college from here. You should put some of your divorce money into this place."

Her sister laughed. "According to Mom, Dad left her penniless, remember?"

"Enough, you two. When you inherit the place, you can do what you want. Tonight, I'm turning up the heat."

She stopped at the bottom of the stairway and gazed back at her daughters—her treasures. They were the one good thing that came from her marriage to Sam Simonetti. Well, that and a $65,000,000 property settlement. "Good night, my loves."

"Goodnight, Mom."

"We love you, too."

Two shadows remained in the living room. *Will they never go to bed?* The wind had dried the trespasser's pants, but the tumbling temperature made him shiver. *I should have brought a warmer coat. Who knew that September could be so goddam cold up here?*

It had been warmer three nights earlier when he picked the lock on the old mansion's basement door. He had waited three hours after the lights went out before making his stealthy invasion. All he had needed was access to the basement. Tonight, maybe he wouldn't have to wait that long.

In the upstairs hallway, the mistress of the house paused in front of the thermostat. *Sixty-eight ought to do it with a blanket.* She switched the thermostat to *heat* and set the temperature.

On the way to her room, she pulled an old woolen blanket from the linen closet in the hall.

Downstairs, one of the sisters switched off the TV. "Too bad Dad and Mom got a divorce."

"Yeah, but at least we're still his daughters and when he dies, he'll leave us money and we can fix up the house."

"Are we gonna be spinster sisters and live here together until we're ninety?"

"I'm gonna live to be a hundred and five."

"Okay, you win. You can have the house." The older sister rose from the couch, leaned over, and softly kissed the top of her sister's head. "Good night, Sis. I love you. I'm off to bed."

"I'm right behind you. Love you too."

The last lights went out on the second floor.

Finally. He scrutinized the dark windows through his binoculars. He became aroused thinking about the brilliance of his preparations to create the inferno. *Surely, it's cold enough to make that ancient furnace go on. It could be happening right now. Right this instant.*

A light flickered through the small windows of the basement. He imagined the women sleeping soundly, oblivious to the hungry monster below them that would devour the basement ceiling joists as it gained strength and its appetite grew. The windows on the first floor began to glow.

It's happening. It's finally happening.

A flicker in a window on the second floor teased his gaze.

By the time those bitches wake up, the smoke will burn their eyes. They'll panic. They'll try to scream, but the smoke will clog their lungs. He imagined them throwing their bedroom doors open, only to be faced with a wall of flame. *Yes! Yes! Now that's what I call a fire! Ohhhhh, yeah, baby!*

Ten minutes later, sirens howled in the distance. It was risky to stay and watch the orange beast digest the house, but he couldn't leave now that his goal was in sight. That would be like leaving the job half done. He faced the house, enthralled, as the fire engines arrived and the firefighters struggled in vain to get ahead of the flaming monster.

Hunkered down in the azaleas, invisible in the flickering orange light of the inferno, he watched the flames consume the house in front of his hungry eyes. Finally, the roof collapsed and fell into the space inside the stone walls.

In a couple of hours even the glowing embers had faded to black. He felt sated. This was better than sex. *God, now I really need that cigarette.*

He turned away from the husk of the house, feeling depleted. But he always felt like this afterwards. He eased his way silently down the slope to the bottom where he was once again invisible.

Time to make that phone call.

ONE

"Chuck, I may have a client for you." The caller was Victoria Ramirez, an A-list partner with a boutique law firm here in Port City. The clients she had sent me over the last eight months must have been happy with my services.

"Great. Who is it?"

"Ike Simonetti."

I grabbed a notepad and pen from my desk. "Any kin to…?"

"His son."

I whistled and wrote it down. Ike Simonetti's father, Sam Simonetti, had been one of the richest men in Florida. "You sure know how to pick 'em, Vicky. Why does he need a private investigator?"

"Ike's got a big, expensive problem."

That was good. Big, expensive problems require big, expensive solutions.

"This could be a winning lottery ticket for you, handsome. Don't screw it up."

"No way I would let that happen."

"I can list a dozen ways, including your so-called sense of humor. But mainly because Ike Simonetti doesn't think he has a problem."

"Then why does he want me?"

"He doesn't. Lorraine Wallace, his wife, is the one who wants a PI. Ike doesn't want to pursue the issue."

"What issue?"

She told me. I could see why this was an expensive problem. I took more notes. "What did you tell Simonetti about me?"

"That my firm had worked with you many times. And that you were honest, persistent, and tough."

"But not funny?"

"He's not going to hire you for your jokes. You're an acquired taste, big guy."

"Vicky, seriously, I owe you big time. How can I repay the favor?"

"I'll think of something—maybe a foot massage."

Foot massage? I thought. *Where did that come from?*

"He'll be at your office in less than an hour."

"How did he know I would be here?"

"He didn't. My secretary called your receptionist and she said you were in. Ike said, and I quote: 'Might as well get this over with.' So they're on their way."

"They…meaning?"

"Ike and Lorraine Wallace, his wife. Be glad she's coming with him. She's your best ally in corralling his business."

"I'll get back to you on the foot massage," I lied. I knew that I wouldn't.

I Googled Ike Simonetti, then Lorraine Wallace. There were so many citations that a thorough job on either would take hours, maybe days. I skimmed the last twelve months of newspaper and magazine articles about Ike and his famous father and Lorraine Wallace and her medical practice. I skipped the tabloid stories, amusing as I knew they would be.

Glancing at my clock, I saw that I had five minutes before they arrived. I had eaten a lot of rice and beans and ramen noodles while I built my PI business. If I landed Simonetti as a client, that was about to change. I could upgrade to hamburger meat and day-old buns.

I pulled out the bottom left drawer of my second-hand desk, leaned back with my ankles crossed on it, and gazed out the office window while I waited for my ship to come in.

A silver Ferrari slewed into the parking lot and glided gracefully to the far side, away from the other cars. The driver parked diagonally across two slots so no one could squeeze in beside his extravagant Italian beauty and ding those classy Italian doors. He parked the same way I did, although my 1963 Avanti sitting a couple of slots over was worth a great deal less than his Ferrari.

The driver unfolded himself from the low-slung car. I recognized him from internet pictures and gave myself a mental high-five. Ike Simonetti: age forty-three, slightly gray temples, conservative pin-striped suit, regimental tie. His light blue shirt had a white collar and French cuffs. A *Wall Street Journal* fashion columnist would approve of the look. Then I wondered if the *Wall Street Journal* had a fashion columnist. Probably not.

He seemed a little too perfect as the wealthy entrepreneur. Was it a front? Even without the Ferrari, he would impress you as richer than God. Was it over the top?

Simonetti got out of the car. He leaned back inside, said something to the passenger, and slammed the driver's side door. *Ouch*, I hoped he hadn't hurt the Italian beauty. He stomped around to the other side of the car and jerked the door open.

A woman levered herself out of the low-slung sports car—not easy in a pencil skirt and spike heels. Lorraine Wallace, age forty-one. She was as thin as a runway model, but wore a pin-striped blue jacket matching her skirt and shoes. A multi-colored scarf took the place of a man's tie. Businesswoman of the year.

Again, almost too perfect. *Hmm. Stop being a cynic.*

The two of them marched stiffly toward my building without a word or a look. They were together but apart. I noticed a sly smile on her face. Or was it a smirk?

I surveyed my office. Half-full trash can. Stacks of papers on both desk corners. A few pieces of lint on the seats of my office chairs. Not tidy enough to impress Ferrari people. *Better use the conference room.*

My phone rang. "Dr. Lorraine Wallace and Mr. Isaac Simonetti are here to see you, Mr. McCrary."

"Tell them I'll be out in two minutes." I didn't want to appear too eager. Besides, my receptionist would need time to get their coffee.

To kill time, I ogled two young women through my office window as they power-walked down Bayfront Boulevard. As a former cop, I wanted to see if they were engaged in nefarious, felonious, or suspicious activities. As a trained observer, I concluded that walking did their derrieres and my attitude a world of good. Too soon, they passed from sight with no sign of criminal intentions.

Let's go meet the Goose of the Golden Eggs.

I set my laptop on the conference room table as I walked to the reception area.

As I passed Nancy's desk, she handed me two business cards.

I gave Nancy a smile and stuck the cards in my pocket.

The couple eyed me as I approached.

"Dr. Wallace? Mr. Simonetti? I'm Chuck McCrary."

The man stood and we shook hands. "Please, call me Ike. My dad was Mr. Simonetti." He smiled at the old line.

The woman rose gracefully to her feet and extended her fingers with the palm down. More like a duchess than a dermatologist. Maybe she expected me to kiss her hand. "And since you're not my patient, Lorraine will be fine for me."

I resisted the urge to click my heels and bow as I shook her hand.

Wallace looked older than her official age. Maybe a doctor's long hours had taken a toll. Faint wrinkles lined her forehead and the corners of her eyes. Her makeup was the tiniest bit too perfect, in keeping with her model-thin physique. She was the poster child for the motto *You can never be too thin or too rich.*

I thought of a line from Shakespeare. *Yond Cassius has a lean and hungry look, he thinks too much; such men are dangerous.* I figured the same comment applied to women. Lorraine Wallace looked dangerous.

"Lorraine, it's a pleasure to meet you," I said instead.

She painted a smile on her lips as she released my hand. "How do you do?"

"I'm doing well, thanks. May I take your cup?" My offer merited a slightly friendlier smile. I carried her coffee to my conference room. Ever the considerate host, that's me.

I centered the doctor's cup on a coaster and stood across the table, waiting for Wallace to sit.

Ike Simonetti scanned the room. "Where's your desk?"

"In my office, through that door." I tweaked my head that direction. "Most people prefer talking around a table rather than across a desk."

Wallace sat and so did I, but Simonetti remained standing.

His eyes fixed on the ego wall to my right. A photo of my Special Forces unit, the Triple Seven, in Afghanistan. He was reading the citation for my Bronze Star Medal. For a moment, I was transported back to Ghar Mesar, a village in the mountains of Afghanistan. An old scar on my left bicep throbbed when I remembered one team member in particular who hadn't come back.

Simonetti studied my PI license, my criminology diploma, and my honorable discharge. Then his gaze moved to the Atlantic County map on the other wall. He stood there long enough for me to wonder if he intended to memorize it.

Mercifully, Wallace broke Simonetti's trance by clearing her throat. "Dear, perhaps you should tell Chuck why we've come."

He frowned but sat down. "Did Vicky Ramirez tell you about my situation?"

"A little, but, please, assume I know nothing and start from the beginning."

"Okay. I guess you know my father was Sam Simonetti."

"Vicky told me." Every human in the Florida knew about Sam Simonetti. According to *Forbes* magazine, he was the tenth richest man in the state when he died. "I remember hearing about your father's funeral on the news. The governor, both U.S. senators, and three congressional representatives attended. And, of course, the mayor. Sam was well-loved in Port City." It wasn't hard to remember what I had read twenty minutes earlier.

"The politicos didn't come to his funeral out of love, unless it was their love of his money. I'm cynical enough to think those jackals came to get their faces on the news and their hands in my family's pockets."

Imagine that: a politician wanting to get on the news. But I didn't say it.

"What brings you to see me, Ike?"

He drew a deep breath. "Lorraine insists that Ramona—my father's widow—is trying to steal two hundred million from me."

"Two hundred million. As in *dollars*?"

Wallace nodded.

I eyed her. "How does Sam's widow plan to steal your money?"

"It's not my money; it's Ike's. Ramona, Pop's wife, was pregnant when he died. Now she has a three-month-old daughter, Gloria, and claims her child should inherit half of Pop's estate. But I believe Pop was not the father."

I opened my laptop. "Why not?"

"From the baby's birth date, we know Ramona got pregnant while Pop was in the hospital."

A patient can have sex in a hospital bed. I had happily participated in two such events while recuperating from battle wounds in Landstuhl Regional Medical Center in Germany. Of course, I was twenty years old then, not seventy-five like Sam.

Simonetti seemed embarrassed.

"If Sam isn't Gloria's father, you inherit the entire estate?"

"Yes, but if Ramona's daughter gets a share, I get half."

"I read that Sam's estate was worth over a billion dollars."

"Dad left a lot of money to charity. After taxes, and the widow's share of $30,000,000, the remaining estate is only $400,000,000."

I had never heard anyone refer to $400,000,000 as *only*. "The widow's share?"

Simonetti rose abruptly and paced around the room. "Their prenuptial agreement said if Ramona survived him, Dad would leave her $30,000,000, with the remainder to be divided among his children."

"How many children did your father have?"

"When he married Ramona, Dad had three—me and two daughters from his previous marriage to Allison Montrose. Dad made his will right before he married Ramona."

"So, Allison's daughters are your half-sisters?"

"Were. Allison and both daughters died in a house fire six weeks before Dad passed, so he thought I was his only remaining child. He never knew Ramona was pregnant. At least, he never mentioned it."

"And if Sam isn't Gloria's father, you inherit the whole $400,000,000?"

"That's right."

It didn't take a math genius to do the arithmetic. "Hence her 'theft' being pegged at $200,000,000."

Simonetti regarded his wife. "That's why we're here."

I pulled my laptop closer. "What were your sisters' names?"

"*Half*-sisters," he replied, an unpleasant edge in his tone.

His attitude made me appreciate my own sister. Even though she was a busy fashion model in Houston and we lived fifteen hundred miles apart, we telephoned or video-called every couple of weeks and saw each other every Christmas in Texas. Ike's family proved that even the mega-rich suffer their disappointments.

Ike interrupted my reverie. "Their names were Danielle and Melinda Simonetti."

"Did either one have children?"

"No. They were both single."

"As their mother, does Allison step into their shoes as legatee?"

Simonetti shook his head. "Vicky drew Dad's will to include me and my two half-sisters and any heirs of our bodies. Do you know what 'heirs of our bodies' means?"

"I think so. His estate could pass to your children or your half-sisters' children, but not to Allison. And not to anyone an heir married." I gestured toward Wallace. "Like Lorraine."

"That's right. Dad made sure that Allison didn't get any more of his money. Their divorce cost him $65,000,000, and he was bitter about it. With my half-sisters dead, I stood to get the whole caboodle."

"You said Danielle, Melinda, and their mother all died in a house fire?"

Wallace nodded. "Something about faulty wiring. Allison's family built the house in the 1920s, when they first hit it rich, but they never updated the wiring." She lifted her coffee cup, little finger extended, and took an elegant sip.

"Ike, if you suspect fraud, why not go to the District Attorney?"

He shook his head. "Not without evidence. If I'm wrong, I don't want a media feeding frenzy. I can imagine the headline—Millionaire Son Says Billionaire Dad's Merry Widow Has Illegitimate Heir." Simonetti shuddered. "We can't get a DNA test anyway because we don't have Dad's DNA to compare it to."

"They would compare it to your DNA or your half-sisters' DNA."

"Can't. I'm adopted and my half-sisters were cremated, both figuratively and literally. Anyway, Vicky says we can't force a DNA test. The law presumes a baby conceived during marriage is legitimate, absent evidence to the contrary."

Wallace took over again. "First you need to find evidence that Ramona cheated. Then, we'll try to find a DNA sample for Pop and ask a judge to order a DNA test on Gloria."

"If your father wasn't cremated, we could still get a DNA sample." I waited until he took my meaning.

Simonetti shuddered again. "God, no. Even without a media frenzy, I wouldn't exhume Dad's body except as a last resort—that's ghoulish." He stood and walked to the window, gazed out at Bayfront Boulevard, his back to me.

I can take a hint. His body language shouted, *I'm pissed that you even suggested it.*

I tried to recover. "We can get DNA from his personal effects like gloves and shoes, but it's not as legally convincing."

"I would rather this whole paternity thing didn't get out because it would embarrass my family. It's not like we need the money."

"Of course," I agreed.

"If the press gets wind, they'll jump on it like stink on a skunk. I would be happy with half the estate, but Lorraine insists that we investigate Gloria's parentage." He sat beside her. "My wife's a good nag."

Wallace patted his thigh and smiled sweetly. "You bet your ass I am."

"Understood," I answered. "Discreet is my middle name."

Simonetti pointed at my PI license on the ego wall. "I thought your middle name was Andres." He smiled, acting comfortable for the first time since we shook hands.

"So, how can my discretion and I help you?"

Simonetti paced the room again. Not as easy as it sounds. My conference room is larger than a walk-in closet—barely. Simonetti could take three steps before he had to turn around. He stopped at the window. "I want you to know it's not about the money."

My dad always said, "Son, if someone tells you it's not about the money, eleven times out of ten, it's about the money."

Simonetti continued. "I'm not on the *Forbes 400* list like Dad was, but I don't need another $200,000,000—it's the principle of being duped out of our family's money. Vicky thought you could find out who fathered Gloria."

"Perhaps, but do we need to prove the father's identity? Couldn't we just show that it's not Sam?"

"Yes. I looked it up," Wallace said. "We don't need to prove who the real father is."

"If I prove Sam isn't Gloria's father, what good does that do Ike?"

She held up two fingers. "One, Ramona's daughter won't inherit any of Pop's estate, and, two, Ramona will have violated the fidelity clause and she loses everything, including her widow's share."

"Fidelity clause?"

Simonetti paced again. "Lorraine and I knew Ramona was a gold digger as soon as Dad introduced us, so we insisted that he have a fidelity clause in their prenup. If she cheated, Ramona forfeited any claim to Dad's assets."

"I don't see a woman sharp enough to hook your father jeopardizing $30,000,000 for a roll in the hay. Unless she was sure she could get away with it."

"She's also smart enough to figure the odds. If it worked, she would control $200,000,000 for at least eighteen years as Gloria's guardian," Simonetti said. "With that kind of access, I'm sure that even Ramona could steal at least half of it. I know I could."

"What if your father cheated on her? Any penalties for him?"

"Dad wouldn't do that."

"I didn't say he did. I'm asking whether their agreement had a similar restriction on him. I would think any attorney for Ramona would insist on a tit-for-tat."

"I never read their prenuptial agreement."

"I read it," Wallace said. "There was a comparable restriction."

Simonetti raised his eyebrows at her. "You read it?"

"Sure, why not?" She reached up and patted his arm. "I need to know this stuff so I can nag you better."

"Whatever." Simonetti handed me a flash drive as he sat down. "Vicky gave me a list of documents to give you: prenup agreement, etc. It should all be on there."

"I presume I can discuss the case with Vicky?"

Simonetti sipped his coffee. "I have no secrets from Vicky or her father or my personal assistant Tom."

I plugged the flash drive into my laptop. "What's your P.A.'s last name?"

"Collins." Simonetti smiled a little.

I smiled back. "Tom Collins? You gotta like any guy named after a cocktail."

I called Nancy for more coffee while the flash drive loaded.

"Okay," I said to Simonetti. "I see the file saved as *Prenuptial Agreement* and another as *Last Will and Testament.* What's on the JPEGs?"

Simonetti moved to the chair nearest me and pointed at the screen. "That's a scan of Dad's death certificate. Then their marriage license and Gloria's birth certificate. Those files are photos of Ramona and Gloria."

I let my eyes glide around the other icons and captions on the screen. "Where's the autopsy report?"

Wallace answered. "There wasn't one. Pop died in a hospital under a doctor's care. As an 'attended death,' a post-mortem wasn't required. Too bad on the DNA front."

"Any idea who the real father is?"

"I know it's a cliché," Wallace said, "but look at the tennis pro. I saw him and Ramona together at the Wessington Club more than once, and I heard rumors about him from other women members. He even came on to me one time after a tennis lesson."

Simonetti stared at his wife. "You never told me that."

She waved it off. "It was nothing. And I shot him down. Believe me, it was nothing. He is a great tennis teacher, so I let it slide."

Simonetti didn't look any happier.

I changed the subject. "Okay, Ike. Before we talk money, I need to know who the real client is."

"What do you mean?"

"Vicky's law firm hires me so I can claim attorney-client privilege if necessary, but we both know she doesn't call the shots. Who do I take my orders from?"

"Me." Simonetti patted his chest.

"Not you and Lorraine both?"

He patted his wife on her knee. "No, she's just here to nag me."

She smiled that saccharine smile again. A little of her make-up crumbled this time. "You bet your ass I am."

"Okay," I said. "Now let's talk about my fee and expenses."

"Vicky said you're honest; that's enough for me."

Wallace frowned.

"I appreciate Vicky's endorsement, but I keep clients happy by making sure that the amount of my fee is never an unpleasant surprise. I am expensive." I quoted my daily rate and the retainer I wanted. While waiting for Simonetti to arrive, I had calculated the balances on my credit cards. Funny thing, they totaled the same amount as my retainer. "I fly first class if I travel. I stay at four-star hotels unless the job requires undercover work." I waited for him to signal agreement, and I continued. "And that's before my success fee."

"What success fee?"

"It's the bonus I earn if I can help you cut Gloria and Ramona from the will."

"Ramona? This is about Gloria's inheritance."

"If I prove Ramona cheated, she loses the $30,000,000 she would have inherited. In that case, you inherit her $30,000,000 plus her daughter's $200,000,000. If I get that total $230,000,000 for you, what's my share?"

"How much do you want?"

"It's found money, paid from a recovery you wouldn't have otherwise. One percent of the extra, plus my rate and expenses."

Simonetti crossed his arms. "That's more than $2,000,000." He squinted his right eye. "There are a lot of detectives in Port City."

"Must be hundreds of them." I decided this wasn't a good time to tell him that detectives were cops, and that I was a private investigator. Instead, I waited for the counteroffer. There's always a counteroffer.

He stared at me. "I'm sure I could find another private detective to do this cheaper."

"Probably." I returned his gaze. I tried to appear calm and keep my breathing steady, even though my stomach was doing the boogaloo.

He contemplated my ego wall. "I'll tell you what—you prove Gloria is not Dad's daughter and I will pay you a $500,000 bonus."

I gave myself a mental high-five and a chest bump for good measure. "Ike, let's make it an even $1,000,000 and I'll show you a way to make the IRS pay half."

"How's that?"

"Check with your CPA, but if Vicky hires me on behalf of the estate, my fee is an administration expense. It comes out before your distribution. The IRS pays more than half. Win, win all around."

He grinned. "I hadn't thought of that."

Everybody wants to screw the IRS. "Say the word and I'll have Vicky draw up an agreement to that effect, so we avoid any misunderstanding."

"Sure."

"Okay. And I'll have Vicky send me the retainer."

"Right." Simonetti rubbed his hands together. "Now what do you want to know?"

"Let me review the data on this thumb drive and do more research. I'll meet you at your office tomorrow and you can tell me more."

"Tomorrow's no good. How about Saturday?"

"Okay. That'll give Vicky time to get our agreement and retainer taken care of. One more thing: Do you have Sam's computers, cellphones, tablets, stuff like that?"

"Yeah. I'm Dad's executor; I have everything."

"Bring Sam's electronic devices to your office Saturday."

"What for?"

"Many people keep a file on their computer to store their passwords. If Sam did, perhaps it will also have Ramona's passwords stored on it. That will be easier than having my IT guru hack her accounts. Hacking can leave footprints and we don't want that."

"Okay. I'll bring them." Simonetti fished a business card from his wallet. "You have my card, and this one is Tom's. He'll get anything you need."

TWO

M y phone chirped. It was a text from Vicky.

You free tonight?

It was 4:30 p.m. and judges don't work late on Friday, so she wasn't in court. Therefore, following the long tradition of Sherlock Holmes, I deduced that she was in a meeting.

I finished my research and called her twenty minutes later.

"*Hola*, Carlos. Thanks for calling."

"How was your meeting?"

"How did you know I was in a meeting?"

"Magical powers. Yes, I am free tonight."

"Good, I'll buy you dinner."

She probably wanted an update on the Simonetti case. "Where shall I meet you?"

"My condo at 7:30?"

"I'll be there."

"Dress casually."

Dress casually? What was that all about?

Vicky opened the door. *"Buenas tardes."* Vicky and I spoke Spanish when we were alone or with family.

I wore khakis, boat shoes, and a silk shirt. I had expected Vicky to wear *business casual*, but she surprised me. More like shocked me. She wore a short turquoise skirt topped by a sheer cream silk blouse with a low scoop neck. The only women I knew who would wear that blouse in public were working girls I had seen when I'd been a patrol cop. It wasn't transparent, but it was translucent. Being the World's Greatest Private Investigator, I figured we weren't going out to dinner. She also wasn't wearing a bra. As a trained investigator, I notice such things. *Hmm.*

"Something to drink?"

"I'd be a fool not to."

Vicky took my hand and led me into her kitchen. She had never held my hand before. Another clue?

"Chicken Marsala okay?" She pulled out a bottle of wine. "You like Merlot, don't you?"

"I never met a wine I didn't like." I opened the Merlot while Vicky focused on cooking. She studied the recipe lying on the counter; I studied her. Her breasts beneath the translucent fabric put on a mesmerizing show as she reached and twisted and did magical things at the stove.

I stood. "Can I make the salad?"

"Bowls in that cabinet over there. The other stuff is in the fridge."

I pulled the French chef's knife from the wooden knife block. I chopped the lettuce, sliced the tomatoes, and tossed the salad.

Vicky covered the skillet, took a sip of Merlot, and set a timer. "Ten minutes until the chicken is ready."

I grabbed my glass and followed her into the living room.

Vicky sat at one end of the leather couch; I sat at the other.

She rotated toward me, and her skirt hiked up her thighs. She took a deep breath, which caused wonderful things to happen under her blouse. "Hank says you were a good cop."

Hidalgo "Hank" Ramirez was a Port City police lieutenant. He was also Vicky's brother.

"He was disappointed when you quit the force. He can't figure out why you left."

"No big secret. I never intended to be a career cop. I was there to get the experience required for a PI license."

"That was all?"

"I told the recruiting officer that at my interview. She said maybe I would change my mind later." I finished my wine.

"What made you decide to be a PI?"

"Promise not to laugh?"

"Go ahead."

In for a penny, in for a pound. "Hero worship."

"Hero worship?"

"My dad had a shelf full of classic detective stories. They had always been there, but I never paid attention to them until high school."

"What happened?"

"One day I read one of the books and got hooked. I read Sam Spade, Mike Hammer, and Spenser, he-with-no-first-name. Then I discovered Lee Child and the Jack Reacher novels for myself."

"Did you see yourself in them?"

I studied her face. Was she was being sarcastic? She wasn't, so I answered truthfully. "Those men were like knights of old. They did the right thing, whether or not it was legal. I wanted to be like them." I felt embarrassed. I contemplated my empty glass, considered a refill, then rejected the idea. I seldom had a personal conversation with a woman. I may not be able to take the lead with women, but I know how to follow.

"You're an idealist."

When in doubt, crack a joke. "Someone has to make the world safe for democracy." I grinned to let her know I was kidding, I think.

Vicky regarded me with wide eyes. "I never knew you were a romantic."

"Romantic? *Moi?*" In the candlelight, her brown eyes glittered with gold flecks I had never noticed before. Of course, we had never been this close before. We usually saw each other across a conference table or desk. My collar felt tight. Then I realized I was wearing a sport shirt.

"Did you ever tell Hank this?"

"I never told anybody."

"You mean I'm the first?"

I didn't know what to say, so I said nothing.

The timer dinged and broke the awkward silence.

We walked back to the kitchen. Vicky gestured to the big salad bowl. "Why don't you bring the salad?" She dimmed the lights over the island, leaving the dining area lit by candles. She carried our plates to the table and leaned across me to set my plate on the woven-straw place mat.

I felt a spark pass through my silk shirt between her breast and my shoulder.

Throughout dinner, her long candle-lit legs shone golden through the glass tabletop. As we finished eating, she put down her fork and leaned forward. The front of her blouse gaped open. "Would you like more breast?"

I normally react to awkward situations with humor. This time I stared, transfixed by her cleavage. "That's plenty for now," I managed to say.

"You want dessert now, or would you rather wait a bit?" She saw my expression and laughed. "I made a chocolate mousse."

"I could eat or wait—your choice."

"Let's go to the living room." She glided to the liquor cabinet as smoothly as a sail boat, placed two snifters on the bar, and poured Calvados.

Vicky settled back on the couch and pointed her knees at me. Her skirt hiked up higher this time.

"Chuck, can I ask you a personal question?"

"Sure. Although I reserve the right to ask for an attorney."

She laughed politely; it wasn't that funny. "How long have we known each other?"

Why is she asking this? She knows the answer.

"Seven years. Hank and I came home from Landstuhl Medical Center on the same plane, and you came to meet him at Dover Air Force base."

"That meeting doesn't count. You went off to college, and I didn't see you again for four years. I meant how long have we known each other *well?*"

You don't know me well, Vicky, I thought. *At least not yet.*

"Since I moved to Port City and started hanging out with Hank, three years ago."

"In three years, why haven't you ever asked me out?"

Somehow, I knew she had planned that question all evening. Truth was, I had never asked *any* woman out—at least, not the first time. I couldn't admit that, so I told a little white lie. "Until tonight, I never thought about you romantically."

Okay, so that was actually a big white lie. I had thought about her often, usually when we sat close enough in a meeting for me to smell her perfume.

"Does that mean that you're thinking of me romantically now?"

I grinned. "I'd be a fool not to. But the first time we met at Dover, you were my commanding officer's older sister." Hank was a Captain in the Special Forces; I was a sergeant. Really just a grunt.

Her eyes sparkled. "Do you think that it's okay for a man to date a younger woman?"

"Of course. Happens all the time."

"Then shouldn't a woman be able to date a younger man? After all, this is a democracy."

I lifted my glass. "To democracy."

We clinked glasses.

"In the spirit of gender fairness and making the world safe for democracy," I said, "I could also ask why you never asked *me* out."

"But I did ask you out, when I texted you." For a mature woman, she was acting almost coquettish.

"That doesn't count. I figured your invitation was for an update on the Simonetti case. After all, I received the retainer check and fee agreement you sent me by messenger this morning. Either that or you wanted to call in my marker for that foot massage."

She laughed. "You noticed that remark, did you?"

I took a leap of faith. "I was kinda looking forward to rubbing your feet."

She lifted her feet and stretched them across my lap. "Now's your chance."

Her skirt finished its climb to the top of her thighs, and I pondered the double meaning of her remark. I placed my snifter on the coaster and massaged her feet with both hands.

Vicky closed her eyes. "*Mmm.*" She opened her eyes a little. "Chuck, I don't need a serious relationship right now. I just want some fun with a man I admire. You know, 'friends with benefits.' How would you feel about that?"

In truth, I had mixed emotions. I wanted a family of my own. Last Christmas, Dad reminded me that he and Mom already had two children when he was my age. Mom said that their friends were starting to have grandchildren, and she only had one, my niece Rebecca. No pressure there.

On the other hand, my profession made it difficult to have a relationship that might blossom into love and a lifetime commitment, *i.e.*, marriage. My Asian girlfriend was one failed example. We met in the mystery section of a bookstore. She asked me out for coffee to discuss the finer points of Robert B. Parker's *Sunny Randall* series and Sue Grafton's *Kinsey Milhone* mysteries. After a couple of dates, I realized we had nothing in common. When she broke up with me, she confessed that she had gotten the idea to pick up men in a book store from an article in *Cosmopolitan* magazine. She was really more into Paranormal Romance novels than mysteries.

I wanted to find a wife and mother of my children; she wanted to get laid.

Well, it could have been worse. At least we had a good time for a couple of weeks. Maybe reading the Paranormal Romances had improved her performance in her own romance.

Even if Vicky was not interested in marriage, she was a strong, smart, beautiful woman. After all, I am a normal human, sort of.

I kept rubbing her feet as I answered. "You mean no commitments?"

"None, either way."

"What about Thanksgiving and Christmas? I always go back to Texas for those."

"Nope."

"What about exclusivity?"

"Definitely not." She grinned. "You won't always be available."

"What if later on you or I find a real romance with someone else?"

"We go on professionally as before, no problem. I expect the same from you if I became involved with someone else."

"Just so you know all the relevant facts, Vicky. I want a wife and kids. Every woman I date, I ask myself would she be a good wife and mother."

"No problem. I hope you find a girl like that someday."

Vicky eased her feet from my lap and stood. "Just not right now."

I grinned. "What's not to like?"

I stood also.

She set her Calvados on the table and took both my hands as she stepped toward me. "Then let's have dessert."

The silence somehow got quieter. Her breath caressed my lips as she lifted her face. She wrapped her arms around my neck and I felt her body from my chest to my knees. I breathed the fragrance of her perfume. It reminded me of the times I had thought about her in the past.

She guided my face into a warm, slow kiss, then leaned her head back. "Let's leave the mousse for later. I suddenly want a different dessert."

We ate the mousse for breakfast.

THREE

The parking garage was nearly empty on Saturday, so I didn't feel guilty hogging two spaces for my Avanti.

I touched base with the guard in the lobby of the Simonetti Tower, and he made a short phone call. "You know where Mr. Simonetti's office is?"

"No."

"Thirty-eighth floor. Take a left off the elevator. Mr. Simonetti said to take the door behind the reception desk. He'll hear you."

As I approached the elevators, I glimpsed familiar red hair—Renate Crowell, a reporter with the *Port City Press-Journal*. What the hell was she doing downtown on Saturday morning?

I twirled away, hiding my face.

She could smell a story like a hog rooting for truffles, and I was smack in the middle of a front-page scandal.

I hoped Renate hadn't seen me, or, if she did, hadn't recognized me.

The elevator took forever to arrive, but Renate didn't notice me. I exhaled after the door closed.

A minute later, the panel flashed *38*, the door opened, and I stood face-to-face with an upright grizzly bear, ready to attack. Without thinking, I pulled my Glock and sidestepped as I aimed the pistol at the bear's chest.

The bear didn't move. It was a hunting trophy. I holstered my sidearm and glanced around to see if anyone had noticed my reaction. My face felt flushed from embarrassment. Fortunately, the hall was empty.

The bear had been stuffed with his paws up in attack position. He had to have been eight feet tall. I presumed Simonetti didn't do much business with animal lovers.

A moment later, Simonetti came through a door. He greeted me in a blue golf shirt and gray slacks with scuffed boat shoes. Casual Saturday. "Morning, Chuck. Lorraine's in my office."

"Am I late?"

"No, Lorraine and I were early. I made coffee. Want some?"

"Sure."

As we left the office kitchen carrying our coffees, I stopped Simonetti in the hall. "Ike, did you bag all these animals?" The heads of a variety of deer, antelope, and even a moose lined the walls.

He raised both arms as if sighting a rifle. "Every single one. I nailed that elk in Canada two years ago. Hit him in the heart from three hundred yards with that Ruger Hawkeye with a Leupold scope." He pointed to the rifle displayed in a locked case on the wall beside the elk trophy. "Wait 'til you see my office."

Ike's private reception area was larger than my three-room office suite. It must be nice to own your own skyscraper. He had probably spent enough just mounting his trophies to fund my entire retirement plan.

Maybe I should have held out for the two million on the success fee. On the other hand, Ike didn't get rich by overpaying for things.

A gigantic mounted sailfish on the left wall behind an empty secretary's desk faced an equally impressive mounted hammerhead shark on the right wall above a green leather couch.

"Where did you catch those?"

"The hammerhead off the coast of Baja." He viewed the trophy with approval. "Landed the sailfish off Acapulco. I went down there to decide whether to move to Port City to join Dad in business. I go fishing or hunting when I need to clear my head or make a big decision."

"I go for a long run to think things over."

"To each his own." Simonetti led me through another set of double doors into an office the size of Rhode Island.

Coffee in hand, I greeted Wallace, who could have stepped from an ad in a yachting magazine. Once we were seated, Simonetti raised his eyebrows. "Where should I begin?"

"Tell me about Sam's first three wives."

I booted up my laptop as Simonetti began. "I was adopted by Dad and Willamina Warner, his first wife. She died of cancer when I was two; I don't even remember her. Then Dad married Yvette Forsythe. Yvette is the only mother I ever knew."

"What about your biological parents?"

"Tried unsuccessfully to find them. The adoption agency lost some records when they moved to new quarters thirty years ago. They weren't computerized back then, so they had no backup. Too bad." He didn't seem disappointed.

I felt lucky to have had my normal middle-class family in small town Texas.

"What happened to their marriage?"

"They were not a good match."

"How so?"

"Dad and I liked to hunt and fish. Yvette thought hunting and fishing were cruel."

"I can relate. My mother's a veterinarian." I had hunted deer in

Texas, but we always ate what we killed. Mom would kill me if I ever trophy-hunted. Something about the row of stuffed heads in Simonetti's hallway was off-putting. Mom would have hated them.

"Anyway, Yvette loved opera and Dad thought those huge halls with comfortable seats were a great place to take a nap. She loved art museums. Dad supported her by writing large checks, but he refused to go to gallery shows and pretend to like what he called 'pretentious grifters who have bamboozled the public.' He and Yvette were great friends, but they didn't have much in common other than me."

"So, Yvette and your Dad were on good terms after their divorce?"

"Oh, yeah. At our wedding, Yvette sat with Dad as mother of the groom."

At least Ike had enjoyed that much normalcy.

"Yvette always came to Houston for Thanksgiving with Ike and me," Wallace said. "Pop always joined us. After we moved to Port City, she came for Thanksgiving with Pop and us until Pop married Ramona."

"Did Yvette ever adopt you?"

"Not that I know of." A frown. "What's that got to do with anything?"

"I don't know. Sometimes things connect with other things; sometimes they don't. My motto is *Nothing succeeds like excess*. I collect lots of information, even though most of it will be useless. Otherwise, I might miss something that turns out to be important. Rule Six: *You never know what you'll need to know*."

"What's Rule Six?" Wallace asked.

"I have some rules I follow in my investigations. Rule Six is *You never know what you'll need to know*."

Simonetti shrugged. "Okay, I guess."

"Did Yvette and your father divorce while you were at the University of Texas?"

"I never told you I went to UT."

"I researched you on the internet."

"If you already knew, why ask?"

"It's the way I work, Ike. Pretend I didn't know. Did they divorce while you attended UT?"

"Yes."

"What did you study?"

"Didn't you look that up too?"

"Ike, let's make a deal: I won't tell you how to explore for oil and gas or develop real estate, and you don't tell me how to run an investigation. Okay?"

He rolled his eyes. "Okay. I studied petroleum engineering."

"Got it." I entered that on my laptop. "And that's how you wound up in Houston?"

"It's a big oil center. Also, my mother was from Houston, so I have family there too."

"The Warners?"

"That's right."

I noted that and signaled him to continue.

"After he divorced Mom—"

"You're referring now to Yvette Forsythe?"

"Yeah. After he divorced her, Dad dated different women from the Port City Social Register every month or so. After a couple of years, he settled down and chose a trophy wife from an old-money family in Cleveland."

"Wife number three," I confirmed.

"Allison Montrose," he said. "The Montrose family money was so old it was becoming extinct."

"Extinct?" I asked.

Wallace answered. "The Montrose family had lived off their capital for decades." She said "lived off their capital" like it was an STD. "Their core principal was nearly exhausted. Of course, Pop didn't know Allison was a fortune-hunter until after they married."

Simonetti frowned at Wallace. "Do you tell this, or do I?"

She made an "after you" gesture, then walked to the window wall and faced the bay, her back to us.

He continued. "Allison inherited a few million dollars from her father, but she wanted to marry someone disgustingly rich like Dad."

Over her shoulder, Wallace interjected, "A classic gold digger."

Simonetti winked in her direction. "I called Allison the *sports model* to piss her off. Dad was fifty and Allison was only a few years older than I was."

"What about her daughters?"

"Allison wanted children. For reasons I couldn't understand, so did Dad. After all, he had me to carry on the family name. Why would he need more? Anyway, she had the two daughters pretty quick."

"How did you and the daughters get along?"

"Badly. They were a generation younger—and they were spoiled, ball-busting bitches. I lived in Houston and they lived here in Port City, so we didn't see each other much. When we gathered at Christmas or Thanksgiving, they were insufferable brats. It was Dad's fault; he let them get away with murder. Then Dad caught Allison cheating and divorced her. He didn't mind paying child support, but Allison nailed him for $65,000,000 in a property settlement. No prenup."

"What happened to her money when she died?"

"I don't have a clue. I guess she had other family."

"What happened to Allison and the girls after the divorce?"

"They moved back to the Montrose family home in Cleveland."

"She moved in with her mother?"

Simonetti sighed as if I was boring him. "No, Allison's mother died while she and Dad were still married. After the divorce, the house was still empty, so she and her daughters moved in."

I entered that into my laptop. "How did your father meet Ramona?"

"A mutual friend at the Wessington Club introduced them and they dated for a couple of months. Then boom! Dad had a heart attack. He was in his seventies, and it scared him. Hell, it scared us too. Dad decided he needed someone to look after him other than Lorraine and me. He had dated Ramona casually before the heart attack, but she stayed with him constantly in the hospital while he recovered. I guess he figured she was loyal enough."

"Where did Ramona's money come from?"

"She told us she inherited it from her father," Wallace said. "He had a lot of property in Spain."

"How well do you two get along with Ramona?"

"Surprisingly well. I was Dad's best man, and Lorraine was Ramona's matron of honor."

"Ramona doesn't have any other family?"

Simonetti frowned. "I didn't think anything of it at the time, but she doesn't. Isn't that weird that she didn't have any family at their wedding?"

Wallace left the window wall and stood behind Simonetti. She placed her hands on his shoulders. "Be that as it may, Ike and I are Gloria's godparents, and Ramona even named us in her will as Gloria's guardians."

"Is Ramona a U.S. citizen?"

Simonetti twisted to look at his wife. "Lorraine, would you please sit down? I can't see you back there."

She took a chair. "I presume she's a citizen. But she told us she was born in Spain."

"Where in Spain?"

"A little town we had never heard of. I don't even remember the name. Do you, Ike?"

Simonetti shook his head. "'A little village,' I think she called it. The village was on her father's land, like he was a nobleman or something. I think maybe he owned the whole village."

"How long were they married?"

"A little over a year. I remember we celebrated their first anniversary in Dad's hospital room."

"What did he die of?"

"Cardiomyopathy," Wallace answered.

"And, in English?"

A tolerant grin. "A heart attack."

"Any foul play suspected?"

"None," Simonetti said.

Wallace frowned. "With the benefit of hindsight, Ike, I'm not so sure."

Simonetti held a palm up. "But at the time he died nothing was suspicious. Dad was seventy-five years old, for God's sake. He had felt poorly for months while Ramona cared for him at home. And the man had a long history of heart trouble."

"Let's keep Ramona in the dark as long as we can," I said. "She shouldn't get defensive if she doesn't know you suspect Gloria's paternity. Lorraine, with your medical practice, can you take time off to visit Ramona and Gloria?"

"I'm a dermatologist, so we don't have many emergencies. I, or we, can visit Gloria anytime we want."

"Good. You two try for two or three times a week, just casually. Now, let me change the subject. Ike, you were in the oil business?"

"Well, technically, petroleum exploration and production."

"Why move back to Port City?"

"I was tired of the whole energy industry and Dad wanted me to take over his company here so he could retire."

"Your dad was in real estate development?"

"Redevelopment—office buildings, shopping centers, golf course communities. We buy distressed properties and whip them into shape."

"Is that how you met Vicky and Don?"

"They were Dad's attorneys," Simonetti answered, "so they became mine. When Don cut back his hours, Vicky continued to handle my affairs."

"Lorraine, we'll need a sample of Sam's DNA from somewhere. Would his doctor have one?"

She frowned. "He might. His name is Virgil Norris. Ask Tom for his number and address."

"Okay. We don't have to prove who fathered Gloria, simply that it wasn't Sam. As I mentioned before, without your Dad's certified DNA, we have to rely on Sam's personal effects that may contain his DNA. Again, think of that as circumstantial, not conclusive, evidence. It might not be legally sufficient and, if not, we'll have to positively prove who did father Gloria. That's a big haystack."

Simonetti grinned. "That's why you'll have to earn that bonus we talked about."

"Agreed to, actually. How about a photo of your father?"

Simonetti canted his head. "I can get you one from the *Forbes* spread, but why? What does Dad's picture have to do with Gloria's paternity?"

"Maybe nothing; I don't know at this point. I ask questions; that's my job. Rule Five: *You can never have too much information.* I want pictures of your father, of you, and of your half-sisters, their birth certificates and yours, your father's marriage licenses for all four weddings and both divorce decrees. I want death certificates for Willamina, Allison, and her daughters, and a lot more I'll think of later."

"Are you sure you're not doing this to pad your fee?"

I thought back to Vicky the night before. "I'd be a fool not to."

"Okay, now I know you're kidding."

"Ike, I'm serious when I say I never know what's important until I find it."

He shrugged. "At least your fee's tax deductible."

Like I said, everybody wants to screw the IRS.

FOUR

Wallace had suggested I start with the tennis pro. That was as good a place as any. Reynaldo Mateo was the head professional at the Wessington Club, 250 bucks per fifty-minute lesson. Wallace claimed he spent his free time shtupping female students.

It must be nice to be Reynaldo.

I called my research guy, a techno-geek with the handle Flamer21. He didn't fit any gay stereotype I knew, but that was irrelevant. I had never asked why he picked the handle. "I need your magic background check on one Reynaldo Lopez Mateo, a tennis pro at Wessington Country Club."

"Spell it."

"Sure. W-E-S-S-I—"

"Always with the jokes. Can you spell 'asshole?' No, I meant the guy's name."

I spelled it.

"How deep you want to go? Quick and dirty, or you want his nanny's name when he was a baby?"

"Quick and dirty. I'll tell you later if I want deeper."

"When you need it? Yesterday like usual?"

"Of course. Stream it to my email as you get it." I could check it on my phone or tablet from my car.

Data started to flow as I drove to the club in my Avanti. I parked a block from the entrance and reviewed the info on my tablet, including a criminal record and Mateo's picture from the Wessington website. In his tennis whites with the Wessington logo, he depicted the perfect Latin movie star—straight white teeth, wavy black hair, dark tan.

Mateo was thirty-six years old and had a sealed juvenile record from nineteen years before. His adult rap sheet had two arrests for domestic violence against women who wound up in the hospital. One had two cracked ribs. She told the emergency room doctor that she fell off a ladder changing a light bulb. Six months later another woman claimed she fell down a flight of stairs, but her broken humerus with a spiral fracture meant that someone had twisted her arm.

I knew about spiral fractures from a case I had taken four months before. The client's ex-husband repeatedly ignored a restraining order. To get him to stay away from her, I had to negotiate with a head butt and a kick to his balls. The negotiation was successful. Abusers make my blood boil.

Both of Mateo's police reports said that he had cuts and bruises on the knuckles of both hands. At least the women had fought back. Both times the complainants changed their minds and failed to press charges. Was it guilt or shame? Who knows? If it were me, I would have done anything to put the bastard in jail, but that's me.

Mateo looked like a movie star, but he was an abuser.

Maybe it wasn't so nice to be Reynaldo, after all.

I spoofed my way into the Wessington Country Club by pretending to be interested in joining. Throwing Ike Simonetti's name around got me past the gatekeepers and onto the tennis courts.

Mateo was lobbing balls to a blonde Barbie practicing her overhead smash. The thirty-something woman wore her too-blonde hair in a long ponytail. Her Wessington-logo white top was soaked in sweat and clung to her like she was in a wet tee-shirt contest. Unfortunately, she wore a bra. But that was okay; I have a vivid imagination.

I watched the Barbie from the stands until Mateo finished the lesson. I have had worse stakeouts.

Mateo approached the net and kissed her hand with gallant flair. I almost thought he was going to bow.

She giggled. Mateo released her hand. "Until later, then." He blew a kiss and, despite the long workout, the Barbie headed into the women's locker room with a decided spring in her step.

I walked out onto the clay.

"I'm a friend of Ramona Simonetti's. Chuck Andrews." We shook hands. "I believe she takes lessons here?"

Mateo paused a second too long before he answered. "Yes, but not for eight or nine months. She took lessons three times a week. She got pregnant and had to quit. Doctor's orders." His smile seemed forced. Was there something there?

"Did she take lessons from you or one of the other pros?"

He studied my face. "From me. I'm the head pro." His unspoken message: I'm the best. I would have expected him to smile when he bragged about being the head pro, but he didn't. He stared at me.

"How long did you teach her?"

He stepped back and put his hands on his hips. Not easy to do with a water bottle in one hand, but he managed. "Why do you ask? What difference does it make?"

"I played a little in college years ago. I want lessons too."

"That's good, but why all the questions about Mrs. Simonetti?"

"No particular reason, just making conversation. Is she a good player?"

His eyes narrowed. "If you know her, you should know the answer to that."

"Actually, I was more a friend of her husband, Sam. I haven't played with Ramona yet. She any good?"

He waggled his hand back and forth in a "so-so" gesture. "She's better than when she started. But if you were on a college team, you could beat her blindfolded."

"That's a relief. I'd hate to let a pretty girl beat me at tennis."

Back on familiar turf, his smile broadened again. "We have at least two professionals always on duty seven days a week. When would you like?"

"I'll check my calendar. When are you here?"

He told me. "Call the pro shop; they handle all the schedules. Tell them you want Rey for the lessons."

We shook hands again. He grabbed his racquet and walked like a loping panther toward the locker room. Still moved like the professional athlete he must have been. Hell, if I were a woman, I might fall for him too.

Ignoring the recycle bin, he tossed his water bottle near the trash can. It bounced on the clay, but he ignored it. I really hated him now. I retrieved the empty bottle with a handkerchief, stuck it in my pocket, and left.

Mission accomplished: I had Mateo's DNA and fingerprints from his left hand if I ever needed them.

I drove straight to the lab and left the water bottle for DNA analysis.

I told them to get the fingerprints too, but keep to them on file JIC (just in case). Rule Six again.

I changed vehicles and returned to the Wessington Club in my white Dodge Grand Caravan. I call it my invisible minivan because white vans are as common as waves on the ocean. They attract as much notice as an extra bucket of water over Niagara Falls. That's why I drive one for business. My Avanti is mainly for fun.

After watching Mateo smooch Barbie's hand, I figured he would leave early for a booty call.

I called a friend at the DMV. She gave me the description of Mateo's car and its license number, TNNS PRO—what else? It also helped that Mateo drove a red Mustang. I cruised the employee lot and found his car. I parked across the street. While I waited, I changed shirts and reviewed the rest of my info on him.

In less than an hour, Mateo wheeled out of the lot. I stayed two cars behind his Mustang.

It's easy to follow someone who doesn't suspect. My DMV lady friend had also given me Mateo's registered address, but I didn't expect him to go there—not with Barbie waiting for him. Sure enough, he passed the turn to his apartment and continued toward the fancy suburbs.

When you follow someone on a busy street, the traffic hides you. It's tougher in a residential neighborhood. By the time Mateo turned into the last residential street, the other traffic had dropped off. I was a hundred yards behind him for the last three blocks. That would be too much coincidence, so when he drove into a cul-de-sac, I went straight. I parked at the curb, grabbed a clipboard, and quick-stepped back to the intersection in time to see his Mustang turn into a driveway a block down the street. He drove out of sight to the back of the property. It was too far away for me to be sure which driveway.

I waited two minutes. Then I walked up the street with my clipboard. You can get away with anything if you carry a clipboard. People assume you have the right to be there. Otherwise, why would you be carrying a clipboard?

I worked my way up the street to approximately where the Mustang had disappeared. At first, I didn't see Mateo's car. I was frustrated until I spied the last two feet of a red Mustang sticking out behind one of the houses. *Bingo.* I couldn't see the license plate, but what were the odds? I photographed the house and address number and walked back to my minivan.

I U-turned the van to watch the intersection and waited for Mateo's Mustang to reappear.

I passed the time with a medley of oldies on my cellphone while I reviewed the info Flamer had sent me. Twilight fell, and I had worked my way down to "El Paso" by Marty Robbins by the time Mateo's Mustang appeared under the streetlight.

I paused Marty. He didn't mind; he died before I was born. I concentrated on following the Mustang. Darkness was a mixed blessing. It's easier because all they see in the mirror are your headlights. It's harder because you can't see car color from a distance, and oncoming headlights blind you.

I lost him, but I figured he was on his way home. I had input his home address to my GPS while I waited. I caught up with him as he turned into his apartment complex.

Mateo's apartment was on the third floor at the end, separated from the next apartment by an exterior hallway. Any noise wouldn't be heard next door. I wasn't sure about the people downstairs; if it came to rough stuff, I would have to take my chances. Maybe they would think the guy upstairs was moving furniture.

I checked both ways down the walkway; I was alone. I knocked three times. The faint light through the peephole darkened as someone peered through it. "Who is it?"

"Adolph Throttleback," I said.

"What? I can't hear you."

"The atomic number of gold is seventy-nine," I said, but louder.

I heard him unfasten the door chain. As soon as the door cracked, I beamed and stuck out my hand. "Hey, Rey. Chuck Andrews. I have more questions about the tennis lessons."

When someone smiles at you and extends a hand, you naturally shake hands. It's a conditioned reflex that I counted on. Mateo shook my hand as I stepped into the room. He seemed puzzled. I closed the door behind me. "I have a couple more questions for you."

His face lit up when he recognized me. "You're the guy from the tennis courts this afternoon." He smiled for real.

Foolish man, I thought.

I decided not to speak Spanish. The less he knew about me the better.

"Let's sit down." I sat on his living room couch before he could react.

"How did you find my address? I'm not listed."

"I followed you from the club."

"You what?" he asked.

"I followed you from the club."

"I left there over two hours ago."

"Yeah, I know." I gave him a conspiratorial smile. "You have a lot of stamina, you sly dog."

"What did you say your name was?"

"Don't ask; I'll lie."

"You mean you were not interested to join the club?"

"Nope."

"You lied to me?" Mateo may have been handsome, but he was not the brightest bulb on the porch.

"If it's any consolation, I feel bad about it. Now, I know you're shtupping that blonde I saw you with this afternoon. Are you still shtupping Ramona Simonetti too?"

He pointed at the door. "I don't have to talk to you; get the hell out!"

"Rey, I don't go anywhere until I get answers. Are you still boinking Ramona Simonetti?"

"Get out, or I call the police." He picked up the phone.

"Yeah, Rey, why don't you do that? Tell the police you let me in here. Tell them I asked about your affair with a married woman, a member of the club that employs you. I'm sure the Wessington Club would love to hear about that. Go ahead and call. I'll wait."

I leaned back and spread my arms across the back of his couch. The unspoken message: *I ain't going anywhere. I have all night, buddy.*

He stared at the phone and swayed back and forth. "Screw you." He slammed the phone down. He charged and swung at my head—an easy target since I was sitting on his couch.

I leaned sideways and shot a left jab to his crotch that knocked him on his butt. He groaned and rolled onto his side, holding his groin.

He glared up at me. "That was a sucker punch."

"I guess that makes you the sucker. Sit down; let's talk."

He struggled to his feet and came at me again.

I didn't need to get up to jab him in the ribs.

He fell down again.

"Stay down, Rey. I can do this more times than you can."

He got up slower but staggered toward me.

This time I stood. "What are you, a slow learner?" I punched him in the ribs on his other side, the better to distribute the bruises artistically. "How many times do we do this dance, Rey?"

He started to get up again, thought better of it, and sat on the floor. "Who are you? What do you want?"

"Tell me about your relationship with Ramona Simonetti. Rey, I don't need to embarrass you at the club. But don't even think about lying to me, because I know all about you. I don't care who you ride off into the sunset with—the blonde from this afternoon or anybody else. I want to know about Ramona."

He raised his hands in surrender and sat in an easy chair. "I teach tennis; that's all."

I could practically hear the wheels turn in his head as he searched for a believable lie.

"Cut the crap. I followed you today and waited over two hours while you did the horizontal hula with that bimbo from the club. I don't care about that. I want to know how long you have been screwing Ramona Simonetti, and is it still going on?"

"The woman this afternoon, she came on to me; I swear it. You saw her. Could you turn her down?"

"Of course not. No red-blooded man would turn her down. I got excited just watching her practice this afternoon. But, Rey, you're not paying attention. Read my lips: I. Don't. Care. About. Her. I want to know about *Ramona*."

"Did her husband hire you?"

I snatched him off the floor by the front of his shirt. "Let's get our roles straight, Rey. I ask the questions; you answer them. How long have you been screwing Ramona?"

I tossed him down and waited while he took a long breath. He eyed me, watching for an opening.

Apparently, this guy's elevator didn't go all the way to the top. I slapped him with both hands, right, left. The fight went out of his eyes.

"Mateo, you're outclassed. You can beat up a hundred-twenty-pound woman, but I'm a professional thug. I don't like to hurt people, even assholes like you, but I will. Accept that you will tell me; you'll save us both time and energy."

Mateo got the point and started talking. Ramona had been a naughty girl.

FIVE

lamer's research on Ramona Gamez-Cristobal Simonetti yielded a dozen items, mostly news articles about charity events attended with her prominent husband, Sam Simonetti. Flamer sent me a separate email with an item from a tabloid newspaper that claimed Ramona was a direct descendant of Grand Duchess Anastasia, the youngest daughter of Tsar Nicholas II, the last sovereign of Imperial Russia. Wow. I wasn't sure how to use that undoubtedly reliable information.

There was no mention of her in either the traditional press or the tabloids before she and Sam announced their engagement. One society column called Ramona a mystery woman who came from nowhere to be "swept off her feet" by Sam Simonetti. The official story was that she came from a prominent family in Spain or Brazil. Flamer had searched websites in Spanish and Portuguese. Nothing. Curiouser and curiouser.

The logical explanation was that Ramona Gamez's identity was a fiction. She had been born under another name.

I called Tom Collins, Simonetti's PA.

"Good morning. How may I help you, Mr. McCrary?" I had used the phone that let Collins see my caller ID.

"Call me Chuck. Mr. McCrary is my Dad."

He laughed politely at the old joke. "Sure, Chuck. If you want Ike, he left yesterday to go fishing in northern Manitoba. No cellphone service."

"What do you know about Ramona's background?"

"Nothing. I met her once, at Sam's funeral."

"I tried to find background info on her, and there's nothing before she met Sam."

"Join the club. I tried an internet search before Ike hired you. It's like she materialized on the planet the day before she met Sam."

"Any evidence she changed her name?"

"None that I found, but I'm no expert. That's why Ike hired you."

"Good point. You know any connections Ramona may have in California? Friends, relatives, jobs, a former address, anything like that?"

"California? No, that's news to me. Why California?"

"Her Social Security number was issued in California a month before she met Sam."

"How do you know that?"

"I have magical powers. So why was she in California?"

"Beats me," Collins answered. "How did you get her Social Security number?"

"Professional secret. If I told you, I would have to kill you. Can you get me an appointment with Dr. Virgil Norris?"

"Who?"

"Virgil Norris. He was Sam's doctor."

"Sure. I'll text you."

I always check clients' backgrounds. I want to know who I'm working for. When Simonetti did business in Texas, he crossed swords with the EPA over disposal of oil exploration by-products. He paid three hefty fines. He also lost two lawsuits from landowners who claimed he cheated them out of leasehold royalties. Three other suits were dismissed when the landowners dropped their claims.

Simonetti hadn't told me that, but then I hadn't asked. So, he wasn't as clean as driven snow. Neither was I.

Wallace was born Lorraine Huddleston. She married Walter Wallace while she was in med school in Houston. Walter Wallace was a third-generation doctor. Their marriage lasted seven years until he died. Three years after that, Lorraine married Ike. I presumed she kept Wallace's name because that was the name on her medical practice and licenses.

There was one background check I didn't think to run until later. It nearly got me killed. My only excuse was that I was still new at private investigating.

Rule One: *When in doubt, ask questions.* I needed to interview Ramona.

Since she didn't know me, I didn't call ahead. Why give her a chance to say no? I drove to the mansion that Sam bought before his wedding to Ramona.

An honest-to-goodness butler answered. "Good afternoon, sir. How may I help you?" A British accent topped it off.

I handed him my engraved Carlos Calderone business card. "I have come to pay my respects to Mrs. Simonetti. I was a friend of Sam's. I have been in Chile the last few months and I did not learn of Sam's passing until last week." With my other hand, I held the flowers I had brought.

The butler eyed me from top to bottom, then evaluated my Avanti parked behind me. I passed inspection because he nodded and swung the door wide. "I'm Howley the Butler." He said "Butler" with a capital B.

"I'll take those flowers, sir."

I handed them over.

"Please, come in, sir. Make yourself comfortable. I'll tell Madam you're here." He carried the flowers from the room.

I visualized my impending meeting with Ramona. I can't take the lead around women when I act for myself. But when I'm in private-eye mode, it's like another person takes my place. Maybe I'm a natural actor. I didn't anticipate any problem. Ike and I had brainstormed this meeting. He had sketched out a couple of Sam's deals for me to mention that would explain how I knew Sam. I visualized the details Ike and I had discussed.

I made myself as comfortable as I could in a room with furniture that cost more than the GDP of a small, emerging-market country. The gold-trimmed double doors with gold-veined mirrors opened, and I stood to greet Ramona.

Showtime.

Nope. It was Howley.

He wheeled in a silver cart with my flowers, now looking much better in a vase, and a silver coffee service on it. He bowed. "I thought you would want to present the flowers to Madam yourself, sir."

"Thank you, Howley. That's very thoughtful of you."

I poured coffee and positioned my cup on the antique table. Of course, I used a coaster; I wasn't raised in a barn. I was raised *near* a barn, but not in it.

Seven minutes later, the double doors opened again. I rose again to greet Sam's widow. This time Ramona entered.

"Mr. Calderone, how nice of you to come."

"*Señora* Simonetti, *Discúlpeme, Señora.*" I explained in Spanish that I had been in Chile when Sam passed away and just recently learned of his death. "I brought flowers for you," I continued in Spanish. I bowed and gestured at the flowers. "Howley put them in a vase."

Ramona answered in Spanish without hesitation. "Thank you, Mr. Calderone. I know you would have come if you had known." She gazed at me intently and frowned slightly. "You are much younger than most of Sam's friends. How did you meet him?"

"Please, call me Carlos. Sam and I did business together. I found the Fifth Avenue Tower deal for him as well as the Port Henry Golf Club."

"Really? Sam told me he learned about the Fifth Avenue Tower foreclosure from his banker."

Oh, shit. Obviously, there were important details Simonetti hadn't told me. "I'm the man who told the banker about it. He put me in touch with Sam." *Please, God, don't let her know who the banker was.* I made a mental note to get more details on the deal from Simonetti in case it came up again.

"So, you know Eduardo Dominquez at First Continental?"

When you think things can't get any worse...Bam! "Not very well. My contact at First Continental was Henry Smith." *There's got to be a bunch of Smiths at First Continental.* "Henry and I had lunch with Eduardo and Sam at the Wessington Club where we discussed it."

"And what did you think of the Fifth Avenue deal?"

Thank God Simonetti and I had discussed that answer. I waggled my hand. "It analyzed so-so at first, but Sam renegotiated the terms with the mortgage holder. It worked out okay in the end."

She seemed satisfied. "Please sit down, Carlos." She poured a coffee for herself. "I don't know much about Sam's businesses. Only what he mentioned at the breakfast table. Sam's son, Ike, runs those for me now, of course. And please, call me Ramona."

"Of course, you wouldn't know, Ramona. Sam wouldn't bore a beautiful woman with such details." I favored her with my best smile. It had been several months since Sam's funeral, and she might feel a little flirtation was okay.

She blushed right on cue. "You are too kind, Señor. You were in Chile you say?"

"Chile and Mexico. An extended business trip."

Her carefully concealed native accent was Mexican, not Spanish. "Sam and I loved Chile. We visited Santiago on our honeymoon and then cruised from Valparaiso around Cape Horn to Buenos Aires. It was October here but spring down there. What do you do in Chile, Carlos?"

"I own a copper mine in the Andes."

We discussed our favorite restaurants and tourist sites of Santiago and Valparaiso. I used Mexican rather than Spanish slang and she didn't notice. I spent two summers during college backpacking around Spain, so I knew the regional accents and idioms. My mother had been born and raised on a *rancho* near Mexico City. As a boy, I spent a month there with my grandparents every summer. Ramona's accent would fool most people, but not me.

She was Mexican, not Spanish.

What else had she lied about?

"But my life is boring, Ramona. I would rather talk about you and Sam. Didn't someone tell me you were from California?"

"No, I'm from Spain. What gave you the idea I was from California?"

"I don't recall. Perhaps Sam told me?"

She shook her head. "No, Sam knew I was born in Spain. I came to the United States three years ago. Then I met Sam and decided to stay."

I pumped Ramona discreetly for as much personal information as she would give me, which was practically none.

She lied well, but so do I. With me, it's an occupational requirement. I didn't know what Ramona's excuse was. My knowledge of Santiago and Valparaiso came from the internet. Simonetti had told me his father had honeymooned in Chile. I had prepared for this meeting by reviewing honeymoon photos on Sam's computer that Ike had loaned me.

I entertained Ramona with true stories about my summers in Spain while we finished our coffee. Unlike our earlier conversation about Chile, she ignored my attempts to compare various Spanish cities.

Every wealthy Mexican family travels extensively in Spain. After all, it's the Mother Country. I concluded that she knew almost nothing about Spain. That indicated that she did not come from a monied family.

After a while, I asked about the baby. "I would love to meet your daughter."

"Gloria's taking a nap. Perhaps you could visit us another time? She's awake in mid-morning." She stood and extended her hand. "Thank you for coming, Carlos. These flowers are beautiful." When she shook my hand, she placed her left hand on my right. And didn't let go.

I had hoped to take something with Gloria's DNA on it, but no such luck. I tried another tack. "Ramona, I would love to come back and meet Gloria. I know the perfect occasion. If Sam were alive, and if I had been in the country, I know he would have invited me to her christening. I would like to get a christening gift for Gloria. Would you please write down her baptismal name so I can have it engraved?"

"That's kind of you, Carlos." She selected pink personal stationery from a burled walnut, antique writing desk that was worth more than my Avanti. She wrote on the engraved sheet with a gold pen. "You are too kind," she said as she handed me the paper.

I took it by a corner and placed it in my jacket pocket, breathing a quiet sigh of relief.

Mission partially accomplished—no DNA, but I had Ramona's fingerprints. Or would as soon as my lab processed her stationery with ninhydrin.

SIX

It was mid-afternoon and Kennedy Carlson was manning the front desk at Jerry's Gym. "You have the place to yourself except for a woman you straight guys would call hot." Ken was gayer than a pocketful of posies and he wasn't shy about it, but he didn't broadcast it either. "You may have seen her around for the last couple of weeks. She recently joined the gym. Want me to spot for you?"

"I'm good. Thanks anyway." I locked my weapons in Ken's desk, changed, and got to work.

The woman eyeballed me from the leg press station. That wasn't significant; there were only the two of us in the room.

Ken was right; I had watched her from a distance ever since she started coming to the gym. I had seen her when the gym was crowded, but I was too nervous to strike up a conversation. She peeked my way as I finished the bench presses. I gave her my third-best smile, the one for social occasions with strangers.

She smiled with recognition and moved to the stair-climber. Her shorts fit so well that I knew she wore bikini underwear, not a thong. After all, I am a trained observer.

I started my leg presses and contemplated the situation with Ramona.

Point one—Ramona Gamez-Cristobal was not her real name. Otherwise, internet searches would show something from before she met Sam.

Point two—she wasn't from Spain, even though her marriage license indicated she was born there. Nobody in the county clerk's office verifies that data. She could have said she was from Antarctica and no one would have checked. She also was not familiar with Spanish cities and tourist attractions.

Point two-and-a-half—she was from near Mexico City. She appeared to be late twenties or early thirties, which conflicted with her birth date on the marriage license. The birthday on her marriage license would make her forty-two. Why would she lie about her age? Stranger yet, why would she lie and say she was older. When women lied about their age, didn't they claim they were younger?

I made a mental note to discuss that with Vicky Ramirez. She knew more about women than I did. Actually, everybody but a hermit crab knew more about women than I did.

Point three—if she came to the States to run a scam on Sam, she could have learned her trade in Mexico. If so, perhaps she had a record in Mexico. But, without a name, I had to rely on her fingerprints.

Point four—I had her fingerprints on the paper with Gloria's baptismal name.

I decided to call my Uncle Felix with the Mexican Federal Police as soon as I finished my workout.

The woman had moved to the leg extension machine near the entrance to the men's locker room. As I passed, I upgraded to my second-best smile. She smiled back through her timed breaths.

That seemed like an invitation, but I didn't know how to handle it. I can field-strip an M249 SAW—squad automatic weapon—in the dark, blindfolded, but I didn't know how to talk to women.

I stopped a short distance away and watched. I could do that much without looking like a weirdo, right?

She watched me watching her. The sweatband that held back her hair dripped from perspiration, and her tee-shirt showed sweat patches. I could smell her femaleness where I stood. She was no dilettante. She was working out when I started and when I finished. Was she a gym rat like me?

In my line of work, I get few opportunities to meet what I think of as "real women." I watched this real woman while I tried to think of something to say that wasn't lame. My mind was as constipated as a prehistoric chunk of dinosaur feces. I turned to leave.

She paused to catch her breath. "I joined the gym."

I stopped in my tracks—deer in the headlights. What was I supposed to say now?

When I didn't say anything, she continued. "Ken said you've been a member here for some time." Interesting. Either she had asked Ken about me or Ken had mentioned me to her. Maybe Ken had used me a reference when she expressed an interest in joining. Or maybe he was playing matchmaker.

Okay, I knew how to answer a question—even one from a pretty woman. "About three years. It's convenient to my office and townhouse."

"I take it Ken owns the place?"

I nodded. So far, so good.

She shook her head and little sweat droplets flew off her hair. "Why does he call it Jerry's Gym?"

"Ken bought it from a guy named Jerry. Ken jokes that he was too cheap to spring for a new sign. But the name had goodwill."

She kept working the leg machine. "Makes sense. If it ain't broke… You said your office is near here. What do you do for a living?"

"I'm a private investigator."

She stood. "What a coincidence; I'm a cop." She wiped her hand on a towel and stuck it out. "Teresa Kovacs."

We shook hands.

"Chuck McCrary. North Shore precinct?" I asked.

"How did you know?"

"Lucky guess. It's a few blocks from here. You must know Lieutenant Weiner. Mother Weiner was my training officer." We called her "Mother" because she had a Jewish mother attitude. She pretended the nickname annoyed her, but I think it secretly pleased her.

"Mother's my training officer too. Small world. When did you leave the job?"

"Eight months ago, when I became a PI."

"I started at North Shore right after you left. Why did you leave? Not enough money?"

"No, I make less now, but I have hopes." *Okay, boy, nothing ventured, nothing gained. If you don't ask; you don't get. No guts, no blue chips. Stop thinking in clichés. You're stalling. She's sending all the right signals; make your move.* "It's a long story. You free for coffee after we shower? Separately," I added.

She laughed. "I was beginning to think you'd never ask. Meet you in the lobby in fifteen minutes?"

Whew. She said yes. "Make it twenty," I countered.

"Done."

I made it in fifteen. I retrieved my guns from Ken's desk and waited for Teresa. The after-work crowd began to file in while Ken and I shot the breeze.

Teresa came out after twenty-five minutes. The way she looked made it worth the wait.

"Sorry I took so long, Chuck."

"No problem. I used the extra time to teach Coach how to tie his shoes." Ken had been a strength coach for the Pittsburgh Steelers before moving to Port City.

Teresa eyed Ken. "Is he always like this?"

"No. Sometimes he's worse."

Teresa grinned and faced me. "How about that coffee shop across the street?"

"Java Jenny? One of my favorites." I grabbed her gym bag and threw it over my shoulder.

"Good idea." She took my arm. "We don't want to invest too much effort in a first, almost date."

This was good. She called it an *almost date*. I gave myself a mental fist bump.

We stashed our gym bags in our cars and dodged the traffic to Java Jenny's. I picked a table in front. "What would you like?"

"Iced coffee, large and black."

I brought back two iced coffees. I prefer a little creamer, but I ordered mine black like hers. Maybe to show we had something in common? I wasn't very good at this. Correction: I was terrible at this.

She rested her drink against her bottom lip. "Okay, as I was saying at the gym, why did you leave the job?"

"Never intended to stay. I worked there for my experience requirement for a PI license."

"Why a PI?"

"I've wanted to be a PI since high school. Private investigation lets me indulge in things I like to do."

"What sort of things do you like to 'indulge' in?" She made air quotes.

"Oh, the usual: consorting with lowlifes, asking embarrassing questions, solving puzzles. And there's always the chance for an occasional gunfight."

She raised an eyebrow. "You've been in gunfights?"

"No, no. I was joking. Had a fistfight a couple of days ago, but I have never drawn a gun in the line of business. Hope I never do."

"I hope I never do, either."

Then I added, "Besides, my mission is to make the world safe for democracy."

"You're kidding." She saw my face. "Oh, you are kidding. Do you make jokes out of everything?"

"It's a curse."

"I'll have to learn to tell when you're joking, won't I?"

"If you do, you can teach me."

We both laughed. I felt better than I had any right to.

"What about you, Teresa? Why did you become a cop?"

"Family tradition. Dad and Gramps were cops, and Mom is a dispatcher. We're big on law and order in the Kovacs family."

"My parents are farmers. Mom is also a large-animal veterinarian. No one in my family has been a cop except Uncle Felix."

I liked her. We talked about pirates and poets, walruses and walnuts, coal-heavers and confectioners. The tail of the afternoon raced by as I bought us giant chocolate chip cookies and more coffee.

Vicky had invited me to dinner that night, so I had to bring the "almost date" to a close. I gave her my best smile. "As far as I'm concerned, Teresa, this first almost date is a roaring success. How do you feel about it?"

"Pretty good. I give it a B minus." Her eyes sparkled.

"B minus? How does a guy get an A?

She laughed. "He asks me to dinner."

Dumb, dumb, dumb. "Oops. I have plans tonight."

"I didn't say it has to be *tonight*. I just said he asks me to dinner."

Dumber, dumber, dumber. "I'm normally not such a dim-wit, Teresa. How about dinner tomorrow night?"

"It's a date. And my friends call me Terry." She handed me a Port City Police Department business card. "Hand me your phone; I'll add my number to your contacts."

I did, and she entered her number. "Okay if I use your phone to call mine so I'll have your number too?" she asked.

"Are you always this much of a take-charge person?"

"She who hesitates is lost." I wondered if she had gotten this whole phone number routine from *Cosmopolitan.* It sounded very slick, almost well-rehearsed.

I made an after-you gesture. "Go ahead."

She made the call and handed my phone back.

"Thanks. Here's one of my cards," I said.

As we approached Terry's car, she clicked her remote. I opened her door with my left hand and extended my right. "Terry, this is the most fun I've had in two hours."

She squeezed my hand and kissed me on the cheek. "Chuck, that line deserves a double-entendre reply, but I can't come up with a worthy one. I look forward to tomorrow night."

My mother was the oldest of five children. Her brother Felix was the youngest. As a result, Felix was seven years older than I. During the summers I spent in Mexico, Felix and I became as close as brothers. The summer after high school graduation and before I entered the Army, we chased girls together and closed more than one bar. Actually, Felix did the chasing and I just tagged along.

I called him as soon as I got home. "Felix, this is Carlos. I need a favor."

"Sure, *gringo*. How much money you need?"

I never knew what Felix would say when I asked for a favor. "I'm sending you a partial set of fingerprints I got off her personal stationery. See what you can learn. She goes by Ramona Maria Elena Gamez-Cristobal Simonetti. She says she is forty-two, but she looks about thirty. I think she's a criminal, maybe a confidence woman."

"Send it to my personal email. I'll do it tonight after work."

"*Muchísimas gracias, Tío.*"

The next day, the late afternoon rain ended as I pulled into Terry's parking lot. She lived on the second floor of a three-story garden apartment. I skipped the elevator and climbed the stairs two at a time, as eager as a kid on Christmas morning.

Terry opened the door. Her yellow silk blouse had a scoop neck that revealed the swell of her breasts. I inhaled the bouquet of her fragrance. After I regained consciousness, I beamed my best thousand-watt smile and stood speechless like a doofus.

She smiled back, showing a cute dimple in her left cheek. Her eyes twinkled. "Hello, handsome. My, you certainly clean up well."

"You smell a lot better than you did yesterday. Oh, shit. Did I say that out loud?"

She laughed.

"I meant to say that you smell even better than you did yesterday. Yeah, that's it: 'even better.' Did I recover? Or should I go back to my car and start over?"

"I'll take either one as a compliment. Come in for a drink?" She led me into her apartment. The view of her derriere beneath the white linen knee-length shorts was inspirational. She stopped at the kitchen counter. "What's your pleasure, Chuck?"

I knew she enjoyed the double entendre from the twinkle in her eye.

"What a great question, so non-directive. You asked that yesterday, and I let you pick. That worked out so well, why don't you pick again tonight?"

She opened a cabinet. "Merlot or Cabernet Sauvignon?"

"Blindfold me and I wouldn't know them apart. But then I'm a barbarian."

"I'm counting on it." She chose the Merlot. "What shall we drink to?"

"What does one drink to on a first-and-a-half date?"

Terry pursed her lips in mock thought. "I'm pretty sure this is our second date. But I haven't decided yet whether to upgrade yesterday's almost date to a full date or not. I'll tell you later."

"In that case, let me rephrase that. What does one drink to on a probably second date?"

She clinked my glass. "To us."

"To us," I echoed.

She grabbed my hand. "Let's go to the living room." She sat on the couch and patted the cushion next to her. She kicked off her sandals and swung her legs across my lap.

After my experience with Vicky, I figured she wanted me to rub her feet. I did.

She sighed. "So, Chuck, tell me everything." We exchanged stories from our personal lives as we sipped the wine. When we had emptied our glasses, she raised an eyebrow. "Another?"

"I'm driving. I'll have another at the restaurant."

My favorite Chinatown restaurant is Nine Dragons. Terry and I rode the elevator to the twelfth floor. As we approached the host stand, I saw a familiar face with a warm smile. "Mr. Chuck, how nice to see you again. And what a beautiful lady you bring to grace my restaurant."

"Great to be here, Jimmy. Teresa, may I present Jimmy Wang, the owner. Jimmy, Teresa Kovacs."

"So nice to meet you, Jimmy."

Jimmy took her hand. "You decorate my restaurant with your beauty." He bowed to me. "Your table ready soon. I show you place in bar. Come." He led us to a table overlooking Chinatown. He gestured a server over. "Take good care of Mr. Chuck and Ms. Teresa."

Terry ordered the house Chardonnay. I ordered coffee, and I noticed the surprise on her face. "I'm driving. I'll have one glass with the meal."

She put her hand on mine and lifted her glass. "To new beginnings."

"New beginnings." I lifted my coffee.

Jimmy appeared and bowed. "Table ready. You follow me, please."

The rest of dinner was a blissful daze of smiles, winks, laughter, and one glass of wine.

Terry finished the last of her dessert. She gazed into my eyes as she licked the spoon. Twice. "This is the most fun I've had in two hours."

"Better than yesterday's probably-first date?"

"Yes, so far this date earns a B plus."

"So how does a fellow get an A?"

She grinned. "I'll tell you later. Better yet, I'll show you later."

I signaled our server. "Check please."

She burst out laughing.

My Avanti has bucket seats, but somehow Terry sat closer on our way back. When I wasn't shifting gears, we held hands. We soon found ourselves standing at her door. She handed me her key and I opened the door. She led me inside. "Would you like a drink?"

"Better make it coffee; I'm driving. I know how big the Kovacs family is on law and order."

Terry put her arms around my waist. "What if you didn't have to drive until tomorrow?"

"That would be different."

"Then I'll show you how to get an A. And this is definitely our second date."

"Why are you sure now that yesterday was an official first date?"

She closed one eye in a slow-motion wink. "Because I don't put out on the first date."

SEVEN

R ule Two: *When in doubt, follow somebody.* I followed Ramona, or tried to.

Monday at 7:00 a.m., I parked my invisible minivan across from Ramona's house and listened to music. Marty Robbins still sang about El Paso and still got shot from his horse for love of a Mexican girl. I could relate: Dad did the same thing—fell in love with a Mexican girl, that is. Getting shot from a horse is not an occupational hazard for farmers. Stepped on by a cow maybe, but not shot.

I pulled out my laptop and reviewed the files on Ramona as I listened to my music.

At nine o'clock, Ramona came out the door pushing Gloria in a jogging stroller. They took off up the street. I knew she wouldn't be going far pushing Gloria, so I waited. She returned at ten.

"Jogged for one hour," I wrote.

At 11:30, a dark-blue Kia sedan drove through the gate. I snapped a picture, put the van in gear, and idled forward for a better look. I snapped a telephoto picture of the license as the Kia drove up the driveway. The sedan parked in front of the garage and a young, nanny-looking woman got out. I zoomed in and snapped another picture and video as I cruised past the gates.

If Ramona was waiting for the nanny so she could leave, I might see action soon. I drove around the block and parked up the street. I didn't wait in front of the same house where I had earlier; the homeowner might get suspicious.

My earlier research with a contact at the Department of Motor Vehicles had disclosed that Ramona owned a silver Mercedes CL600 Coupe, a red Cadillac XTS sedan, and a black Lincoln Navigator. The silver Mercedes glided down the drive and sped past. Funny how silver looks different on a Mercedes than it does on a regular car.

When I had picked my surveillance spot, I gambled that she would turn right. I guessed wrong, so my Caravan faced the wrong way. If I made a U-turn to follow her, she might see me in her rearview mirror. I waited until she turned the corner and raced to follow the Mercedes, but she was already out of sight.

I drove by Mateo's apartment on the remote chance that she was going to see him. I drove past every car in the parking lot. No luck.

I ordered a sub sandwich and a diet Dr Pepper to go and went back to the street near Ramona's house. I had lots of practice waiting when I was in the Army. Ramona returned at 5:38 p.m. If she had been to see Reynaldo Mateo, I had missed it. The Kia left at six o'clock sharp.

I called Terry. "This is Meals on Wheels. Did you expect a Chinese food delivery tonight?"

"That depends. Will it come from Nine Dragons?"

"Is there something special about Nine Dragons?"

"Yes, I ate there the other night. An hour later, instead of being hungry, I was horny. I wound up naked in bed with a stranger. I suspect their food is an aphrodisiac. I want to see if their takeout food has the same effect."

"I'm forty-five minutes away. Why don't you call our order in and I'll pick it up."

"Okay. But I must warn you; if their takeout has the same effect, I might tear your clothes off and jump your bones. You willing to take the risk?"

"Risk is my middle name."

"Okay, you have been warned. By the way, who is this?"

After dinner, I helped scrape the dishes and load the dishwasher. "Terry, I'm working a case I could use a woman's perspective on."

"I can give you a woman's perspective on anything, anywhere, anytime." She licked her lips and winked.

"Hold that thought. First let's discuss my case. Can you keep this confidential?"

"Sure."

"Okay. A young woman marries a wealthy old man in poor health who doesn't have long to live. Their prenuptial agreement limits her to a small portion of his estate. A large portion by anyone else's standards, but a small percent of the whole. She wants to get pregnant so she can claim a share of his estate for her child. But he can't perform, or can't perform very well."

"I hate it when that happens."

"I would bet you've never faced that problem."

"Not yet, anyway, but I don't know any wealthy old men in poor health."

I finished loading the dishwasher.

Terry said, "Let's sit on the balcony."

We sat in the dimness, lit by light escaping from the apartment swimming pool. Terry poured us each a glass of wine. "Go on with your story."

"Let's assume she got him happy hard-on pills and jumped his bones every time he could get it up."

"I'm sure he hated that."

"His health was poor, but he wasn't dead. Believe me, she's as hot as Las Vegas in August. If you were her, and you wanted to hedge your bets about getting pregnant, who would you choose as auxiliary sperm donor?"

"If she's as hot as you say, lots of men would take her offer."

"Her prenup cuts her off if she roams off the ranch. She stands to lose $30,000,000."

"Thirty million dollars is a small portion of the guy's estate?"

"Yeah."

Terry whistled. "So, the hard part is not finding a man, but keeping the affair secret."

"So how would you do it?"

She sipped her wine. "It should be a man she sees anyway. That attracts less suspicion."

"Like the swimming pool man?"

"Or the gardener, or the butler, et cetera."

"She's a snob, not the type to shtup the hired help. How about her tennis pro?"

"Is there a golf pro, a masseur, a personal trainer?"

"Not as far as I know."

"She take tennis lessons?" Terry asked.

"She used to. Three times a week until she got pregnant."

"Three times a week sounds suspicious all by itself. Is the tennis pro shtup-worthy?"

"He looks like a Latin movie star."

"Then I vote for the tennis pro." She took another sip of wine.

"That's what another of the tennis pro's customers told me. She claimed he made a pass at her too."

"There you have it. Case closed. It must be the tennis pro." She set down her wine glass. "Speaking of shtupping…"

I raised a hand. "Okay, next question. She put a birth date on her marriage license that says she's forty-two years old, but she looks thirty. I know that some women lie about their age and say they are younger. But why lie and say you're older?"

"You said this May-December marriage was late in the millionaire's life?"

I decided not to tell her he was a billionaire. "A little over a year before he died."

"If she were a true gold-digger, she probably lied to reduce the age difference so the marriage wouldn't look so suspicious. If she had been fifty-five, no one would have said a thing, right?"

"I see. She knew she couldn't get away with adding twenty-five years, so she added enough to make her over forty."

"Probably." She sat in my lap. "Now that we have solved your case, let's play a different game."

I traced the license plate of the blue Kia. It belonged to a college student. She had to be the nanny Simonetti mentioned. The Kia showed up again at 11:30.

This time I parked facing the other way.

Fifteen minutes later, Ramona's Mercedes rolled down the driveway and sped away. I followed at a discreet distance. Three miles later, she entered Crosstown Parkway.

I called Flamer on my hands-free. "Send me all the activity of Ramona Simonetti's SunPass accounts on all three of her cars for the last ninety days. Can do?"

"When you want it, Chuck? I'm at lunch with a friend."

"This afternoon will be fine."

The phone went dead. No "yes sir," no "screw you," and no "good-bye." That was Flamer all right. His truculence had distracted me and I had lost Ramona's Mercedes.

I didn't want to waste the rest of the day and start all over tomorrow tailing Ramona. After a minute's befuddlement, I decided to think like Ramona. If I were a tabloid-newspaper-worthy fashionable woman with an afternoon to kill, where would I go? The answer hit me: the Galleria, an upscale mall where rich people prove they can afford to pay $400 for $50 sneakers.

I took the gamble and arrived as Ramona's Mercedes pulled into view.

I let two cars in between us and followed her into the parking garage. Naturally, she stopped at valet parking. After all, no one could expect her to park her own car. What would the tabloids think?

I parked a floor above and walked down the ramps until I found her parked Mercedes. I stood behind a concrete column until a valet had locked another car in a spot near Ramona's and entered the elevator. Glancing to make sure I was unobserved, I stuck a GPS tracker under the rear bumper.

I retrieved my van and parked across the street where I watched both garage exits. By then, Flamer had sent me three months' toll charge details on Ramona's SunPass account. SunPass transponders work on any toll road in Florida and integrate with the parking garages at the major airports. Her SunPass account statement would show me every entrance and exit she had made from any toll road or airport parking garage in the state.

I punched up the SunPass toll road map on my laptop and studied where she had driven, and in which cars, for the previous three months. As I wrote down the trips, I recognized patterns. A dozen Wednesday and Friday trips began at the Marshall Boulevard entrance after 3:00

p.m. If she left her house right after the nanny arrived, she must have spent a couple hours somewhere else before she got on the toll road.

The key question: Where did she go on those days before she got on Crosstown Parkway at Marshall?

She wasn't going to the Wessington Club; it was the other direction. Besides, she no longer took tennis lessons and didn't use the club much anymore. I made a note to have Flamer analyze her Wessington Club account charges to see when she had lunched at the club.

When she exited the garage, the back seat of the Mercedes held enough packages to intimidate Santa Claus.

I followed her home.

The next day I took up my post near Ramona's gate at 11:00. The Kia showed right on time, and Ramona's Mercedes came out right on time. No surprises. That was not good. Now that I knew her routine, I wanted her to do something different, a change of scene.

My wish came true. She bypassed Crosstown Parkway and stayed on JFK Boulevard. Twenty minutes later, she drove down Lexington Avenue and parked her Mercedes at Gino's Takeout Pizza. She must have called her order in, because she came out in four minutes with a pizza box and a sack that might have been drinks.

Underway again, I figured she was close to her destination. I saw her use her cellphone for a short call. In the next block, she pulled into a two-lane driveway between the Guiding Light Rescue Mission and the Payday Pawn Shop. I waited for her car to disappear, then followed.

The driveway crossed the rear alley and fed into a parking lot behind some apartments a block off Lexington. I drove into the alley and squatted in a loading zone behind the Guiding Light Rescue Mission. *No deliveries between 11:00 a.m. and 2:00 p.m.* I took the sign at its word and blocked their loading zone with my Caravan.

I watched Ramona's Mercedes in my mirror. She locked the car and walked to the apartments.

I grabbed a clipboard and followed at a safe distance, pausing to snap a picture of her car and the apartments.

She climbed the stairs at the left of the courtyard and walked toward the middle of the row of apartments. I lurked in the shadows, pulled out my clipboard, and pretended to take notes. She stopped at a door, knocked twice, inserted a key, and entered without waiting. I snapped a telephoto of the door. Number 212.

I returned to the mailboxes. Number 212 had a plastic stick-on label reading *R. Gomez*. Ramona's maiden name was Gamez. *Hmm. Gamez* and *Gomez*. Rule Seven: *There is no such thing as a coincidence—except when there is*. I texted the name and address to Flamer.

I went to my van and killed two hours listening to my stomach growl. Note to self: Next time take a sandwich when you're on a stake-out. I was still new at the PI business and still learning.

The dashboard clock indicated fifteen minutes had passed. I spent another two hours imagining animal shapes in the clouds as they formed and moved across the midday sky. My clock said twenty minutes had passed. I pictured Terry naked. Before I knew it, two o'clock came. I couldn't block the loading zone any longer. I backed my van into a visitor's spot forty yards from the Mercedes. More waiting. For variety, I pictured Vicky naked.

About 3:30, Ramona's Mercedes backed out of her parking space. If her pattern held, she would enter Crosstown Parkway at Marshall Boulevard. She did.

I texted Flamer to check her credit cards for charges at Gino's Takeout Pizza. I also asked for a report on R. Gomez in apartment 212. Twenty minutes later, he emailed me her credit card data, which showed charges on the same days she entered Crosstown Parkway at the Marshall Boulevard entrance. The report on R. Gomez would take a little longer.

After dinner at my townhouse, Terry and I lounged on the back deck, sipping my special Mexican Sangria. Terry gestured at my boat, moored behind my townhouse.

"Chuck, you said you made less money as a PI than you did on the job. But you live in a waterfront townhouse and own a nice boat. I'm a flatfoot, not a fancy detective like you were, but what gives? Are you rich or something?"

"I wish."

"Then how come you have a place like this and a boat like that on less money than you made as a cop?"

"The townhouse is simple. When I finished college, Port City was in one of its real estate busts. This townhouse was worth half what it had been three years before."

"I remember a similar situation in Gainesville when I was at the University of Florida."

"My landlady had her entire nest egg invested in this row of townhouses. She couldn't sell any of them for enough to make a profit. I offered her a deal."

"What kind of deal?"

"I signed a five-year lease for the prices in effect four years ago, about half what these go for now."

"What about the snazzy boat?"

"The boat sank in Palm Beach during Hurricane Dominic three years ago. The insurance company declared it a total loss, paid off the owner, and wound up with the title to the sunken boat. The owner of a boat sunk in navigable water is responsible for clearing the waterway.

The insurance company didn't want to be bothered. They sold it to me for one dollar on the condition that I remove it from the waterway. I spent every weekend for two years repairing it."

"You did the work yourself?"

"I'm good with my hands."

Terry smirked. "That you are."

"All I paid for were parts. I did the labor. Voila! A nearly new boat for practically nothing."

"So, you're not rich?"

"Sorry to disappoint you."

"That's okay. I only want your body anyway."

The next morning, I called Ramona's house on my Carlos Calderone phone. The butler answered. "This is Carlos Calderone, Howley. I want to make sure my christening gift arrived. Is Mrs. Simonetti in?"

"I'll see if Madam is in. Would you hold, please?"

A moment later, Ramona answered in Spanish. "Carlos, how nice of you to call."

"Good morning, Ramona." After a few pleasantries, I asked, "Did Gloria's gift arrive?"

"Yes. And I did not expect anything so...," she paused for a moment, "...extravagant."

"It's a sincere gift from a friend of Sam's. I never know what to get a baby. I figure if it's for a female of any age, you can't go wrong with Tiffany's. I ordered it from their website, so I never saw the cup engraved. Does it look okay?"

"You can see for yourself, Carlos. Why don't you join Gloria and me on our morning jog one day soon?"

"I would love to. How about Saturday?"

We made the date.

Next, I reviewed the information on R. Gomez that Flamer had lifted from the apartment management company's computer system. Foolish company. Flamer penetrated their system like a bee sucks pollen from a flower.

R. Gomez's full name was Ramon Gomez. Ramon *Gomez* and Ramona *Gamez*. I would bet a Super Bowl ticket against a sub sandwich they were connected. Ramon had lived there twenty-five months on a month-to-month lease. He paid his rent in cash. Ramona had used her credit card to pay his rental deposit—the card she still had in her supposed maiden name. That linked Ramona to Ramon for at least the last twenty-five months.

I needed DNA from baby Gloria, Ramona, and Ramon Gomez, but how to get it?

I staked out Ramon's apartment.

I parked at one end of Ramon's parking lot. Flamer's data showed that Ramon Gomez bought a pickup truck when he rented the apartment. I noted the truck's description and license and went to reconnoiter. That's army talk for "look around." I located an empty space in the parking lot with *212* painted on it. It was the middle of the afternoon, so Ramon might be at work. Flamer hadn't yet found Ramon's employment data.

I parked close enough to watch Ramon's parking spot and waited. It rained again, so people wouldn't hang around to notice me lurking.

Shortly after six p.m., Ramon's pickup pulled into space 212. He ran through the rain toward his apartment. I waited ten minutes before I started to snoop.

I peered in the pickup's window. A pair of well-used work gloves lay on the passenger seat. A toolbox sat on the floor behind the driver's seat. I noted the inspection sticker and license plate expiration dates. Florida license plates expire in the owner's birth month—Ramon's license plate expired in July. I didn't have a birth date for him yet, so that could be a clue.

I was alone in the lot, so I stuck a tracking device inside a rear wheel well. By eight o'clock the rain had stopped.

I was ravenously hungry but I had forgotten my own advice: I hadn't brought a sandwich. Note to self: Next time read the "Note to self."

At 8:10 p.m. Ramon got in his truck and drove away. With the tracking device, I followed him from two blocks behind.

He drove to El Rodeo, a cantina in Little Mexico. I gave him two minutes and followed him inside.

The dim room reeked of tobacco smoke. A Port City ordinance forbids smoking in restaurants, but I guess El Rodeo patrons don't mind, and the cops don't pay attention. I could hold my breath for a couple of hours. Or not.

Ramon stood at the bar. I paused at the door for my eyes to adjust to the light in the smoky, dim room. An old man in a faded *Dos Equis* tee-shirt and worn blue jeans brought him a Corona and a menu.

I went to the other end of the bar, ordered a Corona, and watched the *futbol* game along with half a dozen other customers.

Ramon finished his second beer and ordered a third, along with an order of *enchiladas de puerco*. Chips and salsa were insufficient to soak up my alcohol intake, so I ordered *tacos al carbon* and guacamole. Besides, I was far beyond hungry. Try *famished* or maybe *voracious*. But then, I'm always hungry.

The bartender picked up Ramon's empty beer bottle and brought him another. He stashed the empty on top of a case of empties to be recycled. When he passed through the kitchen door, I leaned over and wedged a finger into the neck of the bottle, lifted it over the bar, and slipped it into an inside pocket unobserved. Now I had both DNA and fingerprints on Ramon Gomez.

The *tacos al carbon* was delicious.

Saturday morning at 9 o'clock, I locked my weapons in the car at Ramona's. I didn't expect any gunfights in her mansion.

Howley opened the door as I climbed the steps. "Good morning, Mr. Calderone. Nice to see you again, sir."

"Howley, I would ask you to call me Carlos or Chuck, but I know you won't. And I would shake your hand, but you would find that inappropriate, right?"

"Yes, sir, I'm much too proper for such familiarity with Madam's guests." He winked. "Won't you come in? Madam is expecting you."

Howley showed me to the parlor. The flowers I had brought on my first visit had wilted a little, yet Ramona hadn't thrown them out. That was a good sign.

As Ramona walked in, I noticed that she had dressed up for me—another good sign.

"Would it be terribly low-class to whistle?"

"Probably, but do it anyway."

I did, and she responded with a grin. "Carlos, you are such a character."

"I try my best."

She held up the Tiffany Baby Bows silver cup I had sent Gloria. As she kissed me on the cheek, I smelled her perfume. "Here is that lovely cup from Tiffany's. See how beautiful the engraving is."

I read *GES* for *Gloria Elena Simonetti*. "It's beautiful. Thanks for showing me."

"I'll get Gloria." She carried the cup from the room and returned pushing Gloria in the jogging stroller. "I brought an extra water bottle for you."

My heart did a double flip when I saw Gloria. She reminded me of my niece in Texas whom I had not seen since Christmas. I wanted to pick her up, but I didn't want to push too fast with Ramona. I squatted by the side of the stroller and rubbed the back of Gloria's hand with the back of my index finger. "She's gorgeous."

"Thank you. I think so too, but I'm prejudiced." Ramona pushed the stroller to the front portico.

"I'll help you." I grabbed the stroller's front rail and held it level as we lugged it down the steps.

"Thanks, Carlos. Off we go." Ramona took off at an easy pace to Pennington Park and we looped the track for a half-hour. Then she stopped and extended a water bottle to me. "Water?"

I took it. As I drank, I wiped my sweaty face with the towel I had slung around my neck.

Ramona drank a long pull from her own bottle. "Let's get you some milk, *muñequita*." She pulled a baby bottle from the stroller and picked up Gloria.

"Can I feed her? It's been months since I've seen my niece Rebecca, and I miss her." That much was true, even if the rest of my time with Ramona was an act. "Hey, pretty girl, come see Uncle Carlos." I smiled at Ramona. "How old is she? About three months?"

Ramona raised an eyebrow. "For a man, you know babies; she's three-and-a-half months." She handed me a burp diaper, followed by Gloria.

"My niece Rebecca was that age last time I saw her." While I fed Gloria, we talked about the weather, the baby, and the high cost of hiring good domestic help. I put Gloria over my shoulder and pulled my towel so the edge was exposed under Gloria's burp diaper. I patted her back until she burped. She spit up a little and I wiped her mouth with my towel. I burped her again and handed her back to Ramona. "Thanks. I miss Rebecca. My sister tells me she's almost walking. Would you like me to take your water bottle?"

"Thanks. The recycle is over there." She drained the last few ounces.

When we jogged back to Ramona's home, I pushed the stroller.

"Ramona, thanks for a lovely morning. And thanks for introducing me to Gloria. She is lovely—like her mother."

This time Ramona gave me a real kiss on the mouth. "Why don't you come see me again, perhaps tomorrow? We can lunch by the pool. One o'clock?"

"It's a date."

Ramona squeezed my hand at the door and kissed me again.

My phone whistled as I walked to my car. The text from Uncle Felix announced

Results are in. No joy.

I called him. "Felix, what'cha got?"

"Nothing, *gringo*—nada, zilch, bupkis, zero. She's never been arrested in Mexico City."

"What about outside the city? Don't you have a national fingerprint network like our AFIS?"

"Theoretically, but it's incomplete. Smaller cities don't have the budget to integrate with the database. Are you sure she's from Mexico?"

"She tries to disguise her accent, but I can tell you, she's as Mexican as you are."

"Well, *gringo*, we bring additional cities online to the database all the time. I'll check again next week."

"Thanks, Felix."

I returned to the Pennington Park recycle bin. I had twisted Ramona's bottle into a spiral before I tossed it in. It stood out like a corkscrew among knitting needles. Now I had DNA samples for both mother and daughter.

I drove to the lab and dropped off their samples and the one for Ramon Gomez.

Midafternoon, I rapped on Teresa's door. "Hey, gorgeous. You look good enough to eat, like a vanilla ice cream cone."

"You don't eat ice cream, you lick it."

"I stand corrected. You look good enough to lick."

"I'll hold you to that later." She put her hand through my arm as we walked to my car.

We drove to North Beach—Terry's favorite. She had no tan lines above her waist and, trained observer that I am, I figured she frequented our local topless beach.

Terry piled her blouse and shorts on her sandals on a corner of our blanket. Then dropped her top on the pile of clothes. *Oh, my.* She stretched her arms overhead and twisted one way and the other as if stretching before a golf shot. She touched her toes and peeked sideways through her sunglasses. "Are you staring at my boobs?"

"I am a trained investigator; it's my job to notice everything. One never knows where one will find a valuable clue." I tossed my shirt and shorts onto my own sandals.

"Are my boobs a clue?"

"You bet. I plan to study your boobs thoroughly."

She wiggled her shoulders. "See that? They're too small."

"*Au contraire, ma petite.* A wise Frenchman once said 'More than a mouthful is wasted.' I would say yours are the queens of boobs." I watched with interest as she applied sunscreen.

We spent a pleasant few hours dozing, chatting, and watching sea birds and beach people. When the shadows reached us, Terry put on her top and we climbed the wooden stairs to the Thirsty Marlin, a thatched roof bar/restaurant overlooking the beach.

Terry ordered a margarita; I had iced coffee. When our drinks came, I raised mine in a toast. "To the queens."

"And the king." Terry reached under the table to pat my groin.

I put my coffee down and placed both hands on hers. "Terry, are we a couple?"

"A couple of what?"

I groped for the right adjective. "A couple in a relationship. You know, as in Chuck-and-Terry."

"You mean Terry-and-Chuck." She grinned.

"Whatever. Are we a couple?"

"Do you want us to be?"

"Yes."

"What brought that up now?"

"Our love making is terrific, Terry. But, in the long run, I want something more serious and exclusive."

She pursed her lips in thought. Then she squeezed my hands. "Chuck, do you remember that old Cyndi Lauper song from the 80s, 'Girls Just Want to Have Fun'?"

"One of my favorites."

"That song could have been written about me. I want to have fun. Let's compare you and me. You have lived on your own since high school, right?"

"My parents offered to send me to college when I graduated."

She waved me off. "But you didn't accept their offer. You joined the Army, for God's sake. You fought bad guys in Iraq and Afghanistan. Then you used your Army benefits to put yourself through college. No money from Mom and Dad."

"Almost true. Mom and Dad covered everything the Army didn't, so I didn't have any student loans."

"Money isn't the point; it's independence. My parents saved for my college from the time I was born. They paid for the whole nine yards. I depended on them the whole time. See the difference?"

"Right."

"Then you went to Iraq and Afghanistan. The one foreign country I have seen is a little piece of Canada when we took a vacation at Niagara Falls."

"What about the Bahamas?"

"I've never been."

I gestured to her straw beach bag with *Nassau Bahamas* on it. "That is what we professional sleuths call a clue."

"Found it at a garage sale."

"Oops. Anyway, you say you've lived a sheltered life?"

"Sort of. You have been out of the nest for years. How much did you change in the Army? Were you the same kid that graduated Theodore Roosevelt High School?"

"No, I was different after basic training and even more so after Iraq and Afghanistan."

"And what about college? Did that change you?"

"I came back from Afghanistan with a pretty grim view of mankind. College reminded me that people can be civilized."

She put a hand on mine. "Chuck, you saw college through adult eyes instead of schoolboy eyes. You have had a decade to live as an adult. I've lived independently for one year. You are more..." she searched for the right word "...fully formed than I am."

"In my expert opinion, you are the most fully-formed woman on the beach."

She smiled politely. "I appreciate the compliment, but the point is that you know yourself better than I do. I don't know who I'll be in two or three years. I'm a work-in-progress. See my point?"

"I see both your points."

Terry snickered. "Oh, you really are a male, chauvinist pig. I can't tell if you're joking or serious."

"Neither can I."

She shrugged. "I'm serious...maybe too serious."

"Babe, I concede your point; you wouldn't feel right making a commitment because you don't who you'll in a year or two."

"Right. Hell, I might decide to move to Wyoming just for a change. I can be pretty wild."

I grinned. "Tell me about it."

"For now, let's see where this goes." She sipped her margarita, then she winked. "Right now, I hope it goes back to my place."

"Instead of dinner?"

"We can eat later. And I have something that reminded you of an ice-cream cone you can lick for dessert."

I held up a hand and waved for our server. "Check please."

EIGHT

I convinced myself that lunching with Ramona, I might learn something to break the case. The fact that she looked as hot as a new frying pan was merely coincidental. Okay, not really.

I had left Terry's earlier that morning after a goodbye that curled my toes and straightened other parts of my body. I recover quickly though, so I could do justice to Ramona should the occasion demand it. Anything for the cause.

I parked the Avanti in front of Ramona's at 12:55. I took the steps two at a time with my beach bag and rang the bell. I heard the familiar Westminster chimes from the inside.

Seconds later, Ramona opened the door wearing a pink and white tropical silk ensemble. She struck a pose and did a model's pirouette. The pink sarong was decorated with hibiscus flowers embroidered in shades of pink and gold. The sarong hung so low on her hips that it defied gravity. Gold sandals peeked from under her sarong. Her fingernails and toenails were the same pink as the sarong. The sheer white halter top had two matching hibiscus flowers embroidered strategically over the breasts. It was definitely not designed to wear on a public beach unless it was a nude beach.

"You look so lovely that you brighten even a sunny day." I had rehearsed that line on the way over.

She gestured me inside and closed the door. "I gave Howley the day off, the cook is in the kitchen, and Gloria is with the babysitter." She stood on tiptoes as she leaned into me and kissed me softly on the lips, her breasts pressed firmly against my ribs. It was more than a social greeting.

She grabbed my hand and led me across the polished marble floor to the French doors standing open across the foyer. We stepped onto a wide marble loggia overlooking the pool and fountains.

Four deck jets spouted majestically from each side of the forty-foot pool and met in the center. A three-tiered waterfall fountain highlighted the deep end and flowed into the sparkling water. A dozen chaises awaited us around the pool, waiting for a party to break out. An assortment of bougainvilleas in half a dozen colors decorated the grounds behind the fountain.

Ramona led me by the hand to the curved marble stairs down to the pool deck. A green and white striped awning sheltered three white wrought-iron tables with glass tops and matching chairs. The last table would seat four but was set for two. Ramona led me to the matching wheeled serving cart with a pitcher and two stemmed glasses. "I made a pitcher of Bloody Marys. Would you like one, Carlitos?"

"I'd be a fool not to." I set my beach bag on the deck.

Ramona leaned far over the serving cart to grab the pitcher and made sure to show me she was naked beneath the halter top. As she sat on the wrought-iron chair, her sarong draped open and revealed her bare, tanned legs. She kicked off her sandals and crossed her legs in my direction, which hiked her sarong so high it was illegal in most Middle Eastern countries.

We worked our way through the Bloody Marys with Ramona doing most of the work. I sipped sparingly, both because I would have to drive later but also because I might be called upon to pay for lunch by servicing the hostess. It was a tough job, but someone had to do it.

Ramona flirted and pumped me for information. The conversation was like a tennis match: I lobbed a subject over the net, and she changed it to me and hit it back.

"Carlitos, tell me more about yourself. What do you do in Chile?"

"There's not much to tell. I'm developing a new copper mine in the Andes. I have forty men working way back in the jungle. It's forty kilometers to the nearest town. Did you and Sam see much of the Andes on your honeymoon?"

"No, we stayed at lower altitudes because of Sam's heart. I see that you don't wear a wedding ring. Have you ever been married?" She refilled her glass and added a quarter-inch to mine.

"I haven't found the right woman. With my travel schedule, it's difficult to maintain a relationship. How did you and Sam meet?"

"A mutual friend introduced us. Do you have a home here in Port City?"

The conversation whipped back and forth with her drinking and me pretending to sip my Bloody Mary. My stomach growled. Was the cook really in the kitchen preparing lunch?

"No, I borrowed the home of a friend who is in Europe for the summer. Did you and Sam ever get to visit your hometown in Spain?"

Before Ramona could answer, the cook appeared with a serving tray that held two large quesadillas and assorted toppings.

"Thank you, Melissa. Make us another pitcher of Bloody Marys, then take the rest of the day off."

"Yes, ma'am."

Ramona refilled her glass, added another quarter-inch to mine and served the quesadillas, leaning farther over the table than necessary. *Wow.*

Throughout lunch, Ramona took every opportunity to touch my

hand when she spoke. Her bare legs were completely visible through the glass tabletop. "Carlitos, I can see that it must be hard to have a girlfriend when you spend so much time in the wilderness."

"I go for days with no one to talk to but the other miners."

She poured the last of the first Bloody Mary pitcher into her glass. Her words came a little slower and she seemed to concentrate when she spoke. No wonder; she had polished off three-quarters of a pitcher of Blood Marys.

"You must get lonely."

"I stay pretty busy."

"But don't you get *lonely* lonely?" She winked at me.

Any fool could see where this was leading. "Of course, lovely lady." Sigh. Poor lonely mining mogul.

Melissa delivered the next Bloody Mary pitcher and silently disappeared, telling Ramona that she would see her tomorrow.

Ramona refilled her glass, ignoring my nearly-full glass this time. "When I said that Gloria was with the babysitter, I meant that I took her to the babysitter's house." She placed her hand on mine and swung her legs out from under the table. She pointed her perfect knees in my direction. She blotted her mouth with the linen napkin, careful not to smear her lipstick. "Carlitos, it was fate that I met you here. I too am lonely since Sam died. I've lived like a nun. I love Gloria so, but I have no social life. Perhaps you could take me dancing sometime?"

Ramona was checking me out as her next rich husband, but I figured she really was lonely too. I hadn't come here to get laid necessarily, although that seemed likely, but I did want to become her next targeted husband. "I would love to. Perhaps in a couple of weeks?"

"What about tonight?"

I smiled sadly. "Tonight I have a meeting. People are flying from Mexico City to meet with me at the airport. I can't cancel it."

"Oh, well. I'll take you when I can get you. Now," she stood up abruptly and swayed a little, "let's go for a swim." She held both hands out.

I grabbed her hands as I stood. "Where can I change into my swimsuit?"

She pulled my arms around her waist. She stepped into me and pressed her breasts against my ribs. She raised her lips to my face as she released my hands and wrapped her arms around my neck.

Her kiss was very soft, very wet, and very long. Then I repaid her kiss with one of my own.

She stepped back and grinned. "Who said anything about swimsuits?"

She unfastened her halter top, slipped it over her head, and dropped it on the deck. She reached to her waist and the sarong surrendered to gravity and dropped to the deck.

"I prefer to swim like this. I hope you will join me."

I bowed to the inevitable.

I called Uncle Felix. "I need another favor."

"Sure, *gringo*, whose car you want me to steal?"

"I have more fingerprints for you. At least two sets from a beer bottle. One set is from a waiter. I don't care about him, but you may have to run him through AFIS in the USA to eliminate his prints. The other set is from a man named Ramon Gomez. He's in his fifties or sixties. He may have been born in July."

"Any connection between this guy and the lady you asked about last week?"

"Ramon may be her father. I ordered a DNA test. I'll let you know when I get results. If she doesn't have a record, maybe he does. Okay if I email them to your personal account again?"

"Sure, *gringo*. I'll check them tonight."

I took up my post on Ramona's street again. If she was seeing Mateo, I hoped to catch them together. Sam's death had ended the fidelity clause, but proof that she had a romantic relationship with Mateo could help persuade a jury if the paternity case ever came to trial.

After the nanny arrived, I followed Ramona on another day of lunch at a charity fashion show, shopping at another pricey mall, and visiting the Wessington Club. At 5:50 Ramona arrived back home. I was off duty.

I love to check the mail. It's like a treasure hunt when I get a check from a client. Today it paid off. I made a bank deposit with my cellphone app and paid bills online.

Now that I had done the merely urgent stuff, I worked on more important matters. I listed what I knew and what I needed to know.

Then I made a time line:

- April two years ago, Ramona's Social Security number issued in California
- June 1 two years ago, Ramona rents a waterfront condo
- June 4 two years ago, Ramona pays deposit for Ramon Gomez's apartment
- June ?? two years ago, Ramona meets Sam at Wessington Club
- October 20 two years ago, Ramona and Sam marry
- June 30 last year, Sam goes into hospital.

- July, maybe August? last year, Ramona
  learns she is pregnant?
- September 27 last year, Cleveland house
  fire.

I underlined *Cleveland house fire.* I stared at it, then continued writing.

- November 6, last year, Sam dies
- Thanksgiving, last year, Ramona tells Ike
  and Lorraine she's pregnant
- April 5, this year, Gloria is born

Some facts created more questions. What was Ramona doing in California? When did Ramona join the Wessington Club, and who introduced her to Sam? Did they set Sam up? When did Ramona learn she was pregnant? When did she stop seeing Mateo? He claimed it was last year. Perhaps that was because Ramona got pregnant and didn't need him anymore.

I called Snoop Snopolski. "Hey, Snoop, how about lunch at Florentino's?"

"Before I check my appointment book, who's buying?" Snoop never says no to a free meal.

"I'm buying."

"I'm available."

Raymond Snopolski had been a Port City police detective for over thirty years. Everybody called him Snoop. The nickname fit him. He could spend two minutes at a crime scene and remember every clue, and he could shoot the eye of a fly at thirty yards. When Snoop's partner was killed, Snoop's wife Janet took it hard. She insisted the job was too dangerous.

Snoop became my partner. Actually, I was his partner. Snoop taught me more about being a detective in the year I spent with him than I learned in the police academy or during the years I studied criminology at the University of Florida.

It took her a year, but Janet convinced him to take early retirement. He got a PI's license more to have something to do than for the money. Janet still worked as an office manager for a construction company. Snoop did field work for lawyers, and I hired him for surveillance and legwork. If I needed backup, I called Snoop.

I never met a better cop nor a better mentor. I relied on him more than people realized. I was still green, and he was often the brains behind my brawn and balls.

Snoop sauntered into Florentino's six minutes after noon. He saw me wave. I shook his hand as he sat.

Snoop held his palm a foot over the table. "I want a draft beer this tall and Boy Wonder will have unsweetened ice tea," he told the server. His idea of exercise was to lift a beer mug with one hand.

I waited for the server to leave. "Snoop, I want to hash this thing over with you. See what I've missed."

"Sure, bud, hit me."

I pulled out my notes and listed the people who could have been involved in the fire or Ramona's fake identity or Gloria's paternity. "The deaths of Ike's stepmother and his half-sisters were convenient for both Ike and Gloria. What do you think?"

Snoop sipped his beer. "Gloria's a little young to be planning murders. The timing is suspicious. They died pretty soon after Ramona would have found out she was pregnant. But Ike says he didn't know Ramona was pregnant?"

"Yeah, Ramona told him and Lorraine that she was pregnant last Thanksgiving." I went to the next item on my list. "Ramona first appeared in the United States two months before meeting Sam. Where did she come from, and what was her background?"

"One way to check would be to find which Social Security office issued her card and then go to that town and show her picture around at hotels, bars, and so forth. But it's been two years, and you got two chances of finding anyone who would remember her—slim and none. What else you got?"

"She's never had a job. She must have been wealthy before she met Sam because she maintained an affluent lifestyle while she chased him. She told Ike and Lorraine that she inherited her money from her father, a wealthy Spanish nobleman. That's bullshit, because there's nothing about that on the internet. Where did her money come from?"

"Where does she bank? You could trace her deposits. Probably take a court order or a good hacker."

"Ike's PA can find out where Ramona banks. The estate sends her a monthly allowance, and they would know where she deposits the checks. I have her passwords. I'll have Flamer get all the data." I made another note.

Snoop grunted and took a bite of his Fettuccini Alfredo. "Of course, Ramona might not have banked there two years ago. She might have had an account in California."

I sampled my ravioli. "Yeah, but I gotta start somewhere."

"If Ramona changed banks, you could check when she opened the account and see if she opened it by a transfer from her old account. Then you could check out her old account."

"I didn't think of that."

He grinned. "That's why you have me—to teach you stuff. If you made a list of all the mistakes it's possible to make as a detective, I have worked my way two-thirds of the way down the list. But each mistake teaches you something. The more mistakes, the more you learn. *¿Comprende?*"

"Ramona was screwing her tennis pro, but he told me she dumped him ten months ago. Why did she start the affair? And why did she stop?"

"You already know that one," Snoop said. "She screwed him to get pregnant and stopped when she had a bun in the oven. Was there any other reason to take up with him? Was it just to get pregnant? Or maybe her husband couldn't hoist the sail, and she screwed the pro for fun— pregnancy an unplanned side effect."

"It's a moot point. She did have the affair, and she did get pregnant. Did Ramona know the terms of Sam's will? If she did, she had a motive to get pregnant."

Snoop shook his head. "*Nah*. She didn't need to know the terms of his will. Anybody knows that a baby will be included in a dead parent's estate."

"Yeah, that's right. In addition to Ramona's personal $30,000,000, her baby would inherit over a $100,000,000 and Ramona would be her guardian. And, if something happened to Sam's daughters, Ramona's baby would inherit an extra $100,000,000."

"You gotta check out the half-sisters' deaths. But, if Ramona had them killed, why didn't she go after Ike too? Then her baby would inherit the whole estate."

"Maybe she did go after him and failed. I'll ask Ike if anything suspicious happened to him around the time Allison and her daughters died." Another notation.

I reviewed my list of questions. "Ramona visits Ramon Gomez every week and brings take-out pizza. What is her relationship to Ramon? I have ordered DNA tests. I'll have results in a few days."

Snoop read his notes. "I've been tailing Gomez like you asked. He's an electrician at the Humbolt Tower they're building in Humbolt Springs. He spends several nights a week at El Rodeo. It's his second home. He likes Corona even more than I do. He was back at El Rodeo on Friday, Sunday, and last night. He drinks beer and watches Mexican *futbol*. Saturday night he took a woman to a country music nightclub and back to his apartment. I'll stay on him when he gets off work this afternoon."

"Don't bother. I know all I need to know about him until I get the DNA results."

Back in my car, I reviewed my list.

Dennis Howley—I needed to interview him. I called Tom Collins to set it up. I reminded Collins that Howley knew me as Carlos Calderone.

I peered in my mirror before I backed out. A dark blue Nissan Altima with two men in it lurked at the end of the lot. If I hate anything, it's a car that lurks. As I drove to Jerry's Gym, the blue Altima stayed three cars behind me. The Altima had followed me from my office to Florentino's earlier. I pulled into Jerry's parking lot, and the Altima continued down the street. Dried mud obscured its license plate.

I decided the next time I saw the Altima, I would turn the tables and follow it.

After my workout, I ran ten miles in the neighborhood surrounding the gym while I watched for the Altima or anything else out of the ordinary. The Altima was a no-show. I showered, changed, and fired a box of shells at the shooting range. Then I visited Dennis Howley.

The Howleys lived in Wekita Springs, a middle-class Port City suburb. If you looked up *suburbia* in the dictionary, you would find a picture of Wekita Springs. Neat streets, neat houses, neat gardens.

I parked the Avanti in front of their well-trimmed lawn. The two-story house was painted pale lavender with darker trim and shutters. Plumbago hedges separated the spotless flower beds from the house. As I climbed the porch steps, the door opened and Dennis extended his hand. "Mr. Calderone, we have been expecting you. Please come in."

"Thank you, Howley. Now that you're off duty, can you call me Chuck?"

He laughed. "Of course, Chuck. And I'm Dennis. Can I get you something to drink?"

As we entered from the foyer, a slim, middle-aged woman with salt-and-pepper hair walked into the living room. "Ah, here's my wife now."

Dennis stretched a hand toward her. "Margaret, I should like to introduce Carlos Calderone, a friend of Ms. Ramona."

Her smile froze, partly-formed, and she stopped dead still, her hand half raised.

"He is also a friend of Mr. Sam and Mr. Ike."

The wife's smile resumed, and she shook my hand. "Welcome, Chuck. Any friend of Mr. Sam's is a friend of ours. I poured Dennis and me a sherry; can I get you something?" She had the same British accent as Howley.

"Thank you, Mrs. Howley. Anything non-alcoholic. I'm driving."

"It's Maggie for my friends. Coffee okay? How do you take it?"

I told her and she left.

"Dennis, did Tom Collins tell you why I wanted to talk to you?"

"He told me you would visit and said Mr. Ike wanted me to cooperate." He raised one eyebrow. "You know that I don't work for Ms. Ramona, right?"

"No, I didn't know that. And, if I read Maggie's reaction right, your wife doesn't care for her, does she?"

"Nor do I."

"So, who do you work for?"

"I worked for Mr. Sam for twelve years, and now I work for Mr. Sam's estate. My duty is to care for the house—not Ms. Ramona. Ms. Ramona assumes I work for her. Until now, the distinction has been moot. Since I do not work for Ms. Ramona, I have no duty of loyalty to her."

"And that means…?"

His lips lifted at the ends in a faint smile. How very British of him. "Since Mr. Sam's untimely passing, my duty is now to his estate and to

Mr. Ike, as executor. And since Mr. Ike asked me to cooperate with you, I take it your interest in Ms. Ramona is more than social."

"In fact, Dennis, I have no social interest in Ramona at all."

Howley's eyes narrowed. "*Hmm.* How may I help you?"

"Was Ramona having an affair while Sam was alive?"

"I take it from your question that you're a private detective engaged by Mr. Ike?"

"Technically, detectives are sworn police officers; I'm a licensed private investigator. And because of my 'duty of loyalty' as you put it, I can't tell you any more than that or even confirm who my client is."

"No matter. If I were a betting man, I would bet that your client is, in fact, Mr. Ike, and that he has engaged you to discover the identity of Gloria's true biological father."

"I can neither confirm nor deny that."

"I understand. As to whether Ms. Ramona had an affair, I have my suspicions, but I have no proof."

"What suspicions?"

"She took a lot of tennis lessons, and one time she invited the tennis pro to lunch at the house. Nothing untoward happened in my presence, but I saw a look pass between them, and they did disappear before I left the house to run errands. When I returned two hours later, the tennis pro had left. However, I get off around 5:00 or 5:30 each day, so I don't know what she does at night."

A few more questions yielded nothing else useful. I declined Maggie Howley's invitation for dinner and left for home.

The sun had sunk low on the horizon. It flashed in my rearview mirrors as I turned into my driveway.

Bra-a-ap, Bra-a-ap.

Automatic gunfire raked the Avanti. My rear window exploded simultaneously with my front windshield.

I jerked open the door and dove from the moving car. I pulled my Glock as I rolled toward the boxwood hedge between the street and the driveway. The bushes wouldn't stop a bullet, but they would hide me from view. I squeezed off four rounds as the Altima sped down the street, tires screeching and burning rubber. The waning light made the license plate unreadable, even without the caked-on mud.

I sprinted into the street and aimed at the rear of the speeding car. *Damn. Oncoming traffic and two pedestrians in the field of fire.* I was forced to lower my weapon.

I heard my Avanti crash behind me. It had plowed into the garage door and come to a halt against the bent aluminum panels. Somehow, it had missed the concrete block walls on either side.

When I holstered the Glock, my hand felt funny. Blood dripped from my skinned palm, knuckles, and elbows. I stared at the shredded, bloody knees of my pants and the torn sleeves of my shirt and jacket. I shook my head, trying to clear my blurry vision.

Days before, I had told Terry that I had never fired my weapon on the job, and I hoped I never would. Now, I had been in my first civilian gunfight.

I was shot at in Iraq and Afghanistan, but I had body armor and a team of Green Berets with me, and I expected bad guys to shoot at me. Here I was caught alone by an enemy I should have expected but didn't. I had been a split second from dead. It was a stupid rookie mistake.

After I called 9-1-1, my breath was ragged and my hand shook from the adrenaline coursing through my bloodstream.

My body shuddered like an earthquake. I staggered toward my front door, leaned against the wall, and vomited in the flower bed beside the steps. I wiped my mouth on the back of my hand and took deep breaths as I waited for my heart rate to return to normal.

While I waited for the police, I disinfected the cuts and applied salve. There was nothing I could do for the shredded slacks or my dress shirt and jacket. They were so bad that I couldn't even give them to a homeless shelter.

The police finished their reports at midnight.

I went to bed but tossed and twisted all night, wondering who wanted me dead. And why.

NINE

D r. Virgil Norris peered at me through tortoise-shell glasses. He started to shake hands when he noticed the bandage. "What happened to your hand?"

"Some men shot at me last night, and I took a dive on the pavement to escape. They missed, but I got skinned up." I didn't want a conversation about the shooting, so I changed the subject. "Did Ike Simonetti's assistant call you before I came in?"

"Please sit down, Mr. McCrary."

I sat across the desk from him.

"Yes, he called. He said you had questions about Sam Simonetti and wanted a DNA sample. Something about the paternity of a baby born after Sam died. Did I get that right?"

"Yes, sir. Do you have a DNA sample from Sam?"

Norris browsed the file on his desk. "Sam died last year. I remember signing his death certificate. But we wouldn't have his DNA."

"Have you retained any blood or urine samples?"

Norris shook his head. "Those go to the lab as soon as they're drawn. We don't keep them. The ones drawn at the hospital go to the hospital lab. Have you contacted them?"

"No, sir. I wanted to ask you first. Whom should I see at the hospital?"

"Harriet Chrysler in the hospital lab. I'll tell her you're coming." He grabbed his telephone, consulted an old-fashioned Rolodex, and punched in the number.

He leaned back in his chair and cradled the phone to his ear. "Harriet, Virgil Norris here. How are you, beautiful?" He listened for a minute. "Listen, Harriett, I have a detective here who needs DNA from one of my deceased patients, Sam Simonetti."

He shook his head. "No, no. It's not that kind of investigation; they need his DNA for a paternity test. The patient died six months ago."

Norris listened for a while. "I thought y'all might have a blood sample in the freezer."

He listened. "Okay, Harriett. G'bye."

He replaced the phone. "Harriet and I go back thirty years. She can get you anything they have. What else can I do for you?"

"You told her I'm a detective, but I'm a private investigator, not a police detective."

"I know that, and you know that. But it won't hurt if she thinks you're a cop. Don't correct her. *Capisce?*"

"*Capisce.*"

"Anything else you need?"

"Sam's widow, Ramona, had a baby four months after his death. Naturally, she listed Sam as the father on the birth certificate. Ike's wife, who is an MD, thinks someone else fathered the baby. What is your professional opinion?"

Norris thumbed through the folder without reading it. I think it was a reflex action. "Theoretically, Sam could father a child even at his age, but since his heart attack, he was virtually impotent. Partly that was a side effect of his heart medication, but also his age. We spoke about it before he got married. I gave him an erectile dysfunction drug prescription for thirty pills and told him he could use one a week. They married two weeks later, and I gave him another physical before the wedding. They planned to honeymoon in South America, and he wanted to visit Machu Pichu."

"What's the altitude there?"

"I looked it up; it's 8,000 feet. I told him not to go above 5,000. His heart wouldn't take it."

"They took a cruise around South America instead."

"I'm glad he listened to me. If he remained in good health, I figured his first ED prescription would last him six months. Did you check if any of the ED drug was left? That could be a clue."

"Good idea, Doc."

"Anything else I can help you with?"

"No, sir." We shook hands. "Thanks for your help."

———

At Port City Regional Medical Center, a hefty, gray-haired woman in hospital scrubs pushed through the door. "I'm Harriet Chrysler, but you can call me Harry." She noticed my bandaged hand. "What happened to your hand?"

"Occupational hazard. I skinned it in a scuffle with a couple of thugs." That was almost true.

"Virgil said you wanted a DNA sample from Sam Simonetti."

"Yes, ma'am. By the way, I noticed Doctor Norris refers to you as Harriet."

"Virgil's old school. He thinks girls should have girls' names. We have a nurse nicknamed Alex and Virgil always calls her Alexandra.

"Anyway, about that DNA, I checked and we don't have any blood samples. Sorry."

"What about urine?"

"Urine doesn't contain DNA, even if we did have some, which we don't."

"Well, it was worth a try. You have anything else that could have Sam's DNA? Anything from the autopsy?"

"There was no autopsy."

"No autopsy? Isn't that required?" Every murder case I had worked as a Port City detective, there had been an autopsy for me to review.

"Common misconception. The law requires an autopsy for unexplained or accidental deaths or where a crime is suspected. Doctor Norris was Simonetti's attending physician. He determined the cause of death, and he signed the death certificate. No autopsy required."

Wallace had told me there was no autopsy, but it never hurts to double-check. Rule Twelve: *People lie. If they don't lie, they can be mistaken.*

Before I climbed into bed, my phone played "Old McDonald Had a Farm."

"Hey, Grandpa. I'm okay. They missed."

"You know how I worry, Chuck."

"Thanks, Grandpa, but I'm fine. Skinned knees, elbows, and a scraped knuckle from hitting the pavement."

"How's the Ghost?"

My grandfather Magnus McCrary had named my Avanti the Silver Ghost back in the days when it had a Citizens Band radio. He bought it second-hand when he mustered out of the Army in the 1960s. He still owned it when I graduated from college. He gave me the Ghost as a graduation present.

"The Ghost was shot up pretty bad, Grandpa. But my classic car guy is fixing her good as new."

"At least you're okay. I love you, Grandson. You know that I want more great-grandchildren. I'm counting on you, and if you get yourself killed, those plans go out the window, right?" He laughed to show he wasn't serious, but I knew that his jokes masked real fear.

"I know, Grandpa. You'll have more great-grandchildren, I promise."

"I got through Viet Nam with two Purple Hearts. You weren't so lucky in Iraq and Afghanistan. Don't get yourself killed, you hear? That could ruin my whole day."

"It wouldn't do much for my day either. Don't worry; I'll be sure to duck. Give my love to Grandma."

At the North Shore Precinct, I stood in the door to Lieutenant Weiner's office until she waved me in.

She put down the phone and side-stepped around her desk for a hug. She slipped into her Jewish mother persona, which was easy to do because she was, in fact, a Jewish mother. "Carlos McCrary. So, where have you been? You never call; you never write. You could be dead, and I wouldn't know, unless I read the police reports about a certain drive-by shooting."

"Mother, I would have called yesterday, but I knew I'd see you today. And I took you to lunch last month."

She gave me a come-on gesture. "Let's hear it, *boychik*."

I told her the little I knew, that the car followed me and I had no license number. "I got off four rounds and I hit the car once or twice."

"Yeah, I talked to the detective in charge of the investigation. He's checking auto repair shops for an Altima with bullet holes."

"I would bet a steak dinner to a French fry that the car is at the bottom of a canal by now."

"Probably," she said, "but you didn't come here to tell me that. What do you need?"

"I have three sets of fingerprints I want you to run." I held out the contact sheets for Ramona Simonetti, Ramon Gomez, and the waiter at El Rodeo.

She didn't take them. "Are these connected with the shooting?"

"Maybe."

She took the sheets. "What's the case? Is there any crime here? Or are you chasing another wayward husband?" She fixed me with her *hard cop* look.

"Mother, there may be a crime. It may involve fraud and there may be three murders in Cleveland." *Or not.*

That got her attention. She pulled a note pad from her desk drawer. "Talk to me."

"Off the record?"

"You know the rules, Chuck. If there's an unreported crime or a crime about to be committed, the answer is no. If lives or property are in danger, the answer is no. You have to trust my judgment. Remember: You're the one who wants a favor. I am but a mere public servant sworn to serve and protect." She bowed with fake modesty—not easy to do while sitting.

I told her everything I knew and most of what I suspected. At the end, she picked up the contact sheets. "I'll see what I can do, *bubalah.*" She wrote a note and paperclipped it to the contact sheets, which she placed in her "out" box.

She leaned back in her chair. "Terry Kovacs tells me she's dating you. That *shiksa* has the hots for you real bad. You could do a lot worse. One thing, though, I guess you know she's a little wild?"

I shrugged.

"Terry's sown her wild oats around the department—nothing that violates the chain of command, you understand. I warned her about that and she's been good. At least she's stayed away from the married ones. Overall, she's a good patrol cop for a rookie; she's coming along fine. She has a good mind. She'll be marriage material someday *if* she settles down. Listen to an old *yenta*: Don't give up on this one. Be patient, and don't let her get away."

"So far, so good, Mother. But she wants to take it slow. I suggested an exclusive relationship and she passed; said she wasn't ready. But I see her again tomorrow night."

"She's kind of 'girls just want to have fun,' you know what I mean, *bubalah*?"

"That's exactly what she told me, Mother."

"I'm not surprised she wouldn't go steady. But keep after her."

"People don't go steady any more. We say that we're in a relationship."

"Relationship, huh? It's still going steady if you ask me."

The next day Lieutenant Weiner texted:

Come see me.

When I walked into her office, she handed me a folder. "The first prints we got nothing on. She doesn't have a record."

"That's Ramona Gamez Simonetti," I said. "One of the other two prints is the waiter and one is the guy I think is her father."

"The waiter had a DUI twelve years ago, nothing since. Here's the rap sheet on Ramon Gomez." She pushed it across the desk. "He was arrested twice in La Jolla, California for burglary five and eight years ago. First time, he copped a plea in exchange for community service and probation. Second time, the assistant DA dropped it because of an evidence issue. They also collared him three times for suspicion of arson, also in La Jolla, all from five to nine years ago. Didn't you mention something about a house fire in Cleveland?"

"Yeah," I answered. "That's the three possible murders I told you about yesterday."

"Ramon's lived in Port City the last couple of years. How does this fit with your other info?" she asked.

"I don't know how the fire in Cleveland started. The fire investigators didn't treat it as suspicious at the time. But I'm going to Cleveland on Monday."

TEN

Before leaving the Cleveland airport, I called the head of fire investigations. "Captain, this is Chuck McCrary from Port City."

"Yeah, Chuck. Lieutenant Weiner from the PCPD called. I have been expecting you."

"Captain, can we see you this afternoon? We're investigating a suspicious death in Port City and it may be connected to a fire here in Cleveland."

"I'm tied up the rest of the afternoon. How about tomorrow morning at 10:30?"

"Thanks Captain, we'll be there."

He gave me directions.

A little before sunset, a shiny new chocolate brown Escalade with orange trim pulled to the hotel curb in front of us. Cleveland Browns colors.

Snoop did a double take when he saw the driver get out. "You're Bob Martinez."

"You must be Snoop. Pleased to meet you." Bob shook hands.

Snoop held onto his hand. "Bob Martinez, first round draft pick of the Cleveland Browns. MVP at the Super Bowl two years ago."

Bob had six inches, a hundred pounds, and thirty years on Snoop, but he couldn't get his hand free. "I see you keep up with your football." He tried to turn toward me again.

"Where do you know Chuck from, Bob?"

Bob finally pulled his hand away. "We played football together at Theodore Roosevelt High School. We won the Texas 3-A championship our senior year." He gave me a bear hug. "Eighty-eight, you're a big-time private eye now."

"Well, I'm a private eye. Not 'big time' yet."

Snoop smacked me on the shoulder with the back of his hand. "You never told me you knew Bob Martinez."

"He's taking us out to dinner. I wanted to surprise you."

"Well, you sure as hell did."

I awoke to the sound of rain mixed with hail beating on my hotel window. It sounded like popcorn popping. Summertime on the Great Lakes.

Snoop and I grabbed a taxi to the Cleveland Department of Fire Investigations. The driver dropped us in front of the entrance and we sprinted through the rain. I shook my umbrella.

Snoop sneered. "Wimps carry umbrellas. I bet Bob Martinez doesn't even own an umbrella. Real men get wet."

"Then you're a real man, Snoop. Here, carry this until it dries." I handed him my umbrella and brushed off the droplets clinging to my pants. "At least I don't wear rubber overshoes."

"You would if they fit in your briefcase."

The receptionist directed us to Fire Captain Jake Crawford's glass-walled office. He was on the phone, but motioned us to come in and have a seat. "And do it ASAP. Get on it now." He hung up and reached across the desk, his hand extended. "I'm Jake Crawford. Which of you is McCrary?"

I shook his hand first. "I'm Chuck McCrary, Captain. This is my associate Raymond Snopolski. Ray's also a former Port City police detective consulting on this case."

"How can I help you gentlemen? Which case we talking about?"

I opened my briefcase and handed him a file. "September 27 of last year, three women died in a house fire at this address on Edgewater Drive."

He opened the file and read the address. He punched the intercom. "Susan? Could you bring me the file on the Montrose fire on Edgewater Drive from last September?"

Crawford read my thin file. "So, what can I do for you?"

"I suspect the fire was arson."

The captain leaned back in his chair. "By whom? And why?"

I told him about Ramona and Gloria and our suspicions about Gloria's paternity. I told him I suspected the fire had been set to kill at least two of the heirs.

"That's a serious accusation."

"It's a suspicion, Captain, not an accusation. We're here to find out if it's true."

"If it's arson, then your client and the baby had the most to gain. Wouldn't that make your client the prime suspect?"

"Yes, but he would be stupid to hire me if he did it. I think Ramona's father, the electrician, came here to arrange the fire that killed those women. With a house that old, the fire caused little suspicion. That's why I want to reopen the case."

Crawford's door opened and a woman brought in a file. "Here's the file on the Edgewater Drive investigation. You need anything else right now, Captain?"

"No, Susan, that's all. Thanks."

He flipped through the file. "The field inspector's notes say the ninety-year-old electrical panel in the basement shorted out. The wooden mounting box ignited and the fire spread to the wooden studs in the walls and the 2 x 10s supporting the floor above." He flipped another page. "Lacquer thinner and old newspapers stored in the basement acted as accelerants. Then the fire caught the heating oil tank and the whole shebang went up." He closed the file. "They didn't have a chance. Old house, no smoke detectors, no sprinkler system, wooden interior walls. A damned shame."

"Any chance the fire was deliberate?"

Crawford flipped through the file again. "Old houses like this are firetraps if they haven't been updated. Nowadays, fire code requires metal electrical panels, flame-resistant walls, and smoke detectors near every bedroom. We require fire-resistant storage for oil tanks." He tapped the file. "This house had none of that."

"So that made it worse?"

He leaned back in his chair. "In the 1920s, electrical wires were insulated with cloth treated with fire retardant. Ironically, the fire-retardant property wears off as the insulation ages and after forty or fifty years, cloth insulation becomes flammable."

He opened the file again. "But this lacquer thinner is suspicious. Without it, the fire would have spread slower and allowed the occupants time to get out. On the other hand, these old houses have all kinds of crap stored in basements and attics—old mattresses, photo albums, clothing. All those things fuel a fire."

"Captain," I asked, "what happened to the house after the fire? Has it been razed or repaired?"

"We require the owners to repair or clean up within six months. But we had budget cutbacks so our enforcement is piss-poor. It could still be sitting there. Who inherited the house?"

Snoop spoke up. "I did an online search and Allison Montrose Simonetti, the dead mother, is still listed as the owner. Apparently, none of her relatives have claimed it yet."

"In that case, maybe the house hasn't been touched since September."

"Can Snoop and I see the site of the fire?"

"Sure. I'll see if the investigator who prepared this report can go with you."

He made a phone call. "Sergeant Saunders will pick you up at 1:30 this afternoon. Gentlemen, I hate to leave you, but I have a lunch meeting."

He handed the file to me. "Study this before Saunders picks you up." He gestured to his left. "Take it to the conference room. Use our Wi-Fi if you need to check your emails or anything. Susan will provide a temporary password. Saunders will need the file, so give it to him this afternoon. If you want lunch, the receptionist can recommend places nearby. My favorite is Cocina Juanita." He grabbed his coat and led us to the conference room.

A tall black man in a navy-blue uniform stuck out his hand. "I'm Ted Saunders."

"Chuck McCrary. This is my associate, Raymond Snopolski."

Saunders shook our hands. "Cap'n asked me to show you folks the site of the Montrose fire."

"We appreciate your help," I said.

Snoop handed him the file.

"No problem. Let's take my car." He led us to the parking lot next door. I took the passenger seat; Snoop got in back.

Saunders checked the side mirror and pulled into the traffic. "You reviewed the file?"

"We read it before lunch."

As he threaded through traffic out to the lakefront neighborhoods, I filled him in on our suspicions. He, in turn, explained how they investigate fires.

Twenty minutes later, he turned onto Edgewater Drive. "The site's a mile down this way." We drove past large, waterfront estates on the left side of the street. The houses across from the lake were nice but not so grand.

Saunders pulled into the circular driveway of a burned-out mansion. "This is the Montrose house. I did a little research before I picked you up; the same family owned it for four generations."

He opened the trunk of the car and handed each of us a hard hat, shoe covers and gloves.

The front porch floorboards had collapsed and green shoots peeked through them, life rising from death. The house was a gutted shell, its once grand double entrance doors now blackened with smoke and soot and charred by the fire within.

We followed Saunders around back and donned hard hats, shoe covers, and gloves. He picked his way down the narrow basement steps to a door in the back wall of the mansion, reappeared a minute later at the bottom step, and waved a flashlight at us. "It's okay, but stay close."

We made our way down to the basement. The heat from the fire had blistered the paint on the door. "Look at that, Snoop. A skeleton lock." Any burglar with a room temperature IQ can pick one of those. Hell, a ten-year-old kid with a paper clip can pick one.

Snoop took pictures of both sides of the door.

Slivers of light from the early afternoon sun leaked through the burned boards of the floor above, piercing the gloom of the smoke-blackened basement. "This is the remnant of the oil tank." Saunders indicated the area with his flashlight beam. "And this is the electrical panel." He stepped over and studied it. "*Hmm*. That's funny."

"What?"

"The short that started the fire looks like the insulation failed on the old wiring. But if you study it…" He aimed his flashlight at the wire. "Is that an abrasion on the wire?"

I studied the spot where the wire fastened to the circuit breaker. The fire had deposited soot everywhere. Faint parallel lines on the copper indicated where a file could have scraped through the cloth insulation.

Saunders switched on the light on his hard hat and slipped the flashlight into a coat pocket to free both hands. He positioned the inspection file in the beam from the hat and flipped pages. He frowned. "Chuck, I am professionally embarrassed. At the time, everything pointed to this being an accident, so we didn't examine it as closely as we might have. I can't tell if it was arson, but it's possible. I need to reclassify the origin of this fire as suspicious."

"Ted, I'm no expert, but that abrasion looks easy to miss. If it was arson, how did the fire start?"

"Every fire has an ignition source and sometimes an accelerant. The ignition source can be a space heater, a match, or a Molotov cocktail. Or, in this case, an electrical short that caused an arc. See the spot on the breaker panel where it melted?"

"Yeah."

"That's where the current arced. Accelerants can be curtains, carpet, old newspapers, firewood—although firewood is harder to ignite than you think." Saunders pointed at the box. "The ignition source here was a spark from this frayed wire. The first accelerant could have been a rat's nest in the breaker box. The nest is gone now, burned up, but that looks like the remains of rat shit there. The spark created a flame. Yep." He pointed.

"I'll take your word for it. This is my first arson."

"As the nest burned, the pieces fell onto this can of lacquer thinner and caught like a torch. These screw-tops are always gummy from the residue of evaporated lacquer thinner. This magazine pile spread it to the oil tank." He shook his head. "Boom, the occupants didn't have a chance."

"No way for the women to escape?"

The light in the basement was dim, but I think his eyes were glistening. "Thank God, they never woke up. We found their bodies still in bed. Smoke inhalation."

There was an awkward silence. I remembered an IED in Iraq that hit a Humvee in the days before we got the armored ones. The gas tank made an orange and black mushroom cloud fifty yards in front of me. I remembered the fiery sensation on my face from the heat of the explosion. Four of my fellow Green Berets never had a chance. We never got justice for them. Maybe I could get justice for three women I would never meet.

I shook my head to clear the phantom image. "The spark happened when an appliance switched on?"

Saunders grunted. "Had to be that."

"What does this wire connect to?"

He scanned the floor with his flashlight. "There it is." He picked up the cover to the breaker panel and studied the diagram on its hinged door. "This breaker is position seven." He shined his light on the breaker cover. "The heat damaged the diagram; I can't read it. But this house has a knob and tube wiring system."

"What's that?"

"They used the knob and tube system until about 1930. The wires are exposed and wrapped around an insulated ceramic tube. Nowadays we use Romex inside walls or run exposed wires in conduit. See the wires wrapped around those exposed knobs up on the joists?"

He swept his flashlight beam along the blackened wire up to the exposed beams and followed it around a corner to the back of the basement. Snoop and I picked our way across the cluttered floor in his wake.

"There." He pointed the light. "The air handler for the furnace. After the insulation at the panel frayed, the next time the furnace came on, the breaker box arced and started the fire."

He walked back the way we had come. "This breaker box should have been grounded. I remember…this box's ground wire was loose. See it? The ground wire screw must have worked loose over the last ninety years."

The soot-blackened ground wire was bent to wrap around a screw, but the screw hole on the breaker panel was empty. "Could this ground have been disconnected on purpose? I don't see the ground screw."

Saunders studied it. "Yep. No ground screw. Someone removed it. Yep. This is arson. But whoever set this fire couldn't have known when the air handler would come on. It might have been days or weeks before it kicked on."

"So, this wire was sabotaged sometime before the fire. Then the arsonist hangs around until the furnace comes on so he knows that he's succeeded in starting the fire?"

Saunders scratched his head. "Yeah, but that doesn't make sense. A professional arsonist wants time to get to safety, but he also wants to make sure the fire starts. Unless he's a firebug, he doesn't hang around the site where someone could notice him. He uses a timing device to control when the blaze starts. Could be a fuse or a punk or a small paper fire to start a larger blaze. Yep. That gives him time to escape, but he knows right then whether the fire started. This method," he waved in the direction of the blackened hulk of the air handler, "leaves too much to chance."

The answer was obvious to me. "He wouldn't have to hang around. He could watch local TV news or buy a newspaper every day or simply drive by to see if it had burned. If you wanted to burn this house down and didn't care how soon it happened, would this method do it?"

"Yep."

"What's the weather like in Cleveland in late September? Do they run the furnace much?"

"September is funny. The highs run in the sixties and seventies, the lows in the fifties. But I once took my kids to the beach the last week in September. You never know."

"What about this house? Is it well insulated?"

"Oh, sure. This house is brownstone—good insulation. The furnace wouldn't come on every night until late autumn." Saunders referred to the file. "This thermostat was set to sixty-eight degrees. It might not turn the furnace on for days after the breaker box sabotage."

"Can you look up the hourly temperature readings for September 27th?"

"What good would that...oh, I get it."

Saunders spread the printout on the fire station conference table. "These are hourly temperatures for the two weeks before the fire."

I scanned them backwards from the twenty-seventh. "The cool snap on September nineteenth reached a low of forty-five degrees. The furnace came on that night, don't you think?"

Saunders studied the printout over my shoulder. "Yep, for sure."

"The sabotage was after September nineteenth." I continued scanning. "The lows were above sixty until September twenty-seventh when it dipped below fifty at 2:00 a.m. That's when the furnace would kick in. When was the fire reported?"

"2:34 a.m. We responded at 2:44 a.m. and the house was fully involved."

I tapped the printout. "We have our window for the arsonist—September twentieth to twenty-sixth."

Saunders led us into Captain Crawford's office. "Cap'n, we have an arson, sure as you're born." He outlined what we had found. "We need a team to go over the site with a fresh eye."

Crawford sighed. "Okay. It's your case, Ted. Keep me in the loop and keep McCrary in the loop too. Call him when you have anything to report."

Snoop and I went back to our hotel where we had checked our luggage that morning. "It's too late to get a flight to Port City today. Let's get a hotel near the airport. We'll catch an early flight tomorrow."

Snoop laid a hand on my arm. "We can't go home yet."

"Why not?"

"We haven't interviewed the family."

"To what purpose?"

"Chuck, who is the arsonist?"

"This is going to be one of your 'teaching moments,' isn't it?"

He laughed. "If you were a police detective and suspected arson, what would be your next move?"

"I already have a suspect—Ramon Gomez."

"And you know what the prosecutor would say if you stopped looking as soon as you had one suspect. I repeat: What would be your next move?"

"I would interview the family."

"And why would you do that?"

I smacked my forehead with the palm of my hand. "To see if there are any other suspects. Duh."

Westminster chimes sounded from behind the oak door. We waited. I was about to ring again when I felt the subtle vibrations of footsteps from inside.

A maid so old that she made both my grandmothers look like kids opened the door.

"I'm Carlos McCrary, and this is Raymond Snopolski. We have an appointment with Miss Yolanda Montrose." I handed her my card.

"She's expecting you. I'm Emma." She gestured us inside. "Before I take you to Miss Montrose, you need to know that she sometimes gets confused. She had a stroke last year, and it affected her memory. Sometimes, she's fine. Other times…" She shrugged. "That's why I live here full time."

"Thanks for telling us, Emma. We'll keep that in mind."

The decades had darkened the mahogany paneling in the sitting room. Yolanda Montrose sat in a chrome wheelchair with an Afghan over her lap and a knitted shawl around her shoulders even though the room must have been 80 degrees.

Emma handed her my business card.

Montrose stared at it like she didn't know what it was.

"Miss Montrose, I'm Chuck McCrary, and this is my associate, Raymond Snopolski. May we sit down?"

Montrose gestured vaguely in the direction of an over-stuffed burgundy couch from World War I, or maybe the Spanish-American War. Teddy Roosevelt would have looked at home on that couch.

"I'll get you tea," Emma said.

"Thank you." We sat.

"We would like to talk to you about your niece, Allison Simonetti."

"Allison's dead, you know."

"Yes, ma'am. That's why we're here. We want to find out what happened to her."

"Are you policemen?"

"No, ma'am, private investigators. We would like to ask you about Allison."

"If you're not policemen, why are you here?"

"Because we believe someone wanted to harm Allison and her daughters. We want to find out who did it."

She put her hand to her mouth. "You mean they were murdered?"

"Perhaps. That's what we want to determine."

She considered that. "What would you like to know?"

"How well did you know Allison?"

"She was my only family, you know—her and her daughters, Melinda and…" She waved a hand in the air, as if she could conjure up the name. It didn't work. "…the other one," she finished.

"Yes, ma'am. I understand that you don't have any children?"

"I never married. In my day, you had to be married to have children, you know. Not like today. Nowadays, nobody cares whether you're married or not."

"Did Allison have any other family?"

Montrose considered this. "She was married for a while. A fellow from Florida, I think. They divorced, you know."

"Yes, ma'am, we know. Did Allison have any other relatives?"

"Well, there was my brother Frank. He was her uncle, of course."

"And where does Frank live?"

She eyeballed me as if I were the stupidest person she had ever seen. "He doesn't live anywhere. He's dead, you know. He died last year—in California." Tears formed in her eyes.

Emma arrived with the tea. Snoop and I drank our tea while Yolanda Montrose composed herself. The hot tea and the hot room double-teamed me; I began to sweat beneath my suit jacket.

"Did Frank have any children?"

"Yes, he had children. They live out West. I get Christmas cards from them. Emma has their addresses."

She placed her teacup on the table beside her. "Allison and Melinda and Danielle burned to death, you know." Tears filled her eyes again. "In the prime of life, they were. Those girls had their whole lives in front of them. They were in college. Allison was young enough; she could have remarried. She was in her forties. She used to come see me every week. We had lunch on Sunday after church."

She faced the housekeeper. "Who would ever want to harm them, Emma?"

Snoop and I attempted to make pleasant conversation with Miss Montrose while we waited for Emma to find the information on Frank's children. We left as soon we could. Our presence had resurrected Miss Montrose's grief.

"Of course, Yolanda's not competent. She shouldn't be living in that house. Emma is not qualified physically or professionally to see that she's properly cared for. Hell, Emma could use assisted living herself." Hale Stevens leaned back in his chair. "I do the best I can, but I'm merely her attorney. It would traumatize Yolanda to have a competency hearing. I can't put her through that. She's got only a few years left. She told me last year before her stroke that she wants to die in her own home."

"Frank's children in California—they the only relatives she has left?"

"Unfortunately, yes. I don't think she's seen them in years. Yolanda was too frail to travel to California for Frank's funeral. They didn't even come to Cleveland for the funerals of Allison and the girls. They're not a close-knit family—never were."

"You have Yolanda's power of attorney?"

"Fortunately, she signed that five years ago before that stroke screwed up her brain."

"Who are Allison's heirs?"

Stevens shrugged. "Allison was a lovely woman, but she was more decorative than useful, intellect-wise. One of my partners handled her divorce and got her a nice settlement. She ignored our estate planning advice and left everything to her daughters in her will. Since they died with her, she might as well have died intestate."

"Is that why the house is sitting there in ruins?"

"Until the probate court determines who Allison's heirs are, no one has the authority to do anything. Of course, it's a total tear-down, so it's not like it's deteriorating any further. The lakefront lot's worth millions, though."

ELEVEN

S noop dropped me at home at 6:00 p.m. the next day.

Mrs. Parker had finished the repairs. I was about to open the door when my phone played "Georgia On My Mind." Terry was from Georgia; the ringtone seemed apropos.

"Hi, doll. I'm walking up to my door. Gotta take a shower and change. I'll be over in about an hour and a half."

"Chuck, I'm on stakeout. Gotta cancel tonight."

"It goes with the job, Queens. How about tomorrow?"

"Okay, King, if this stakeout doesn't interfere again."

I inserted my key in the deadbolt. It didn't turn. I unlocked the door knob and the door opened. I tried my key the other way in the deadbolt and it rotated; the deadbolt had been unlocked when I arrived.

A shiver of foreboding ran down my spine. *Someone has been inside*, I thought. *Perhaps they're still there.*

My guns were in the gun safe. Inside. On the second floor. I mentally kicked myself.

I ducked below the guest room window, dashed across the street, and called Snoop.

"Yeah, Chuck, what's up?"

"Someone's been inside my house, and all my guns are in the safe."

"I'll be right there."

I called my landlady. "Mrs. Parker, this is Chuck McCrary. The outside looks great, even better than before."

"We installed your old locks in the new door, so you don't need new keys. I finished my inspection about four o'clock. How do you like the inside?"

"I haven't been inside yet, Mrs. Parker. Did you lock the deadbolt as you left?"

"I tried the door when I left, but I don't remember locking the deadbolt. Oh, dear, do you think those men have come back? Do you want me to call the police?" Mrs. Parker must have been seventy-five years old. She didn't realize that everyone in the known universe had a cellphone; sometimes two or three like me.

"No, that's not necessary, Mrs. Parker. It's probably nothing. If I need the police, I'll call them myself." I breathed easier. Mrs. Parker must have forgotten to lock the deadbolt.

"Chuck, there's something else I need to discuss with you."

"Yes, ma'am?"

"I knew you were a policeman when I rented you the place, but now that you're a private detective…with hit men and gun battles…"

I decided not to remind her that I was a private investigator, not a detective. No sense pissing her off more than she already was. "Mrs. Parker, that was an isolated event. It won't happen again."

"You can't know that, Chuck. As much as it pains me, I have to ask you to move for the safety of my other tenants."

"I have a lease."

"I know you do, but you're a danger to my tenants. I could break your lease if I had to. But I won't have to, will I?"

This was an inconvenience, not a disaster. I couldn't blame Mrs.

Parker. She was a sweet old lady who really cared about her tenants—even me. Just not enough to let me stay.

"No, ma'am. I understand. How soon do you want me out?"

"The end of next month. I wish it could be otherwise, Chuck."

"Yes, ma'am, I know. Don't feel bad."

Snoop pulled into the driveway and handed me the Browning .380 which he kept in his glove compartment. I usually carry one just like in an ankle holster. Mine was in my gun safe on the second floor. "Take this. I hate to say 'I told you so,' but I told you so. How you want to do this?"

I told Snoop part of my conversation with Mrs. Parker. No point in distracting him with my eviction notice. "She's a sweet old lady, but forgetful. I probably called you for nothing. She was here until four o'clock. It's unlikely the shooters came in the last two hours."

"It was unlikely they would spray your place with bullets last week. Rule Fourteen: *When you think someone is out to get you, they probably are.* If I wanted to hit you, I would have waited down the block until the old lady left. You remember what I said about 'better an old worrier that an optimistic young corpse'? Let's check it out."

"Okay, Snoop. You go around back. I'll take the front. Call when you're in position."

Three minutes later, my phone rang. "Snoop, you in position?"

"Does a frog bump his butt when he jumps?"

I pulled the slide, cocked the Browning.

I pushed the door open and peered down the dark hallway. Nothing.

I switched on the lights. Waited. Listened. Nothing.

The silence was not as comforting as it should have been. I was wired.

Then I smelled it. A trace of tobacco smoke hung in the air. They had been here.

Mrs. Parker would never allow any workers to smoke in her townhouses. She had a no smoking clause in all her leases.

Worst case, the shooters were in my guest room. I slammed open the guest room door hard enough to bang the wall, crabbed sideways along the wall opposite the guest room, surveying it foot by foot as I moved. Nothing.

Next, the powder room. Nothing.

There was no good way to open the kitchen door without standing in front of it, so I eased down the hall to the dining room. Nothing.

I surveyed the kitchen through the dining room archway. Nothing.

I investigated the pantry, the coat closet. Nothing.

The living room stretched the width of the unit in back, overlooking Seeti Bay. I opened a glass slider. Snoop stood on the dock. I waved to him, and he crossed the back grass.

"The ground floor is clear," I said, "but I smelled smoke. If they're still here, they're upstairs."

Snoop winced and signaled me to whisper. "Quiet, kid. This ain't over 'til it's over. Of course, they're here. Why else would they come… to leave you a gift basket?"

I heard a small creak overhead. I pointed up. "How many you think there are?"

"At least two." Snoop glanced at the ceiling. "How you want to handle this?"

"I vote we wait here and starve them out."

Snoop smiled in spite of himself. "You don't have a fire escape. They can't get down unless they use the stairs or jump from a window, right?"

"Right. The front bedroom window opens over the driveway and the other guest room has a balcony. Either way, they land on a concrete driveway. If it were me, I would jump from my bedroom window. They would land on grass back here. They would be less likely to break an ankle."

"What now?"

"Call for backup."

Snoop hurried to the back garden to make the call, glancing up at the windows. He gave me a thumbs-up as he stepped back inside. "SWAT's on the way," he whispered.

I had a disturbing thought. "These guys know that we know they're upstairs."

"You got a 'so what' to go with that?"

"They have no future waiting for the cops; they'll make a break."

"That means Janet's gonna yell at me."

"If you want to bail on me, I'll understand. I don't want Janet mad at me."

"She thinks you hung the moon. It's me who'll catch the flack." He shrugged. "It is what it is. I'll stick around; you'd do the same."

"In Special Forces we had a saying: The buddy system is essential to your survival; it gives the enemy somebody else to shoot at."

"Somehow that doesn't give me much comfort."

"I think they'll try the back."

"Great minds think alike. You're faster than I am, so I'll cover the bottom of the stairs and keep them penned up there while you cover the back."

I stood outside the rear sliders where the roof overhang shielded me from view. An upstairs window screeched open and the aluminum screen fell to the grass. I heard cloth scrape as one of the shooters worked his butt onto the windowsill. Sneakers and argyle socks extended from the khaki slacks as he slid outward, reducing the distance he had to fall.

The first hood jumped, hit the ground, and rolled to the side away from me.

I took the Weaver shooting stance and aimed the Browning at his center mass. "Don't move. You're almost dead."

He kept rolling while he tried to pull his gun into position. I squeezed off two shots. The first caught him in the chest and the second in the neck.

I studied the second-floor window. It was clear. I felt his pulse. He was dead before he stopped rolling. I didn't recognize his face.

I called over my shoulder. "Snoop. Got one. The next one may come your way."

Snoop shouted, "Hold your position."

I heard sirens in the distance. I squinted at the dead man and felt queasy. My second civilian gunfight. No time to be nauseous now. I swallowed hard and steadied my breathing.

A crash came from inside the house.

"Chuck, someone bailed out the front window."

I bolted through the house and burst out the front door right behind Snoop. The SWAT truck and two black-and-whites screamed toward us from the left. Two men ran toward the right like demons from hell were chasing them. "Snoop, stay here and explain what happened."

They had a seventy-five-yard head start. One man ran between the houses across the street. The other fugitive ran up the block.

I'm not a sprinter, but I can run all day, so I kicked my body into cruise control and took off after the second man. Unless he was a marathoner, I had him. By the time he reached the corner, I had cut his lead to fifty yards.

As I reached the corner, the runner took a shot at me. It was a million-to-one shot, okay, a hundred-to-one shot. I juked and kept running. I gained another five yards.

A siren gained on me from the rear. I peeked over my shoulder at the black-and-white as it rounded the corner. I waved it forward with my left arm and focused on the thug ahead.

The black-and-white passed me. Thirty-five yards ahead it bounced across the curb and blocked my way. Two uniforms jumped from the car, guns drawn, and aimed at me. "Freeze. Drop the gun. On the ground. Now."

I stopped, lifted my gun hand in the air, and pointed with my other hand. "I'm the good guy. That's the perp, the guy you want."

"Drop the gun. Down on the ground. Now."

Standard procedure. Police training taught me the same thing. Once you corner the suspect, don't be distracted. I held the Browning in two fingers and pointed it away from the two uniforms. I placed it on the ground, stepped away, and knelt on the pavement, hands clasped behind my neck.

There goes another good pair of pants. Why couldn't these guys attack when I was wearing old jeans?

———————

Lieutenant Weiner wheeled up to my townhouse parking lot where Snoop and I waited. She ducked under the crime scene tape. "Chuck, what happened?"

I told her. When I got to the part about shooting the jumper in my backyard, I had a flashback. I hurried to my front flower bed and puked. *I gotta stop doing that.*

"Take your time, Chuck," she said.

I wiped my mouth on my sleeve. "Sorry, LT."

Mother Weiner patted me on the shoulder. "I pitched my cookies all over my uniform the time I shot a perp. It's a good thing I never had to do it since. Nothing to be ashamed of. I would worry more if you weren't upset. You okay to talk now?"

"Sure."

"So the other perps escaped?"

"Yeah. The one who jumped out the rear window had no ID, but he had a set of car keys. The uniforms are canvassing the neighborhood to find the car and see if there are any witnesses."

The sergeant came out my door. Weiner gestured him over. "Are you in charge of this mess?"

"Yes, ma'am. Ernesto Donatello, ma'am. Those were my guys that made the wrong collar." He didn't look happy.

Lieutenant Weiner sighed. "Sergeant, I put my pants on one leg at a time like you. I don't expect perfection. Don't beat yourself up."

She focused on me. "I'll let you know what we find on the dead guy and the auto when we find it."

I slept like a man in a coma that night. At least I didn't have any cuts or scrapes this time—just another pair of trashed pants.

FedEx delivered the DNA results for Gamez and Gomez, but Ike Simonetti was out of his office until after five.

My cellphone signaled a text from Weiner:

We identified the dead guy. Found the car. Call me.

Since I was near the precinct, I opted for face time with Mother. Besides, I wanted to look at the file; I couldn't do that over the phone.

"The deceased is Vittorio Martinelli a/k/a Victor Martin. Moved here from Newark, New Jersey seven years ago. In Jersey, he was a leg-breaker and then a gofer here in Port City. We arrested him for aggravated assault—twice, but couldn't make the charges stick."

"Sounds like a small-time hood."

"He is. A hit on you is above his pay grade."

"He wanted to advance his career?"

"And maybe he was the driver. After all, he did have the car keys."

"Your message said you found the car."

She read from a file. "An eight-year-old Hyundai sedan stolen from a used car lot, Smiling Eddie's Shiny Spot, over on 87th. We lifted several sets of prints off the car. We're processing them now. Maybe we can get a handle on the other two guys."

Something wasn't right. "Mother, if the car was stolen, how did Victor Martin wind up with the keys?"

"Bingo," the lieutenant answered. "Smiling Eddie says he always keeps an extra set of keys over the visor."

"Kind of a dumb policy."

"Yeah. But that's his story."

Something tugged at my memory. "Where have I heard of Smiling Eddie?"

"You were a damned good detective, *boychik*; you always remember every person you came across professionally."

The light dawned. "The hit-and-run thing three years ago, right after I came on the job. Wasn't the victim from Jersey?"

"That's right, *bubalah*." The lieutenant pulled another file from her drawer. "The victim was a schlub from Hoboken. He was hit by a car stolen from Smiling Eddie's. Two other cars reported stolen from Smiling Eddie have been used in crimes in the last five years."

"What does Smiling Eddie have to say about that?"

"Same old, same old. Not his fault; his lot is in a bad neighborhood; he doesn't know who stole the cars; yada, yada, yada."

"I could pay him a visit and ask him real nice. He might tell me something he wouldn't tell you official types."

"*Bubalah*, you cannot do police work; you're a civilian. You stay away from him. In fact, I forbid you to go see him at 2200 N.W. 87th street. I absolutely forbid it."

I parked my Dodge Grand Caravan near the office at Smiling Eddie's.

A huge man in a red bow tie, white shirt, and red suspenders bounced up to me. He reminded me of a giant Christmas tree ornament. He was nearly as tall as I am, but about a biscuit short of 300 pounds.

"I'll give you $4,000 for that Caravan right now. Whaddya say?"

I shook his hand. "And you are?"

"Smiling Eddie his own self. Pleased to meet you, Mister...?"

"Delbert Dittlefinger. You can call me Del."

"Nice to meetcha, Del, nice to meetcha. What can I show you?"

"Can we talk in your office?"

Eddie spread his hands to show his lot. "My whole inventory is here. What can I show you, Del?"

"Eddie, I ain't here to buy a car...exactly. Can we talk in your office?"

Eddie wasn't smiling now. "What about?"

"It's a delicate matter." I peered over my shoulder. "I am an associate of Victor Martin." I emphasized the name as if it should mean something to him.

Eddie didn't bite. Now he was the cautious rodent, peeking out of the forest. "Who?"

"Victor Martin. He's my goombah from Hoboken."

"You from Jersey?"

"Yeah. Me and Vic go back a ways. He said you could help me out on a delicate matter. Now can we talk in your office?"

"Any guy from Jersey...C'mon." Eddie led the way to the office, once again the confident salesman. He gestured me to sit a side chair. "What's this about? See, I don't know any Victor Martin."

"Well, Vic knows you. I need a car with local plates, but I don't want it registered in my name and I can't rent one for the same reason. Vic told me to come see you."

"What kind of car you need, Del?" Now he was the clinical diagnostician.

"A four-door sedan that don't stand out in a crowd."

"Will I get it back?"

"Yeah. Gimme a few days."

"Can you do it in less than seventy-two hours?"

I paused like I was thinking it over. "Yeah, I think so."

"What shape will you return the car in?"

"Like I got it, Eddie. No damage."

He practically rubbed his hands together. "Okay, here's the deal, Del: You give me a cash deposit for the price of the car, plus $2,000, see. I copy your driver's license and do the paperwork to sell you the car. Nice and legal, see. But the law gives me three days to file the paperwork. If you return the car within seventy-two hours, undamaged, you get the sticker price back. I keep the two grand, see. And you can watch me shred the paperwork."

Eddie held up one finger. "But there's a catch."

"What's that?"

He grinned like the Cheshire Cat. "You gotta steal the car, Del. If it's not back within seventy-two hours, I report it stolen."

"Why you gotta report it stolen?"

He leaned back and clasped hands over his enormous stomach. "I don't want no one to tie me to anything as an accessory to a crime, see. I run a legit business. I'm clean and I stay that way, *capisce?*"

"So, the car won't be registered?"

Eddie shook his head. "It shows as in my inventory. The day before you take it, I move it to the back of the lot and note the location on my inventory. That's why I can claim I didn't notice it was stolen for three days; it was on the back of the lot, see, and I take inventory once a week."

"Wow, Eddie. Vic said you was plenty smart. But I don't know how to steal no car. I'm more the, ah, physical type."

"Piece of cake, I tell ya, Del. We pick an older car without anti-theft devices, see. In five minutes, I can show you how to jimmy the door lock. Once you're in, it's easy. I keep an extra key over the visor so you don't even gotta hot-wire it. Piece of cake, believe me."

I shook my head. "Vic was pretty smart about those things. I ain't so sure I could do that."

"Bullshit, Del. Vic don't know how to break into a car, neither. He's a leg-breaker. I had to show him too. Five minutes is all I need, believe me."

"Did he have two other guys with him when he picked up that old Toyota, Eddie?" I stared straight into his eyes.

"Two other guys? What the hell's going on?" Eddie jumped to his feet, trying to loom over me. "Who the hell are you?" Now he played the irate, innocent, private citizen.

I stood and advanced six inches, close enough to look down at him. "I'm the guy Vic needed the old Toyota for. He and two other goombahs tried to kill me, Eddie—twice."

The whites of his eyes widened. He tried to step back, but his chair was already against the wall. He scanned the room, but I stood between him and the door.

I pushed on his chest. He fell into the chair.

"The first hit didn't take, Eddie, and I made their car, the blue Altima. So they came to you for another car before the next try, which they made last night."

I leaned over him, inches from his face. "Eddie, I shot Vic Martin twice before he could even lift his gun. But I didn't get the other guys. I want their names."

Eddie held up his hands between us. "I never saw nobody but Vic. Honest. All I know is he told me he needed a four-door sedan."

"Show me the paperwork on Martin."

He started to object, and I grabbed the front of his shirt. "Don't give me any bullshit about the car being stolen, Eddie. You still have the paperwork because you expected Vic to bring it back." I pressed my fist against his chest. His heart pounded beneath my knuckles. "Now get the paperwork."

He eyed the door as he walked around me.

"Eddie, Eddie, Eddie. Go ahead and run; I won't stop you. But where would you go? Your inventory is here, remember? Be glad I'm not a cop."

His shoulders slumped like a hot-air balloon whose fire had gone out. "Okay, it's in the file cabinet." He pulled out the file and handed it over. It contained the bogus paperwork and a photocopy of Victor Martin's driver's license with an address the cops already had. They were probably searching the place right now.

TWELVE

I ke Simonetti' desk was slightly smaller than a ping-pong table. He hiked around it to shake hands. "Chuck, good to see you. Lorraine and I are going to a fund-raiser right after this, so she came with me."

"I have news. I don't know whether it's good or bad, but it is news. There have been two attempts on my life since our last meeting."

Both Simonetti and Wallace started to speak and I raised a hand. "The attacks may not be connected to your case, but they could be. The first attack came a couple days after our conference. The second happened yesterday about six o'clock when I returned from Cleveland."

"Cleveland?" they said simultaneously. Simonetti silenced Wallace with a look. "What were you doing in Cleveland?"

"I'll get to that. First, the DNA results. I suspected Ramon Gomez is Ramona Gamez's father. DNA results confirm that."

Wallace said, "That doesn't explain the trip to Cleveland."

"I'm getting to that." I told them about Ramon's criminal record. "My operative followed Ramon, and we learned that he's an experienced electrician. He would know how to set an electrical fire. He was arrested for arson in California four years ago."

Simonetti interrupted. "So you think he…"

"Yeah," I answered. "The fire at the Montrose mansion was an electrical fire. I put two and two together and flew up there." I outlined what I found in Cleveland.

Simonetti followed my report with rapt attention. "So Ramona sent Ramon to Cleveland to burn the house." It was a statement, not a question.

"That's my current theory. They may have a family criminal enterprise. My operative in Mexico is researching Ramona's background. The Cleveland fire department is looking for fingerprints and evidence of arson, but I doubt they'll find anything."

Wallace cleared her throat. "For the paternity case, you don't have to tie Ramona to the fire. If you prove Pop is not Gloria's father, she's bounced from the will anyway."

"True. But if she did it, I would like to prove it."

"But it's not part of the case."

"I want the murderer caught."

"You're a crusader." She smirked. "A do-gooder."

I raised my hands in mock surrender. "I admit it. Truth, justice, and the American way. That's me.

"Well, it's Ike's decision, of course," Wallace said, "but if it were mine, I would concentrate on determining who Gloria's father is. If we can prove that, the rest is moot."

"Yeah. Well, changing the subject…Ike, if Ramona did have Danielle and Melinda murdered, I would expect her to take a run at you too. Did anything strange happen to you around the time of the fire and before your father died?"

"Nothing that I remember."

"What about a near hit-and-run from a car or truck?"

He scanned the ceiling. "No, that was a close call."

"What was?"

"Last fall, a car nearly hit me when I got out of my Ferrari."

"Did you get a good look at the car?"

"Just a car. I didn't notice. I was shook up." He seemed a little embarrassed. "Sorry."

"Any unexplained electrical phenomena around your home like a shock in the bathroom?"

"Nope."

"Any strange happenings at your office?"

"Just that near miss from the car."

I perused my notes. "Okay, moving along. I went to see Dr. Virgil Norris. He gave your father a prescription for an erectile dysfunction drug. Did you find any ED drugs in Sam's effects?"

"I remember a yellow plastic pill bottle in his medicine cabinet."

"Do you have the bottle?"

"Tom would know." Simonetti pressed a button on his intercom. "Tom, can you come in for a minute?"

A side door to Simonetti's office opened and a thirty-something-year-old man walked in. Short brown hair, military cut, with a slight scar on the left side of his chin.

"Good afternoon, Lorraine." He faced my way and extended his hand. "You must be Chuck McCrary."

"You two hadn't met?"

"Not in person," I answered. "Good to meet you." We shook hands.

"Tom," Simonetti asked, "do you have the medicines from Dad's medicine cabinet?"

"I put all of Sam's things in storage, including his medicines."

"Good," I said. "Can you meet me at the storage facility at 9:30 tomorrow?"

"Sure thing." He regarded Simonetti. "Anything else, boss?"

"That's all, Tom. Thanks."

I interjected. "One other thing, Tom. If you beat me there, don't touch anything. I want to examine the bottle and Sam's other personal effects for evidence."

"You mean like fingerprints? My fingerprints will already be on the bottle from when I packed it."

"That's okay. I don't want any *additional* prints or smudges."

The address Tom Collins texted me was a four-story, concrete block building painted beige with *We-Store-More* in six-foot letters near the top.

Collins greeted me in the lobby, wearing jeans and a Texas Aggie ROTC tee-shirt. "You're early."

"I like your shirt."

Collins peered down at the faded maroon shirt. "It's dusty in the storage unit, so I wore old clothes."

"You were in the Corps?"

"And four years in the Army after graduation, but I didn't re-enlist. I had one tour in Iraq."

"I had one of those myself."

"It was no picnic, but I survived." He handed me a key. "This opens the door. I'll show you."

Collins led me down a long hall with concrete floors and dim lighting. I pulled on nitrile gloves, handing Collins a pair also, before unlocking the door. The light in the storeroom was brighter than the hallway. Barely. Scrimping on the electric bill.

I pulled a Maglite from my kit and scanned the piles of cardboard boxes. "Where did you stack the items from the medicine cabinet?"

"The box on the end, on top."

There were three prescription bottles in it. I bagged each one separately.

Collins leaned over my shoulder. "I saw on television where they can get DNA from a hairbrush."

"That's right. Also from a toothbrush." I poked through the

contents. "Like this one." I bagged it. I also collected a bottle of mouthwash, an electric razor, an old-fashioned glass thermometer, and other items that could have DNA on them. "Okay, Tom, how about Sam's shoes and hats?"

"Let me borrow the flashlight." He scanned the boxes stacked against the wall until he found the right ones.

I cut the first box open and bagged a pair of house shoes.

"I don't get it," he asked. "House shoes?"

"House shoes have dried perspiration which contains DNA. And there are epithelial cells inside house shoes and gloves. Also sweatbands, so I'll take a few hats."

I took the DNA goodies to the lab and called Felix.

"*Hola, gringo.* What jail do you need me to bail you out of?"

"I have news, Felix. Ramona Gamez Simonetti is the daughter of Ramon Gomez. Now that we know her birth name is Gomez instead of Gamez, maybe you can find something on her. I have DNA on both if that will help."

"I don't need no stinking DNA. That reminds me: I still haven't heard anything on the fingerprints for the man, either. Let me light a fire under someone."

"Thanks. Keep me in the loop. By the way, I have a date with Ramona tonight. She invited me to take her to dinner."

"I'm sure this is part of investigating your case, right *gringo*?"

"It has nothing to do with the fact that she's as hot as Acapulco at high noon."

"Wear a condom; you don't know where she's been."

"Yes, Daddy, I will."

"Don't enjoy it too much, *gringo*. You may end up turning her over to the cops."

"I intend to do both. And there's one other thing I ought to tell you."

"What's that?"

"Three guys tried to kill me."

"Who wants you dead?"

"Beats me. It could be someone from back when I was a cop."

"Keep your head down, *gringo*. And your pecker up." He laughed and hung up.

My phone played the Dragnet theme and Lieutenant Weiner's picture showed on the screen. "Hello, Mother."

"I sent a team with a search warrant over to the address on Victor Martin's driver license. We collected a lot of prints and we're running them now."

The next day was Saturday, but Mother called me at 8:00 a.m. "If you're not awake by now, you should be."

"I have finished my workout and started my run. What you got, Mother?"

"We got two more hits on the prints from Vic Martin's apartment. The other two shooters are Charlie 'Bones' Bonano and Hector 'Scrambles' Scarpetta."

"They from a mob family?"

"The Santorini family."

"Don't know them and I never heard of the Santorinis. Are they local?"

"No," the lieutenant said. "They're imported talent from Houston."

"Houston? As in Texas?"

"What other Houston would there be?"

"I don't have any enemies in Houston."

"You have at least one. Anyway, we got mug shots from the

Houston PD and we're showing them around town. I'll let you know if we get any hits."

Houston? That was a surprise.

"Mexican Hat Dance" played on my phone and Felix's picture popped up on the screen. "*Hola, Felix. ¿Que pasa?*"

He spoke Spanish. "*Gringo*, it's good you're alive after your date with Ramona."

"I managed to survive."

"How did your date go?"

"Uncle, you always told me that a gentleman doesn't talk about such things."

"I never said you were a gentleman, so how did your date go?"

"It went as you would expect. She seduced me, and though I resisted, I took one for the team. Actually, I took three for the team. Why do you ask?"

"I got your results on both sets of fingerprints. You've heard of a can of worms?" Felix said *can of worms* in English.

I answered in Spanish. "The American idiom. Yes, I know it."

"This is a bucket of snakes. I got a hit on the man's prints yesterday afternoon after you called."

"That's good news."

"Yes, but there's other news that isn't so good. I emailed you the files, but the bottom line is: Ramona is a black widow. Her father is her accomplice, but I can't prove it yet."

"Okay," I replied. "Tell me what you found."

"She is thirty-five-years old, born Ramona Elena Gomez Cristobal in Leon, Guanajuato. At age twenty-two, she married a fifty-four-year-old widower named Alejandro Sanchez Velasquez. She became

Ramona Elena Gomez Sanchez. Ten months later he was killed in a mugging. The mugger was never caught."

"*Hmm*. And you think she or her father had him killed?"

"You don't know the half of it, *gringo*. There's more. She cremated her husband. He was moderately wealthy and had a large insurance policy taken out right after they married. Her father Ramon lived in Leon at the time. He has a rap sheet for bar brawls. He's put several people in the hospital. Also, he has a record for credit card fraud."

"You think the father did the mugging?" I asked.

"No evidence yet, but he shows up at other places where Ramona's lived. If I had to bet, I would say he was involved."

"Okay, go on."

"Then Ramona moved to Veracruz. She married Hector Cordoba Colon, a forty-two-year-old bachelor, never married before."

"That's unusual for Mexico."

"You don't know the half of it. Hector's father owned the controlling interest in a local bank, and Hector had a significant minority interest. She became Ramona Elena Gomez Cordoba. Eighteen months into the marriage, he dies in a mugging outside a gay bar."

"How convenient for her."

"Yeah. The detective who drew the homicide tells me Hector played for the other team. When he reached forty years of age and was still unmarried, the rumors began."

"Ramona was Hector's beard," I observed.

"Apparently you can't be a successful gay banker in Veracruz. Anyway, the cops went through the motions, but there wasn't much evidence. They never caught the mugger. Ramona had Hector cremated. She was the beneficiary of a large insurance policy."

"Let me guess: It was taken out right after they married?"

"You must be psychic. Then she sold Hector's shares in the bank for a small fortune. Ramona's father moved to Veracruz three months before the mugging and got a job in construction. He's an electrician."

"He's working as an electrician here in Port City right now."

"Okay. Anyway, after Hector's death, Ramona moves to Ensenada. A year later, she marries sixty-year-old widower Rafael Gutierrez. She becomes Ramona Elena Gomez Gutierrez. He lasts for over two years. Then he has a heart attack. He had no history of heart trouble. She cremates him. And guess what?"

"She owns stock in a crematorium company?"

"Close, *gringo*, he had a large insurance policy."

"What an amazing coincidence. Did you find anything on the father?"

"He was also in Ensenada working as an electrician for a local company."

"Okay. Anything else?"

"Yes. After the insurance pays off, she puts her late husband's house on the market, over the objections of Rafael's three adult children. As soon as she gets a contract, the children sue to stop the sale. They settle by letting the children buy it. Then Ramona withdraws the money from the sale and disappears."

"How much did she withdraw?"

"The house sold for eight hundred thousand Yankee dollars."

"Quite a house."

"Yeah. Her husband was rich. Anyway, no matter how much she had from the earlier marriages, she had a lot of capital when she arrived in the U.S.A."

"I wondered how she supported herself in the United States, Felix. The house sale plus the insurance proceeds were enough for her to set up shop in Port City and finance her campaign to marry Sam Simonetti."

"Who?"

"I'll tell you in a minute. How come she has no criminal record in Mexico?"

"She's committed no crime. She had three legitimate names from three husbands and lived in three states. We didn't even know she existed until you sent the name and fingerprints of the father. Since we knew the father, we were able to track down his record. Then we got her birth certificate. The rest we did from his employment records and her marriage licenses. As I said, you'll have the email in your inbox. Is she in Port City now?"

"Yeah, and she's a widow again. This time she hit the lottery and married a billionaire. I'm investigating her on another matter. Did she have any children from the other marriages?"

"Let me see—no. Anything else you need?"

"Not right now, Felix. You've been a big help."

"Okay, *gringo*. Now I want a favor."

"Sure. Anything."

"This woman and her father are lethal. Death follows them like stink from a garbage dump. Be careful. Now that we suspect multiple murders, we have a good chance of proving at least one of them. I'll work the murders from this end. You keep me up to date on your end."

"You got it, Felix. By the way, Ramon has a criminal record in La Jolla, California from five years ago, the same time Ramona was marrying the man in Ensenada. But how could he be in two places at the same time?

Felix laughed. "The border between Mexico and California is so porous it's on the honor system. He could practically commute back and forth. I'll contact La Jolla police and get an up-to-date report on him. Thanks for the tip."

"There's one other thing."

"What's that?"

"Two of the three guys who tried to kill me are from Houston."

"Did you leave any girls at the altar in Texas?"

"Nope."

"Any jealous husbands from your misspent youth?"

"None I'm aware of."

"You got any enemies in Houston?"

"At least one."

"So who wants you dead?"

"It could be someone from back when I was a cop."

"Yeah, but that was in Port City, not Houston. Whoever your enemy is, they hired talent from Houston for a reason."

I called Tom Collins to set up a meet with Simonetti for the next afternoon, then I called Snoop. "Have you conned anybody into buying you lunch today?"

Snoop suggested the Fat Tummy, a locally famous greasy spoon restaurant. The food columnist for the *Port City Press-Journal* rated it three heart attacks. Snoop thinks the four basic food groups are fat, salt, chocolate, and alcohol.

I spotted him sitting at a table perusing a menu. I pulled out a chair as a server approached. "Welcome to Fat Tummy. What would you like to drink?" Snoop had a beer, half-gone.

"Unsweetened ice tea."

Snoop said, "I recommend the Heart-Stopper Special hamburger. It has two meat patties, cheese, bacon, and guacamole. Barbeque sauce is optional."

"Don't you ever eat healthy?"

"Do corn flakes count?"

I scoured the menu for something, anything, that wouldn't line my arteries with plaque. I gave up.

"Felix told me that Ramona buried three husbands in Mexico. All rich. All with large insurance policies. He called her a black widow."

The server arrived with my tea. "What can I get you to eat?"

Snoop pointed to a picture on the menu. "I'll have the Heart

-Stopper, all the way, with onions and barbeque sauce. And another beer."

I read her name tag. "Cora, do you have anything that won't clog arteries?"

"Try the Sweep-the-Floor Vegetarian Pizza on whole wheat crust."

"Sweep the floor?"

"It's got all the vegetable items for toppings: jalapeños, mushrooms, green peppers, onions, pineapple, tomatoes, and three kinds of cheese. It's real good."

"Okay, sounds acceptable. I'll have the medium."

I filled Snoop in.

"I have two new mysteries. First, assuming Ramona murdered Sam in the hospital, how did she do it? Second, who ordered the hit on me? I guess that makes three mysteries. Because if it was Ramona who ordered the hit, how did she know my real identity or that I was investigating her?"

"Okay," Snoop said. "Let's take them one at a time. Maybe Ramona didn't off the old man. Maybe he simply died. Rule Seven: *There is no such thing as a coincidence—except when there is*. Old men with heart conditions do die of natural causes. Also, if she murdered him, wouldn't she have had his body cremated like she did the other three? But she didn't do that. Did you think of that?"

"Of course, but we always suspect the spouse first. You taught me that as my first detective lesson. And his death was convenient for her."

"Bud, his death was convenient for Ike too."

"I have doubts about Sam's cause of death. But after I hung up with Felix, I had an *oh shit* moment. I think we have to ask Ike to get an autopsy."

Snoop frowned. "What's this 'we' stuff? This is your baby, and you know what an autopsy means." It wasn't a question.

"They have to exhume the body."

"That's even less fun than a funeral. I had two exhumation cases when I was on the job. Neither family liked the idea. In fact, they hated it, and they hated me for suggesting it. I don't envy you that conversation with the client."

"At my first meeting with Simonetti, I mentioned that we could get Sam's DNA with an exhumation. It didn't go over well. If I tell Lieutenant Weiner about Ramona's history, she'll investigate the cause of death. She'll be the bad guy to request the autopsy."

"Oh, Mother will love that."

"What are friends for if you can't use and abuse them once in a while?"

"How do you intend to approach Mother on this?"

"I'll discuss the dead Mexican husbands with the client first. I'll get his permission to approach the LT. Then the request for the investigation comes from Ike Simonetti, the big taxpayer, instead of Chuck McCrary, the annoying private eye."

Snoop smirked. "If I looked up 'devious' in the dictionary, your picture would be there. I'll bet you won't tell your client that a homicide investigation will involve an exhumation and autopsy, will you?"

"I'm young, Snoop, but I'm not stupid. One thing at a time."

"Okay. Next mystery, who wants you dead? Maybe the hit has nothing to do with the paternity case. You got somebody besides me annoyed with you? You give that any thought?"

"I come up blank. The guys were from the Houston mob. That's all I know."

Snoop frowned. "Well, somebody in Houston wants you dead."

"And if it's Ramona, what's her connection with Houston, and how did she know who I was?"

"You're the world's second-best detective. You'll figure it out."

When I arrived at Simonetti's office the next afternoon, Lorraine Wallace was there. Again. *Hmm.*

We passed a few social pleasantries and sat down.

"I have developments to report. Ramona first. Her name is Ramona Elena Gomez—not Gamez. She changed it when she came from Mexico."

Simonetti seemed puzzled. "She told us she was from Spain."

"She lied on her marriage license application. She was born in Leon, Mexico. She is thirty-five-years old and was married three times before—in Leon, Veracruz, and Ensenada. All three husbands died under suspicious circumstances, and she had each one cremated."

"Is having them cremated significant?" Simonetti asked.

"Cremation destroys most of the evidence," Wallace answere.

"That's right," I said. "Her father, Ramon Gomez, may have been involved in each death."

"He's the electrician?"

"Yeah. He was a bar brawler in Mexico. Two of her husbands died in muggings while Ramon lived in the same cities. The third husband had a convenient heart attack. Each time she inherited substantial assets. My contact with the Mexican Federal Police calls her a black widow."

Simonetti asked, "Why didn't the Mexican police arrest her years ago?"

"The Mexican police didn't even know about her until I contacted them. Her father has a criminal record, but Ramona doesn't. When the Mexicans traced the father for me, they discovered her true identity. Then my Mexican operative discovered the three marriages and three dead husbands."

"Why didn't the Mexicans know about this before? Three dead husbands—that's got to be more than a coincidence."

"The marriages and deaths were in different states. It was like committing crimes in Omaha, Atlanta, and San Francisco. The cops wouldn't tumble to the crimes if they were in the States. It's no surprise the Mexicans didn't either."

Simonetti appeared stunned; Wallace, not so much. She nearly smiled at the news. "I thought Pop's wife was an adulterous gold digger. Now you say she's a murderer too?"

"That's what it looks like."

"We figured Dad's prenup would prevent any financial rip-offs when he died. I didn't think it could be something this bad. Did she murder Dad?"

"I wouldn't bet against it."

"Do we need to go to the police?" Wallace asked.

Simonetti jumped in. "If it's a false alarm, I don't want any bad publicity. So far, all Chuck can prove is that she changed her name and outlived three husbands. The Mexican police don't have any evidence to charge her with the deaths of her other husbands or they would have arrested her years ago in Mexico. Right?"

"Not exactly. Now that they know about the three dead husbands, my contact at the Mexican Federal Police has opened three murder investigations."

"Anyway, there's no proof Pop was murdered," Wallace said. "His death could be a coincidence. Remember he died in a hospital under a doctor's care."

"That's right," Simonetti said. "Ramona didn't cremate Dad. Even if she intended to kill him, he must have died naturally before she could. I would like to keep this crap out of the media. They would love to smear the family name."

I nodded. "Ike, let's tell Vicky about this and ask her if we have enough evidence for a judge to require a DNA test for Gloria. I took Sam's personal effects to the lab two days ago. We'll have DNA test results next week."

"Call Vicky," he said.

Wallace asked, "Shouldn't we wait for the DNA results?"

Simonetti frowned. "Lorraine, we don't have a choice." He pointed to me. "Call Vicky now."

I called Vicky's secretary. "Carmen, this is Chuck McCrary. Ike Simonetti and I need to see Vicky ASAP."

I put the phone on speaker.

"She's in court today and tomorrow, Chuck. How about ten o'clock Monday morning?"

I asked Simonetti, "That work for you?"

He studied his computer monitor. "Okay, Carmen. Chuck and I will meet Vicky then."

Simonetti faced me. "You mentioned you had other developments?"

"The Port City cops found fingerprints in the apartment of the guy I shot. They have identified two gangsters from Houston. They're looking for them now."

"Houston? As in Texas?"

"Both shooters are in the Santorini mob family," I said.

"Why would anyone in Houston want you dead?" Simonetti asked.

"I don't know. It may not even be connected to this case."

Wallace leaned forward in her chair. "Be careful, Chuck. We don't want to lose you."

"Me neither," I said.

THIRTEEN

C *SI found fingerprint. Call my mobile. Saunders.*
Ted Saunders had sent the email from his Cleveland Fire Department email address late the previous day.

I found his number in my phone's contact list. "Hey, Ted, what did they find?"

"Something weird. Our CSIs found one print from a left middle finger of a guy in the FBI data base. That print belongs to a convicted arsonist named Howard Hopper."

"What's weird about that?"

"The guy lives in Houston."

That made no sense. Hiring someone from Cleveland, yes. From Port City, yes. Even from Mexico, yes. But Houston? "Houston, as in Texas?"

"Yeah."

"Has this guy moved to Cleveland?"

"We got no record for him in Cleveland. The notes here say that the Houston cops told our cops that Hopper is on parole, and he checks in with his parole officer every week. At least his parole officer hasn't put out an arrest warrant for him. He must still be there."

"You got Hopper's address?"

"Not in the notes. Our cops will send a detective down there in a couple of days."

"Okay. What about his PO's name?"

"*Nah*. But I got the name of the Houston cop our guys talked to. You want that?"

"Sure."

"Sergeant Humberto Gonzales." Saunders read me Gonzales's phone number.

"Ted, I appreciate this. Thank Captain Crawford for me."

"I hope this helps. We have done our part. It's in the police department's hands now."

"I'll follow it up and let you know if I find anything."

Houston. Might be coincidence. Might be coincidence that streets get wet when it rains.

I pulled out the class directory from my tenth anniversary Theodore Roosevelt High School reunion. One classmate had worked for the Houston PD. I called the number.

"Officer Simpson, may I help you?"

"Bettina, this is Chuck McCrary. We graduated from Roosevelt High together."

"I remember you, Chuck. We slow danced at the reunion last year. You're a detective at the Port City PD. How are you?"

"I'm fine, Bettina. I'm flattered that you remember me."

"Are you in town? I would love to see you again."

"I'm in Port City. But I left the job eight months ago and hung out a shingle as a PI."

"Gumshoe McCrary. You told me you intended to do that. How's business?"

"Pretty good. I have a case that points to Houston, so I may come there."

"When?"

"I need to make a couple of calls to see if the lead pans out. That's where you come in."

"How so?"

"Do you know a Houston cop named Sergeant Humberto Gonzales?"

"We have over 5,000 cops in the department. I don't even know all the cops at my substation, and I have been here six years."

I was disappointed, but not surprised. "It was a long shot, but it was good talking to you anyway." I started to hang up.

"Not so fast, Chuck. Were you planning to see me when you come to Houston?"

I was glad we weren't on a video call, so Bettina couldn't see the deer-in-the-headlights look on my face. The truth was that I had not considered seeing Bettina again. I had no clue how to say that without sounding cold and rude. My throat tightened so much I couldn't speak even if I had known what to say.

When in doubt, answer a question with a question, I thought.

"What do you mean?"

"Were you planning to call me and ask to see me while you are in Houston? Seems like a simple enough question. You are a detective, aren't you?"

"Bettina, I'm seeing someone in Port City."

"Well, we can at least have dinner while you're here. As old high school friends, that's all. I'll cook for you."

"Dinner sounds good, but I don't know when, or even if, I'm coming."

"Call me when you know one way or another. No biggie either way."

"I'll call you when I know one way or the other."

I called Humberto Gonzales. "Sergeant Gonzales."

"Sergeant, my name is Chuck McCrary. I'm a PI from Port City, Florida. I got your number from a contact at the Cleveland Fire Department in connection with an arson case I'm working that could involve Howard Hopper."

"Yeah. A CSI in Cleveland called yesterday about Howie the Hophead."

"Is that what you call him?"

"Yeah. Nobody calls him Howard. He's hopped up on drugs most of the time. I put him away eleven years ago. He got out on parole three years ago. What was your name again?"

"Carlos McCrary; my friends call me Chuck."

"Carlos? Odd name for a guy named McCrary."

"I'm half Mexican."

"Small world; so am I."

I switched to Spanish. "No, I mean that I'm really half Mexican. My mother was born and raised in Mexico. I have dual citizenship."

Gonzales answered in English. "Sorry. In the 1950s, Spanish wasn't fashionable like it is now. My grandfather arrived in Houston and refused to speak Spanish or teach his children Spanish. Three generations in Texas as a Good Ol' Boy, and I've lost the lingo. Damned shame really. I was named after my grandfather. My friends call me Gonzo. So how can I help, Chuck?"

"CSIs found Hopper's fingerprint at a fatal house fire in Cleveland." I filled him in on what I had found there. "I want to know if he was in Cleveland last September around the time of the fire. If you were me, how would you find that information?"

"I would call his parole officer. He has to get permission to take a piss, let alone leave Harris County."

"Would his PO tell me, a private citizen, if Hopper went to Cleveland last September?"

"Probably not. When I call a PO, it's official, but you're a civilian. Tell you what—I'll see what I can find out and get back to you. Give me your contact info."

After lunch Gonzales called. "Howie got permission to go to Oklahoma last September to his aunt's funeral."

"I would bet a case of whiskey against a can of Coke he went to Cleveland instead of Oklahoma. When did he go?"

A pause while he referred to the file. "September twenty-first. He flew back to Houston on September twenty-seventh. Does that help?"

"More than I can tell you. I owe you one."

"Buy me a beer next time you're in Houston."

"I'll be on the next plane. I'll buy you that beer tonight." I got Howie's contact information from Gonzales and headed home to pack.

I needed to get to Howie the Hophead before the Cleveland cops did.

Howard Hopper's registered address was 326 Jackson Village, a housing project. I drove around the four-square-block project to get a feel for the area. Apartment 326 faced the parking lot. I parked my rented sedan in a visitor's spot and knocked on the door. While I waited, an old lady opened the door to 324, which shared the concrete porch. She came out with a shopping bag.

"Excuse me, ma'am. Could you tell me if Howard Hopper is home?"

"Who?"

"Howard Hopper. He lives here."

"Don't know any Howard who stay here."

"Who does live here?"

"Darshonnay Perkins. She stay here."

"Where could I find Ms. Perkins?"

"She there now. She come in at five o'clock this morning. She woke me up—again—with her noise. These walls are so thin you can hear your neighbor tear toilet paper off the roll." She laughed at her own joke. "She sleep it off this time of day. You never see her up 'til afternoon."

"Thanks." I knocked again.

The old woman laughed. "That won't do you no good. She sleep in the back bedroom on the second floor. And she run that old window unit in her bedroom. That noisy thing drown out any noise out here. That's one reason she run it. She don't want no one to disturb her sleep."

"Ma'am, if you were me and wanted to talk to her, how would you go about it?"

The old woman cackled. "Why, mister, I would open the door and walk right in. That lock's been broke for months. Now, if you'll excuse me, I have to go to the market."

"One thing." I pulled out the mug shot that Gonzo had given me the night before. "You know this man?"

She looped the shopping bag handles over her forearm, lifted her glasses into place, and took the mug shot with the other hand. She squinted at me over her glasses. "You a cop?" She gestured at the bulge in my jacket where my Glock 26 nestled in its holster.

"I'm a private investigator. I'm looking for Howard."

She tapped the photo. "This him?"

"Yes, ma'am. Do you know him?"

She handed the photo back. "I seen him around. He call on Darshonnay from time to time. I never knew his name."

"Thank you, ma'am. You have been helpful."

"Good day to you, and God bless you." She plodded down the steps, clutching her shopping bag.

I presumed from the name "Darshonnay" and the makeup of the neighborhood that Perkins was black. Having an armed, white man wake her in her bedroom was not a good way to begin an interview. I considered going in, announcing myself in a loud voice, and hoping she woke up before I got to her bedroom. On the other hand, if Hopper were there, he could be armed. Not a good idea to announce my presence and give him time to prepare an ambush.

I didn't want to endanger Ms. Perkins. But if she were alone and passed out, I would have to wake her anyway…Nothing ventured…

I eased the door open and drew my pistol as I entered the darkened living room. The humidity made the room feel dankly oppressive. I scanned the kitchen. Roaches feasted on empty carry-out boxes on the counter beside an empty rum bottle. Beer bottles and pizza cartons overflowed from a trash can in the corner. The place smelled like it hadn't been cleaned in a long time—maybe never.

I crept up the stairs, stepping on the side edges of the steps. Less likelihood of a squeaky tread. I heard snoring from above. The air conditioner grew louder. So did the snoring. A feeble current of cool air flowed down the stairs. I peered in the bathroom at the top of the stairs. Clear.

The bedroom doors were both open. I examined the front bedroom first. It was dark and empty. So was the closet.

The sweat ran down my ribs under my shoulder holster.

I stepped into the other bedroom. I stood to the right of the doorway and let my eyes adjust to the dim light that leaked around the drawn window shades. The right-hand window held the air-conditioner. It fought a losing battle against the oppressive summer heat.

The odor of unwashed bodies and marijuana was strong enough to set off the smoke detector, if the room had one. Hopper snored loudly on his back, nude. His right forearm lay across his forehead; his left arm draped across a nude woman I assumed was Darshonnay Perkins.

Even in the dim light, the needle tracks on her arms were obvious. Howie's arms and legs were easier to see because he was white. No obvious needle marks. Maybe he had cleaned up his act, or he was afraid of random drug tests. Or he injected between his toes. I couldn't bring myself to get close enough to look. I collected his clothes and threw them onto the stair landing. Nothing makes a man feel more vulnerable than to be naked when everyone else is clothed.

I stuck the Glock under Hopper's chin. "Wake up, asshole. And don't blink, because you're almost dead."

He tried to sit up. I pressed the gun barrel into his throat. He gagged and opened his eyes wide enough to show white all around the iris. Perkins didn't stir.

"Who the hell are you?"

"I'll ask the questions, Howie. Who hired you to torch the house in Cleveland last September?"

"He—," he caught himself. "I don't know what you're talking about."

"Wrong answer, asshole." I jabbed the pistol into his solar plexus. I stepped back when he rolled to the edge of the bed and puked.

"That's strike one, Howie. Do this easy, or do it hard. It's up to you."

Perkins mumbled and rubbed her eyes.

Hopper sat on the edge of the bed, his feet avoiding the puddle of vomit. He mumbled something. I slapped his head above the ear. "Speak up, asshole. Who hired you?"

"I don't know what you're talking about," he shouted.

That got Perkins's attention, and she swung her legs over the other side of the bed and sat up. Her head wobbled. She was still stoned. "You a cop?"

"No."

"What you want with us?"

"I don't want anything with you. Get dressed and go somewhere else while Howie and I talk. Okay?"

She sat motionless for a moment, then stood. "Gotta pee." She stumbled out. I heard the bathroom door close.

I concentrated on Hopper. "Who hired you to torch the house in Cleveland?"

His eyes flicked back and forth. "I told you I don't know what you're talking about."

He lunged for a nightstand beside the bed.

I hit him across the cheek with the side of the gun barrel. A long, red welt oozed blood. I didn't hit him with the gunsight. That would cut him. I wanted to hurt him, not send him to the hospital. I opened the drawer of the nightstand and removed a cheap five-shot revolver. I stuck it in my pocket.

"That's strike two. You want to find out what happens on strike three?"

He held up his hands. "Okay. It was Lenny Lucas."

"Who's he?"

"My public defender eleven years ago when I went to prison. He's got his own law firm now."

That's not all he told me.

I grabbed some Texas barbeque for lunch before driving to Lucas's office. *Leonard J. Lucas, JD*, the sign on the locked door announced. No answer when I knocked. Maybe things were slow today so Lucas took off early. Or maybe he never came in today.

I returned to the lobby and read the building directory for the manager's contact information. I called the emergency number and schmoozed Lenny Lucas's address from the management company.

Lucas's apartment was one step up from the one Howie the Hophead shared with Darshonnay Perkins. A small step. A dirty, rusty sedan occupied his assigned parking spot. I knocked and stood where Lucas could see through the peephole that I wore a suit and tie. The distorted view from the fisheye lens wouldn't show him the bulge of my pistol.

The deadbolt rattled and the door opened a crack. Part of an unshaven face showed above the chain. "Whaddya want?"

"Hello, Lenny. Long time, no see." The afternoon sun behind me hid my face in the shadow of the porch roof.

"Do I know you?"

That was confirmation enough. I rammed the door, pulling the chain from the jamb and flinging it open. I knocked Lucas off his feet with my shoulder. I closed the door and threw the dead bolt. I grabbed his shirtfront, lifted him off his butt, and threw him against the wall. I rammed my forearm across his neck, choking him.

"Lenny, are we gonna do this easy or hard?"

"Who are you? Let me see your search warrant. You got no right…" I punched him in the stomach. He tried to collapse but my forearm pinned him against the wall.

"I'm not a cop. *Capisce?*" Lenny might be more impressed with an Italian-American hood. I pushed harder with my forearm. He struggled. "*Capisce?*" I repeated.

He spat in my face and tried to knee me in the balls.

I rolled my hip against his knee and slammed his solar plexus with my free hand. "I guess we do it hard." I head butted him. "Do I have your attention now, Lucas? I guarantee that you'll tell me what I want. If you make it sooner rather than later, it'll be easier for both of us, but mainly for you." I slammed him into the wall again. This time his head broke the drywall. "I can do this all day."

When he felt the drywall break, his expression changed. I slapped him, then backhanded him to let him know I was serious.

"Are you having fun yet, Lenny?"

He tried to nod. "Okay, okay. You broke my fucking nose."

I threw him onto a sofa in the shabby living room. "That's not all I'll break." I kicked the coffee table out of the way, breaking one of the legs. I tore it the rest of the way off and waved it. "Why did you hire Howie the Hophead to torch that house in Cleveland last September?"

His eyes darted around the room. I swung the table leg against the fleshy part of his left forearm where it wouldn't break a bone. He groaned and grabbed his forearm with his other hand. I grabbed his shirt with my left hand and got in his face. "Don't even think about lying to me."

He reached inside my jacket for the Glock.

I dropped the table leg, twisted his wrist out and back with my hand. I grabbed his shirt again, and pulled him over to a prone position on the sofa. I put a knee in his stomach and leaned. I was calm and matter-of-fact. "Lenny, if I lean harder, your diaphragm won't expand. Your lungs can't fill with air. You'll feel like you're drowning. It's waterboarding without the water. *Capisce*?"

He gasped and his face flushed. "Nod your head if you understand."

He nodded.

"You ready to play nice? Nod your head."

He did.

I pulled over a straight chair from the dinette. I twirled it around and straddled it, rested my forearms on the chair back. "Let's talk."

And we did. Or rather, Lenny did…a lot.

Then I called Flamer with a rush project.

I knocked on Bettina's door at 7:10. She had said sevenish. Ten minutes felt about *ish*.

She opened the door and grinned. Her teeth flared white against tan skin.

I handed her the bouquet I had bought at a supermarket. My parents taught me to take flowers when visiting someone's home for the first time. I hoped Bettina didn't assign the bouquet more significance than I intended. "It's been a while."

"Way too long," she answered as she took the flowers in one hand. "They're lovely."

She positioned her other hand on the back of my neck and drew my head down for a kiss. I expected a kiss on the cheek like she had left me with when we said goodbye at the high school reunion.

Instead, her lips found mine. The kiss was too slow to be merely a friendly hello between old highschool classmates. I had told her I was seeing someone, so I didn't have a clue as to what she expected. I didn't know how to respond to the kiss. I have never been good with women.

Fortunately, Bettina rescued me by taking charge. She stepped back and opened the door wide. "Come in the kitchen while I put these in water." She led the way. A light fragrance followed. She had put on fresh perfume. Forewarned is forearmed.

She pointed to a barstool. "Sit. We can talk while I cook. What would you like to drink?"

"Whatever you're having."

"That would be Pinot Grigio."

"One of my favorites."

She poured me a glass. "How's your case going?" She took out a ceramic vase shaped like a tall wicker basket.

"Pretty good. I had a beer with Sergeant Humberto Gonzales last night—he goes by Gonzo, by the way. He told me where my arsonist lives—his name is Howard Hopper, but everyone calls him Howie the Hophead. Howie was even home."

"Lucky you."

"Howie was sleeping off a drunk or a high or something. We had a fruitful interview. That led me to the guy who hired him, a crooked defense attorney named Lenny Lucas."

Bettina filled the vase with water and cut the ends off the stems with kitchen scissors. "And this arsonist admitted guilt just like that. And then he told you who hired him, huh?"

"Uh-huh." I grinned. "I can be very persuasive. It's one of the advantages of not being a cop anymore."

She grabbed my hand and examined my knuckles. "You don't look any worse for the wear."

I managed to pull my hand loose. "I can't say the same for Howie. Anyway, I found Lucas without much trouble."

Bettina smirked. "You get lucky a lot."

I didn't like the direction her comments were taking. Terry and I did not have an exclusive relationship, but I didn't want to complicate my life by taking up with Bettina, even if it was only a one-night stand. On the other hand, I did not want to offend my host.

"Luck had nothing to do with it. I played bad cop with Lucas, and he told me who hired him. That guy is also an attorney, but a more reputable one. He's named Franklin Turbot. Lucas said that Turbot hired him to kill the sisters, and he didn't care how."

"And Lucas gave you the guy's name? Just like that?"

"I said please."

"Of course. That would do it."

"I haven't talked to Turbot yet, but he'll lead me to the next link in the chain. It's like pulling on a thread and unraveling a sweater."

"Are you going to 'interview' him like you did Lucas?" She made air quotes.

"According to Lucas, Turbot is a partner with a big law firm downtown. Lucas was a lifelong loser and easy to intimidate; Turbot will be made of sterner stuff. I can't barge into his office and rough him up. I need to be subtle with Turbot."

Bettina centered the flowers on the counter. "How can I help?"

"What do you know about Franklin Turbot?"

She frowned while she chopped lettuce. "The name doesn't ring any bells."

"What about Lorraine Wallace? Do you know her?"

Bettina added the bacon crumbles to the mixing bowl. "Nope. Who's Lorraine Wallace?"

"My client's wife. Say, what are you making?"

"Cobb salad. I hope you like it."

"I never met a meal I didn't like."

"Any other names for me?"

"Ike Simonetti?"

"That name's familiar. Isn't he a local oil man?"

"Not anymore. He moved to Port City a few years ago."

"What's his connection to the case?"

"He's the client."

"Okay. Any other names?"

"Compostela?"

"That name I recognize—local crime family." She scraped the chopped olives into the mixing dish. "You're not involved with the Compostelas, are you?" She grated the cheddar over the bowl.

"I sure as hell hope not. I would hate to have a mob family after me. But Gonzo told me last night that Wallace's sister Virginia, who lives in Houston, is married to one of Albert Compostela's sons."

"Your client's wife's sister's husband is a mobster's son?"

"Sounds a little far-fetched when you say it like that."

"Does it sound better if I say 'the sister of the wife of your client is married to the son of a mobster.'"

"Doesn't sound very incriminating, does it?"

I told her about the case while she finished the salad. "Everything connects in Houston. The client and his wife have Houston roots. The arsonist lives in Houston. Lenny Lucas hired him in Houston. Franklin Turbot, a Houston attorney, engaged Lucas, and two of the three guys who tried to kill me are from Houston."

Bettina stopped with her knife in the air. "Someone tried to kill you?"

"Don't worry. They failed." I grinned. "Charlie 'Bones' Bonano and Hector 'Scrambles' Scarpetta, two soldiers from a Houston mob family, took a run at me."

Bettina made a fist and bopped me on the shoulder. "You should tell me these things, hero. You said there were three guys. Were they from the Compostelas?"

"No. The two Houston thugs were from the Santorinis. The third guy was from New Jersey, transplanted to Port City." I told her about their attempts to kill me.

"Geez, Chuck. You remind me of the old Chinese curse 'May you live in interesting times.' You were lucky again."

That was three times she had called me lucky. I hoped she would take the hint that I wasn't interested in a romantic evening.

She picked up the mixing bowl. "Bring those, big fellow?"

I grabbed two salad bowls and followed her to the dining table.

Bettina handed me another bottle of Pinot Grigio. "Open that for me?"

"I'm going to stop with the one glass. I have to drive back to my hotel after dinner. You still want me to open this?"

"Sure. *I* don't have to drive. I'll have another glass, then stick the cork back in."

I started with the corkscrew and she continued. "So, Turbot is the top link of the chain?"

"So far. There must be another link after him."

"Is there a connection between Turbot and your client or his wife?"

"I'm working on it. I hoped you would know something."

"I have local knowledge, sure, but Houston is a big city. Lawyers at big firms specialize in one or two types of law, like real estate or wills or mergers. What kind of lawyer is Turbot? That could give you a clue."

"I don't know yet; I got his name just this afternoon. I haven't even called my own attorney in Port City."

"After dinner, we'll try the firm's website. It should tell you his specialty. You can use my Wi-Fi network."

"Thanks."

I poured the wine for Bettina.

Her fingers slid across the back of my hand. She raised her glass. "What shall we drink to?"

"To old friends from high school. Go Rough Riders," I answered and clinked her glass.

"And I'll drink to an old classmate who is lucky."

So, I was lucky again. Bettina was too persistent for my taste.

She sipped her Pinot Grigio and took a bite of salad. "You know, Chuck, I always meant to ask you—why didn't you play football in college?"

"I was too slow for college football."

"You scored plenty of touchdowns for the Rough Riders."

"We were a small school, 750 students, and we had Bob Martinez as quarterback. Bob made up in talent what I lacked in speed."

"I remember Bob. He was at the reunion."

I decided not to tell her that I had dinner with Bob in Cleveland. Too long a story. "Bob made me look way better than I was. Hell, he carried the whole team."

"Maybe so, but I well-nigh swooned when you walked past me in the hall. But you were so into Liz Johannes that you never noticed me."

"Yeah, Liz and I were a hot item."

"What happened between you two?"

I shrugged. "I was in love; she was in lust."

"In lust?"

"Yeah. From the first time she asked me out, she used me for sex, fun, and parties."

"Most high school boys would like that fine."

"Oh, I felt like I had died and gone to heaven, but I wanted something more. I wanted a wife and children. I planned to propose to her after graduation. Instead, she broke up with me and said she was going to Northwestern University. The whole time we were together, Liz wasn't serious about me. It turned out that I was only a toy to her. That's when I joined the Army."

"Does it hurt to talk about it?"

"Not anymore. Dad told me his heart was broken three times before he found Mom. That put things in perspective."

Bettina took a bite of salad, waved her fork while she chewed and swallowed. "You didn't bring a date to the reunion."

"At the time I wasn't seeing anyone seriously. Now, I have hopes for Terry Kovacs, the girl I'm seeing in Port City." Maybe giving Bettina a name would get her to back off.

"You spent so much time talking football with Bob Martinez that you didn't even notice me until that Ladies' Choice when I asked you to dance."

There it was. I was supposed to say something clever about noticing her. The truth was that she was right—I hadn't noticed her. Not until she asked me to dance. But she would be crushed if I told her the truth.

"I was really glad when you asked me to dance, Bettina."

"To tell you the truth, I asked the DJ to call a ladies' choice dance so I could ask you. I've always had a crush on you. I still do."

I sat there, tongue-tied with a beautiful woman again. I froze like an insect trapped in amber again.

Bettina watched me with obvious amusement.

Finally, I said, "I'm over my head here. What am I supposed to do now?"

She laughed. "Let me clarify things for you. I know that you and I are fated to be platonic friends, at least for this trip. But let me be straight with you, big guy. If things don't work out with you and Terry, the next time you come to Houston—whether it's for business or pleasure—I want you to stay with me instead of at a hotel. In fact, let me change my mind: Even if things *do* work out with Terry, I want you to stay here. If you're still with Terry, you'll sleep in the guest room and we'll be friends. If you're not with anyone, you'll sleep in my bedroom and we'll be friends with benefits. Is that clear enough?"

"Thanks for telling me." I picked up my almost-empty wine glass. "To friendship, without benefits."

We clinked glasses.

Bettina chuckled. "Now finish your salad, and I'll stop hitting on you. After dinner, I'll see if I can help you with your plans for that big firm lawyer, Franklin Turbot tomorrow.

FOURTEEN

Franklin Turbot lived in the heart of River Oaks, an old-money Houston neighborhood whose average income was somewhere north of *Wow!* even for Texas.

Since it was 8:30 Saturday morning, I tried his home. I climbed the brick steps to the double doors of his mansion. I hoped to see him before he headed for the golf course, or beach, or wherever rich, middle-aged lawyers go on a Saturday morning. Maybe they play polo.

I rang the bell and smiled for the security camera mounted above the entrance. A contralto voice drawled from a speaker beside the door. "Can I help you?"

"My name is Burton Pendlebury. I'm here to see Franklin Turbot."

I heard a click and a forty-something matronly woman with blonde hair draped over one eye opened the door. She held a dust rag and wore blue jeans, scuffed tennis shoes, and an old tee-shirt. The dark roots had grown out a couple of inches.

Was she the maid? On a Saturday?

"He's at the office."

I smiled my second-best smile. "Perhaps I misunderstood where we were to meet. I'll see him at his office. Please forgive the intrusion."

"Don't mention it. My husband meets clients here sometimes, but he normally warns me. As you can see, I'm cleaning house right now. Please forgive my appearance."

Mrs. Wealthy Lawyer, who lives in a mansion, cleans her own house? What was that all about? If she was concerned with her appearance, she could have conversed through the speaker and I would never have seen her. Maybe she was simply old school Texas polite.

"Shall I call Frank and tell him you're on your way?"

I pulled out my cell phone. "I'll call him myself. Sorry to bother you, Mrs. Turbot. Have a nice day." I bowed to leave.

"Like I said, don't mention it."

As I drove downtown, I thought about Turbot's sweet matronly wife. Even scumbag lawyers could have normal families. Would I have a sweet matronly wife and children when I was middle-aged?

Why was she cleaning her own house? Didn't rich people have housekeepers? Maybe housework was her hobby. Maybe the moon is made of cheese.

The law firm occupied three floors of the tallest building in Houston.

I handed the receptionist one of the fake business cards Bettina and I had printed the previous night. "Burton Pendlebury to see Franklin Turbot."

"Good morning, Mr. Pendlebury. I'll see if Mr. Turbot is available." She punched her switchboard.

"Janice, Mr. Burton Pendlebury is here to see Mr. Turbot." She listened for a moment, then asked, "Did you have an appointment, sir?"

Mentally I crossed my fingers—it was show time for the bluff I had worked out with Bettina. "Please tell Mr. Turbot I'm a friend of Ike Simonetti and Lorraine Wallace."

She repeated my instructions. Again, she listened, this time a little longer. She smiled at me as she disconnected. "Mr. Turbot will be right with you."

So far, so good. The bluff was working. I had gambled that either Simonetti or Wallace had been a client when they lived in Houston.

I strolled to the wall of windows overlooking the glass canyons of downtown Houston. A flock of vultures wheeled in slow circles a hundred feet below me as they rode the thermals and updrafts. Somehow, it seemed appropriate that vultures circled near the offices of one of the largest law firms in Texas.

"Mr. Pendlebury?"

"At your service, ma'am." I handed her another bogus business card.

"I'm Janice, Mr. Turbot's assistant. Will you come with me, please?" She led me down the hall to an open door. Inside the office, an overweight, middle-aged man marched around a walnut desk as big as New Hampshire to greet me.

Janice handed him my card. He eyed it as he reached out his hand to me. "I'm Frank Turbot, Mr. Pendlebury." His smile was well-practiced. "Any friend of Lorraine Wallace and Ike Simonetti is a friend of mine. Pleased to meet you."

I shook his hand. "Thanks for seeing me without an appointment, Mr. Turbot."

Turbot and I performed the banal trivialities: first names, coffee order, and the *de rigueur* How-do-you-know-Ike-and-Lorraine? Finally, we got down to business.

Turbot eyed me expectantly. "How can I help you, Burt?"

"Frank, a rather delicate family matter has come up." Bettina and I had discovered the night before that family law was Turbot's specialty.

"When I mentioned my situation to Ike and Lorraine, they both recommended you."

"Actually, Burt, I represented Lorraine. Ike was represented by another attorney whose name escapes me." He shrugged. "It was years ago. I came to know Ike during the course of the negotiations, and I am pleased he was happy with my representation of Lorraine. I try to be fair to both sides in prenuptial matters. In fact, they even invited me to their wedding."

Bull's-eye. Lorraine Wallace was the client, not Ike Simonetti.

"By the way, Lorraine and Ike said to tell you hello. I was in Port City on business last week when I saw them. Lorraine mentioned she hadn't seen you in a long time and she hoped you were well."

"They were here last September, the week after Labor Day. Please give them my best."

My mental wheels were turning, and I missed Turbot's next few words. To process this new information without distraction, I needed peace and quiet. I must have responded with the right answer, because he said, "Good, good."

Then he leaned forward and clasped his hands together. "So, Burt, have you proposed to the young lady yet?"

I returned my rented car at the airport and headed for the airline's first-class lounge. I blocked out the world with my ear buds and closed my eyes as my mind meandered through the meadow of facts, theories, and wild-ass guesses.

If Wallace was Turbot's client, then Wallace was the final link in the chain that led to arson. What was her motive? She wasn't Sam Simonetti's heir; her husband was. Had she gone to see Turbot to arrange the Cleveland murders?

Turbot said he saw her the previous Labor Day. Or did he? I played back the audio recording I made of the meeting. He hadn't told me which one he had seen, or if he had seen them both. But he did say that Wallace was his client and not Simonetti.

Wallace was the one who hired the hit men. And Labor Day was three weeks before the arson in Cleveland.

While I waited for the flight to Port City, I sent Ted Saunders a long email covering everything I had learned about the fire and Howard Hopper. I asked him to forward it to the Cleveland cops who were coming to shake the bushes in Houston.

After the thugs from Houston ambushed me, I was as antsy as a Puritan preacher at a nudist convention. I wouldn't be surprised again.

Sunday afternoon about two, I parked the minivan and walked across the parking area toward my front porch. I eyeballed the garage door and jerked to a stop. Something seemed amiss. I had replaced the garage door after my Avanti crashed into it. It should have been perfectly aligned.

The top panel of the garage door leaned back from vertical. The bottom of the door lacked a half inch of reaching the pavement.

I walked around my townhouse to the boardwalk and docks in the back along the shore. I greeted a couple of neighbors walking and two teenage boys fishing. My glass slider at the back of the house still had the pine needle I stuck across the bottom with tree sap before I left for Houston.

Moving back to the front, I mounted porch steps. The hair I fastened across the front door with a drop of spit was also undisturbed. No one had entered the front. All was normal.

Except my new garage door was ajar.

I returned to the Caravan and moved it to the far side of the parking area, beyond my estimate of the blast radius if there was a bomb connected to the garage door. That time of day, there were no other vehicles close to my garage. I punched the garage door button in my van.

I drew my Glock 17 as the door whirred open

No *boom*. So far, so good.

Then I opened both of the van's sliding doors and sat in the second row behind the driver's seat.

The early afternoon sun left the garage interior in shadows despite the door opener's built-in light. The forty-watt bulb was no match for the sunlight reflecting off the pavement. I couldn't see into the garage, but anyone inside would feel exposed.

I tore off a few sheets from the yellow pad I keep in the van and rolled them into a tube like a kid's telescope. The shaded interior of the van blocked the sunlight, the tube blocked the remaining glare. I stared into the garage, watching for motion.

A neighbor pulled into the parking area. "Hey, Chuck, how's it going?"

I concealed the Glock. "Fine, Sandra. How are you?"

"What're you doing in the back seat?"

"Cleaning out candy bar wrappers, empty cups, and so forth. I need to rake it out once in a while. Have a nice day."

She drove into her garage and her door came down.

My garage door opener light had gone out after four minutes.

I retrieved the Maglite from the toolbox in the minivan and shined it with my left hand as I crossed the parking area, the Glock concealed against my right thigh. Dropping to one knee in front of the Avanti, I shined the Maglite beam under the car. Nothing.

The motion sensor on the garage door light clicked on as I entered. Other than the Avanti and me, the garage was empty.

I searched under the Avanti with a mirror on a stick from my minivan. The bomb was stuck under the engine compartment. I called the PCPD bomb squad.

Until I got these bombers sorted out, I would look under my van and Avanti every time I started either.

My landlady was going to love this.

Sharon Farragut's industrial metal desk at her lab was clear; her credenza and shelves were neat and tidy. She perused the file. "DNA from the toothbrush, two hats, the house shoes, the boots, and one pair of gloves were all from the same person. We presume that proves the DNA is from Sam Simonetti."

"That's good news," I offered.

She flipped several pages in the file, then gave me a puzzled look. "You wanted to prove that Sam Simonetti was not Gloria Simonetti's father?"

"Yeah."

"Then I have more good news. Sam Simonetti is not Gloria's father."

"Great. Did Gloria's DNA match Reynaldo Mateo's?

Sharon referred to the file again. "No, it's not his, either."

I had a sinking feeling in the pit of my stomach. "Then who is the father?"

"Beats the hell out of me. It's no one in our data base."

I telephoned Vicky on the way to our conference and left a detailed voice mail.

Traffic was light and I arrived early. She came to reception to fetch me. "We can make out in my office until Ike gets here."

"I think Lorraine's coming too."

"They'll have to find their own place to make out. My office is reserved for me and my current lover. Which, in this case, is you."

"Lady, you have me at a loss for words."

"That must be a first. Follow me." She paraded down the hall like she was on a fashion runway. She peeked over her shoulder and smiled as she gave me a good view of her backside.

She stopped at Carmen's desk. "I expect Ike Simonetti and maybe Lorraine Wallace soon. When they arrive, call me, then take them to the small conference room. Chuck and I will meet them there."

"Right, boss."

Vicky led me through the door and closed it behind us. She put her arms around my neck, pressed me with a full-body hug, and kissed me. She gave it her thorough attention for a moment, then backed off. "That's all we have time for."

"Your loss."

"I got your voice mail. I listened to it three times. It's hard to believe."

"Believe it. Both Lorraine and Ike went to Houston over Labor Day last year and stayed until the following Thursday. I accessed Lorraine's bank account online. She wrote a large check to Franklin Turbot. The following week, Turbot hired Lenny Lucas to kill the sisters. Their mother was collateral damage. We need to talk to Ike alone about this Franklin Turbot thing. Lorraine can't learn that I know about Turbot or the fire. Not until we talk to Ike alone. Agreed?"

"Right."

As I finished outlining my plan, Vicky's intercom dinged. She pressed the button. "Yes?"

"Mr. Simonetti and Dr. Wallace are both here. I'm going to fetch them now."

"Thanks." Vicky took a deep breath. "Is that everything?"

"Yes. You ready?"

"Luckily, I'm a good liar," she said.

"Well, you are an attorney."

Vicky shot me the finger. At least she smiled when she did it.

We got to the conference room as Carmen arrived with Simonetti and Wallace. We gave Carmen our coffee orders, and sat at the walnut table.

Vicky opened. "Okay, Chuck. What's this about?"

"There's been a development that Ike suggested we get your take on, new information I learned this morning. I came from the DNA lab. They extracted Sam's DNA from the items of clothing I collected. They compared that DNA to a sample of Gloria's that I obtained. Sam was not Gloria's father."

Simonetti sighed. "I shouldn't be surprised, but it's a disappointment to confirm that Gloria is not related. Lorraine and I have grown real fond of her."

Wallace slapped the table with both hands. "Then that's it. Case closed. Gloria gets excluded from Pop's estate, and Ike gets it all."

Simonetti raised a hand in a stop gesture. "Chuck, tell Vicky about Ramona's history in Mexico."

I told Vicky about Ramona's first three husbands. Vicky acted like she was hearing it for the first time. Then I summarized my interview with Reynaldo Mateo where he admitted his affair with Ramona.

Simonetti said, "She risked millions of dollars if she were caught with Reynaldo."

"Yes," I agreed, "but think what she had to gain if she produced an heir for Sam. Of course, she had to get pregnant. She counted on Reynaldo to do the job. That's why she had the affair."

"So Reynaldo is the father?" Wallace asked.

"No."

"Then who?"

"I don't know yet."

"We don't need to know who the father is if we can prove it wasn't Dad, right? And you proved that."

"I proved it circumstantially but not legally," I said. "Vicky, why don't you explain?"

"The DNA samples Chuck obtained from Sam's personal effects may not be legally sufficient to prove Sam isn't the father."

"Why not?"

"Because DNA from hat bands and house shoes is circumstantial. They don't prove to a legal certainty that the DNA Chuck collected was your father's. Ramona could claim that the DNA was someone else's who tried on that hat or those shoes, such as a gardener."

Simonetti said, "I think a jury would say that your evidence was sufficient."

Vicky spread her hands. "You said you wanted to keep this whole question out of the news. You can forget that if it goes to trial. We might win a jury trial, but taking this to court could take years. While I butted heads with Ramona's lawyers, she would control Gloria's half of the estate. The surest way to prove that Sam isn't the father is to exhume his body and take a DNA sample."

Simonetti's mouth compressed into a thin line.

"I believe Ramona set up her most ambitious black widow murder yet," I explained. "First, she gets pregnant with an heir. We found an erectile dysfunction drug in Sam's personal effects. I'm sure that Ramona had sex with Sam as often as she could, hoping to get pregnant. There were five pills missing from the ED drug bottle."

Simonetti scowled.

"Doctor Norris told me Sam was nearly impotent at the time of his wedding. As a backup plan, Ramona selected Mateo to impregnate her in case she didn't succeed with Sam. The first part of her plan worked —she got pregnant."

Wallace spoke up. "But you told us Reynaldo is not Gloria's father."

"That's right. Ramona needed to get pregnant, but it didn't matter who the father was," I said. "She must have had a Plan B. She also slept with someone other than Reynaldo Mateo. Hell, she might have been sleeping with any man she could find."

"But who?" Wallace asked.

"I intend to find out. I'll have to get more DNA samples. Eventually, I'll find a match."

Simonetti frowned. "You said getting pregnant was the first part of her plan. Then what?"

"When Ramona confirmed the pregnancy—which could have been in August—phase two was to increase the share of the estate for her baby by murdering your half-sisters. Her father Ramon set the fire in Cleveland. Phase two worked."

Simonetti said, "So Ramon did set the fire in Cleveland?"

"We still have to prove it. After the sisters were dead, she could execute part three—kill your father. We don't know if that part worked or not."

Vicky raised a hand to stop me. "Why didn't Ramona try to kill Ike too? Then she would control the entire estate."

"That puzzles me. If Ramona killed Ike before Sam died, Gloria would get the entire estate because Lorraine could not inherit from Sam under his will. As it is, Gloria inherits half."

Wallace said, "Two hundred million dollars should satisfy anyone. Maybe Ramona didn't want to raise suspicions by killing Ike."

Vicky shrugged. "This new information about the fire means Ramona may have murdered Sam."

"Should we go to the police?" Simonetti asked.

"Yes," Vicky answered. "We have enough to ask the police to open a homicide investigation."

Wallace turned to Simonetti. "To open a homicide investigation requires an autopsy, honey. And an autopsy means they have to exhume Pop's body."

"If the medical examiner exhumes the body, we get Dad's DNA sample at the same time. Right?"

Vicky nodded. "Yes."

"I guess we don't have a choice. How do we do this, Chuck? Do I call the cops or do you?"

"I'll call my old boss, Lieutenant Weiner. I'll put the wheels in motion."

Snoop had taken the same table at the Fat Tummy. "So, you found two bad guys: Ramona Simonetti and Lorraine Wallace?"

"Yeah. Wallace hired Turbot to arrange the murders of Ike's half-sisters. She may plan to whack Ike later and become a wealthy widow. Ramona murdered her first three husbands. She may have intended to kill Sam too, but nature beat her to it."

"So, what's Lorraine's motive?" Snoop sipped his beer.

The server showed up and I ordered.

"Ike Simonetti is rich, but he's not super-rich. Maybe Wallace wants her husband to be super-rich."

Snoop set down his beer. "Wallace didn't know Ramona was pregnant until Thanksgiving. When she arranged the murders in September, Wallace thought she had raised Ike's share of the estate from one-third to the whole shebang. How much is the estate worth?"

"Over $400,000,000 after taxes and charitable gifts."

"That's a lot of motive, Chuck, even if it's second-hand money."

"Yeah, but when Gloria was born, Ike was cut back to $200,000,000. And Wallace must have felt that she indirectly lost out on the other $200,000,000."

Snoop frowned. "Now Wallace can murder Ramona *and* Gloria, and Ike would inherit everything. Then Wallace waits a couple of years and Ike has a convenient heart attack. Bingo. She's an extremely wealthy widow."

"Do you think Lorraine plans to eventually kill Ike? That doesn't make sense. She needs somebody to enjoy the money with."

Snoop's face fell. "Maybe she would rather enjoy that money with someone other than her husband."

"You'd better check that out. Tail Lorraine and see if she has something going on the side. I'll have Flamer put a full court press on her bank and financial records. One other thing you should know: Ike is hinky, ethics wise. He faced several business fraud charges and environmental skirmishes in Houston. He pretends to play the business game, but he cheats."

Ike Simonetti and Don Ramirez stood looking over the city and Seeti Bay when Vicky and I walked into Don's corner office. Simonetti shook hands, but he acted a little miffed. "Don says you and Vicky want to see me, but he won't tell me why."

Don put a hand on Simonetti's shoulder. "We've known each other for a long time, Ike. I handled your father's affairs for twenty years, and Vicky and I have been privileged to handle your legal affairs too. You're more than a client. This meeting is because we're friends."

"So why am I here?"

Don squeezed Simonetti's shoulder. "We have things to tell you that we don't want Lorraine to know. Believe me, it pains me to ask a husband to keep secrets from his wife. Let's sit down."

Don jerked his chin at me. "Chuck, why don't you tell Ike what you learned?"

"Ike, during my investigation, I uncovered evidence of another, more serious crime. I found evidence of a murder—or murders."

"Yeah, you told me Ramona's father burned down my half-sisters' house."

"That was my initial suspicion. That's what I went to Cleveland to investigate. But when I got there, the evidence sent me a different direction. Last week I got a call from the Cleveland fire investigator. Cleveland CSIs found a fingerprint on the electrical panel where the fire started."

"That's good news. Those fingerprints might prove Ramona's father set the fire."

"Yes, if the prints were from Ramona's father. The prints actually were those of a convicted arsonist named Howard Hopper. He lives in Houston."

"Houston? Why would Ramona hire an arsonist from Houston?"

"She wouldn't. The guy was hired by a Houston attorney named Leonard Lucas. This guy gives new meaning to the term 'criminal attorney.'"

"How do you mean?" Simonetti asked.

"I mean Lucas defends criminals, and he's a criminal himself."

"How do you know?"

"I went to Houston, found Howard Hopper, and I asked him who hired him."

"Why would he tell you?"

I gazed at Simonetti for a moment. "I asked nicely."

The light dawned and his eyes widened. "Then I guess you went to talk to this criminal attorney."

"Yes. I persuaded him to talk too. Lucas told me he was engaged by yet another person to hire someone to kill the half-sisters. The other person didn't specify arson, he left the method up to Lucas. It's a coincidence that Lucas hired an arsonist."

Simonetti said, "Whoever's behind this made sure no one traced the murders back to him."

Don spoke up. "That's right, Ike. That person wanted a long and indirect chain."

"And who engaged Lucas?"

I said, "A Houston attorney with a big firm downtown."

Simonetti's face lost all expression. "Who was it?"

"Franklin Turbot."

He frowned. "That name's familiar. Do I know him?"

"He represented Lorraine before you were married."

At first, Simonetti had no reaction. Then his eyebrows shot up. "I remember now. He was Lorraine's attorney." He stopped. "You think that Lorraine orchestrated that fire?"

"Yes. Turbot was her attorney, and he still is."

Simonetti continued. "Before we married, Frank Turbot represented Lorraine in negotiating our prenuptial agreement, and he redrew her estate plan. Lorraine had significant assets from her first husband and lots of separate property. In fact, she was nearly as wealthy as I was."

Don asked, "Lorraine was married before?"

"Oh, yes," Simonetti answered. "Her first husband died before she and I met…" His eyebrows climbed toward his hairline. "Oh my God… he died of a heart attack."

I nodded. "My background check on Lorraine revealed that."

"You did a background check on Lorraine?" Simonetti asked.

"I did one on you too. Routine on all clients."

He frowned but said nothing.

I continued. "Lorraine went to Houston to see Turbot last September, right after Labor Day. That's when she must have asked him to find someone to kill your half-sisters."

"We went to Houston to visit family. She said she had Turbot change her will to add charitable bequests."

"Whatever else she hired him for, that gave her cover for the real purpose of the trip, which was to arrange your half-sisters' murders. Obviously, she couldn't do it over the phone."

Don spoke up. "You see why we don't want Lorraine to learn that we know all this."

Simonetti paced the room. He stopped and gazed at the street, spoke without turning around. "Guys, I don't know what to do now." He faced us. "What happens now?"

"Ike, there's more," I added.

"What's worse than my wife having three people murdered, plus her first husband?"

"Lorraine is on staff at Port City Regional Medical Center."

"So?"

"Sam was hospitalized there, treated there, and he died there. Lorraine can come and go as she pleases without suspicion—any hour of the day or night."

Simonetti stopped me. "I don't like where you're going with this."

"I don't like it either, but you need to hear this. Shall I continue?"

I gave Simonetti a moment.

"We've been married for ten years. I've slept beside her nearly every night. We have breakfast and dinner together nearly every day. We have cried together over her not getting pregnant."

He scanned each of our faces in turn. "Now you all think she murdered my father."

Vicky put a hand on Simonetti's arm. "Ike, we don't know that Lorraine murdered your father. We know she had the skill and the opportunity. Chuck just discovered Turbot's connection to the fire last weekend."

"That's right, Ike. I still have a lot to investigate. We wanted you prepared for the worst. You have to keep this knowledge from Lorraine. Can you act as if nothing's happened?"

Simonetti stood. "I'm no actor. I can't sleep beside a woman who had three people killed and maybe her first husband. I can't do that, Chuck. I can't go home."

"Then you can go fishing."

"What?"

"Go fishing. Go to Alaska or Canada or anywhere you'll be out of touch."

"I can't run from this, Chuck. I have to do something."

"You have done something; you hired me. Let me do my job." I waited until I had his attention. "I do this stuff for a living. I have Vicky and Don and Tom Collins to help. You have to go somewhere, and it can't be any place where Lorraine expects you to Skype her every night.

You need to be incommunicado in a way that doesn't arouse suspicion. An Alaskan or Canadian fishing trip is perfect."

Simonetti faced Don. "What do you think?"

"Makes sense to me."

Simonetti stoked his chin. "If I go to Alaska, what're you gonna do while I'm gone?"

"I'll try to find out if Sam was murdered. If he was, I'll liaise with Lieutenant Joyce Weiner of the Port City police to find out who did it."

Simonetti raised a finger. "What about Lorraine's first husband? If she killed him, I'm in danger too."

"All the more reason for you to get out of town. While you're gone, I'll get things rolling with the Houston police department to look into the death of Lorraine's first husband. There is no statute of limitations on murder. Second thing to do is consider Gloria. My contacts in Mexico are working to prove that Ramona killed three husbands. After they do that, what do we do about Gloria?"

Simonetti's jaw clenched. "Ramona named Lorraine and me as Gloria's guardians. That doesn't require we be blood relatives, does it, Vicky?"

"No, she could name a family friend or anyone as guardian."

Simonetti said, "So if Ramona and Lorraine both go down for murder, I become her guardian. I'll finally have a daughter, sort of."

"I'll try to help the Mexican police make their case," I said.

Felix answered on the second ring. "*Hola, gringo.* Whose house do you want me to burgle?"

"Felix, I have news about Ramona Gomez."

"Great. I have news too. Tell me your news first."

"I'm afraid it's not good news."

"Like the song says, 'You can't always get what you want.' Tell me."

"We can't get Ramona for murder here in the States. She didn't use her father to burn down the house in Cleveland. A torchman from Houston did it. Lorraine Wallace's attorney found him. We figure Wallace set up the fire."

"Lorraine Wallace is your client's wife?"

"Yeah." I told him the background on the case. "Felix, you have news?"

"I continued my investigations in Leon, Veracruz, and Ensenada. I have enough to charge Ramona and her father with murder if I can get my hands on them."

"It would be tough for you to extradite her because she has a baby who's an American citizen. *Hmm*."

"Yeah, I thought of that. But I heard you say *hmm*. I know that *hmm*. You have something on your sneaky little mind."

"You bet your ass." I told him. After a little back and forth, we worked out the plan.

"Okay, Felix. You know what to do."

FIFTEEN

I called Ramona from my Carlos Calderone phone. "I hope you enjoyed the flowers."

"I got them last week after our date. That night I had a sexy dream about you. When are you coming over?"

"I apologize for taking so long to call you. I was in Mexico City visiting my parents. I hope you will forgive me."

"Of course, *Querido*, but only if you come see me again."

"How about this afternoon?"

"We'll lunch by the pool again. Come over at 1:00."

"I'll be there, Little Flower."

Howley opened the door. "Good afternoon, *Señor* Calderone. Madam is expecting you." He winked. That rascal.

Ramona entered the foyer as Howley showed me in. This time she wore a rather modest (by her standards) white silk sundress with spaghetti straps and a gold chain belt to complement gold sandals and a gold necklace. "Welcome, Carlos." She kissed me on the mouth and I felt her breasts against my ribs as she hugged me.

She frowned when she felt my shoulder holster and stepped back. "Carlos—" she began, but I raised my hand. I tipped my head to indicate Howley standing nearby and then shook my head.

She winked. She led me toward the pool. "Today, I thought I would serve a grilled grouper salad." She spoke to the butler. "Howley, we won't need you for a while."

"Very good, Madam." He disappeared like a whiff of smoke. How did he do that?

When we were seated, Ramona asked me, "Why are you wearing a gun? Are you in trouble?"

"No, but you and Gloria may be in danger. I have come to protect you both." That much was even true.

Instinctively, she put one hand over her mouth. "What kind of danger?"

The cook came from the house with a pitcher of Bloody Marys and two glasses.

"Thank you, Melissa. Bring the salads when they're ready." Ramona waited until Melissa was back in the house. "What do you have to protect us from?"

"From Lorraine Wallace."

"Lorraine? Ike's wife Lorraine?"

"That's right."

"Why?"

"First, there are things about me you need to know. I'm not merely a Chilean miner. I have other interests—a ranch in Mexico, a marina in Fort Lauderdale, a piece of a casino in New Jersey, and another in the Bahamas. Because of those interests, I often carry a gun."

Ramona took a sip of Bloody Mary and gazed over the rim of her glass at me. "Carlitos, are you involved in something illegal?"

I shook my head. "My businesses are one hundred percent legal. But let me tell you the rest, okay?"

"Go on."

"I've had several investments in common with Sam over the years. As a result, I know Ike and Lorraine quite well. Did I ever mention that?"

"No, that never came up."

"I have learned that Ike and Gloria each inherit half of Sam's estate."

"That's what Sam's attorney, Vicky Ramirez, told me. Did she tell you this?"

"I got my information from Ike. He told me Sam had two daughters who lived in Cleveland."

"Yes, Melinda and Danielle. I guess you know what happened to them."

"Ike told me how they died. I deal with many types of people, both good and bad, honest and dishonest. An innocent girl like you—you're a trusting person. I'm not. When Ike mentioned this so-called accidental fire, it sounded suspicious and I decided to look into it."

"But why? That's police business."

The cook returned with our lunch. She dished up our salads and put the remainder on the table near us.

"Thank you, Melissa. Bring out the grouper as soon as it's ready."

I waited for the cook to leave. "As you say, the fire is police business, Little Flower. But the fire investigators in Cleveland classified the fire as accidental and closed the case. I checked into it anyway."

"Why would you do that? It's not your affair."

"*Querida*, I'm blessed with great financial success. Having many resources allows me to pursue anything that interests me. I'm interested in many things other than business." I took both her hands in mine. "One thing I am most interested in is you...and Gloria."

Ramona started to say something, but I placed my forefinger across her lips. "Please, *Querida*, let me continue. I don't want anything bad to happen to either you or Gloria. It would be a pain I couldn't bear." I leaned back. "I hope that's okay?"

Ramona blushed. "Carlitos, I'm flattered you care about me and Gloria. But why investigate this fire?"

"Your stepdaughters' deaths were too convenient for Ike and Lorraine. I checked when the fire occurred. Ike and Lorraine would not have known you were pregnant. His half-sisters' deaths would increase Ike's share of Sam's estate from one-third to one hundred percent as far as he and Lorraine knew. That's a lot of money."

"Tell me—what did you find? Surely Ike and Lorraine didn't conspire to kill his own half-sisters?"

"No, not Ike; it was Lorraine."

"How do you know it was Lorraine and not Ike?"

"I hired a private investigator to investigate the fire." I told the rest pretty much as it happened. I stopped talking when the cook arrived with the grouper.

Ramona waved at her. "Thanks, Melissa. That will be all."

I finished my tale about Cleveland. I didn't mention the men who tried to kill me. "When I discovered that Lorraine's sister was married to a mobster and that Lorraine's attorney had hired the arsonist, I knew what had happened."

Ramona caught on quickly. "Lorraine gains nothing directly because she is not Sam's heir, but she benefits indirectly if Ike inherits a lot more money. If she is the mastermind behind this scheme, then it makes sense she would try to kill Gloria, but only if I am dead first. Otherwise, if anything happened to Gloria, I am her heir. Yes, yes, I see now."

"That's right. In order for Ike to inherit from Gloria, Lorraine must eliminate you first, then Gloria."

Ramona's face congealed to stone. "And later she will kill Ike and inherit it all."

I took Ramona's hands "*Querida*, you and Gloria are in danger. I must take you away."

"But, Carlitos, where can we go?"

"I told my parents about you—about us—when I visited Mexico last week. Even before I knew about Lorraine's involvement with the fire, I told them that our relationship is new but promising. And when I returned to Port City, my investigator told me about Lorraine and about the danger to you and Gloria. I called my parents last night. They have invited all three of us to visit their ranch near Mexico City."

"How long would we be gone?"

"A week at most. My investigator will take his evidence to the police as soon as he ties up loose ends. They'll arrest Lorraine soon. Then the danger to you and Gloria is over, and we come back. Will you come with me?"

Ramona's eyes sparkled. "Yes, I will."

"I don't suppose Gloria has a passport?"

"She's a baby, Carlitos."

"Infants have to have passports. Do you have her birth certificate?"

"Yes."

"Okay, give me her birth certificate. We'll improvise…"

I made a few phone calls. After lunch, I booked three first class tickets to Houston and a suite at an airport hotel.

We flew to Houston, spent the night, and the next morning caught a nine o'clock flight to Brownsville, a modest-sized city at the southern tip of Texas. We took a cab across the border at one of the busiest crossings, which was good for the cabbie because it ran up the meter while we waited in traffic. It was good for us, because no one examined our passports as we left the States. We joined the hundreds of Mexicans who had been shopping in Brownsville and were returning to Matamoros.

Mexico doesn't require infants to have passports so we had no trouble on the Mexican side with me using my Mexican passport. I found it interesting that Ramona had a Spanish passport. I wondered where she had gotten it. I sighed with relief as we cleared immigration.

The taxi took us to General Servando Canales International Airport, where we had lunch before our next flight.

As the wheels touched down at Benito Juarez International Airport in Mexico City, Ramona gave me a big grin. "I can hardly wait to meet your parents. They didn't need to come all the way to the airport to meet us."

"Nonsense. It's 6:30. By the time we get our bags it'll be time for dinner, and my parents have a favorite place in La Zona Rosa to take us. It'll be a big surprise."

Our plane nosed up to the gate, and the seat belt light went out. We were the first ones off. As we walked up the jetway, I carried Gloria in one arm and hugged Ramona with the other. "Just wait, you'll be surprised."

Felix stood at the end of the jetway with two uniformed Mexican police. He walked up to us, pulled out his handcuffs, and announced, "Ramona Elena Gomez, I arrest you for the murder of Alejandro Sanchez Velasquez." He snapped the cuffs over her wrists.

Ramona gawked at me with eyes wide. "What…?"

I smiled. "Surprise."

My phone rang after I got to *Abuelita's* house. The caller ID number had too many digits. Most of the calls I get from numbers like that are robocall scammers, so I was leery when I answered. "Hello."

"Chuck, it's Ike Simonetti."

"Hey, Ike. Where are you?"

"I'm in Anchorage. I'm five hours behind you. I hope I didn't wake you."

"No, I was sitting down to dinner."

"Sorry, I'll keep it brief. You told me to get lost, so here I am. I'll take a float plane tomorrow to go fishing in the bush. There's no cell service or internet so Lorraine won't expect to hear from me. I got a satellite phone so you and I can communicate." He gave me the number. "I called you for an update before I left."

"Okay. By the way, I'm four hours ahead. I'm in Mexico City."

"Why?"

"I'll get to that in a minute, but you're gonna like it. That's the only good news I have. The Atlantic County DA got a court order to exhume your Dad's body so the medical examiner can do an autopsy."

"I guess she has no choice."

"Right. Lieutenant Weiner will have autopsy results soon. Right now, we have no evidence linking Lorraine to your dad's death."

"Chuck, I thought of something. If Lorraine did kill my half-sisters to increase my share of Dad's estate, she may target Gloria too. You must protect her."

"That's the good news; Gloria is safe with me. That's why I'm in Mexico City. I lured Ramona here, and the Mexican cops arrested her for murdering one of her earlier husbands. Gloria and I are at my grandmother's house. *Abuelita*...excuse me, my grandmother, is spoiling Gloria rotten right now."

Abuelita tore her attention from Gloria long enough to look over at me. A wide grin spread across that wrinkled face that I love so much.

I winked at her and continued. "I'll bring Gloria back to Port City tomorrow or the next day."

"How did you get Ramona to Mexico City?"

"I have been courting Ramona for weeks now. I figured the time could come when I would need her to trust me."

"What do you mean 'courting'?"

"I have been wooing her."

"Wooing?" Simonetti said. "Nobody woos a girl anymore."

"Call me old-fashioned, Ike. I'm a wooer."

"Wooer? That's not even a word."

"It is now."

Simonetti laughed. "Ok, you wooed her. Then what happened?"

"Ramona found it impossible to resist my boyish charm and ruggedly handsome good looks. Pretty soon she had the hots for me." *Abuelita* frowned when she heard that. Her English was as good as mine.

I moved to the next room while Simonetti continued. "So how did you get her to Mexico?"

"I lied. I went to see Ramona yesterday, and I explained that Lorraine was a danger to both of them. I convinced her to bring Gloria and stay with my family in Mexico until I could have Lorraine arrested. I arranged with the Mexican police to arrest Ramona when we arrived."

"Who'll take care of Gloria now?"

"I'll arrange for a full-time nanny to stay at Ramona's house until you return. And Howley will be there during the day. I'll have guards around the clock until we arrest Lorraine."

"This is complicated."

"Don't worry, Ike. You hired the World's Greatest Private Investigator."

"Okay, buddy. Thanks."

"One last thing, Ike. Stay lost for a while. I'll handle everything from this end. I'll call you on your satellite phone when it's time to come home."

Before I rejoined *Abuelita* and Felix for dinner, I called Snoop.

"Bud, you know how late it is?"

"Hey, I'm in Mexico City. We eat late. Besides, this can't wait." I brought him up-to-date before giving him further instructions.

"Lorraine told me Reynaldo Mateo makes passes at women tennis students. In fact, he made a pass at her. Now that Ike's out of town, your tail of Lorraine may catch her meeting Mateo. Or anyone else for that matter."

"I repeat: Do you know how late it is?"

"So, charge me overtime."

Abuelita fed Gloria. "Carlitos, I want another one of these. My friends are having lots of great grandbabies and I have only four."

"*Si, Abuelita.*"

"When I was your age, I already had three children." She regarded me over her glasses. "You're not getting any younger, Carlitos. Neither am I. You know I won't be around forever." She crossed herself.

Felix arrived at the breakfast table and saved me any further discussion of great grandchildren. We held a strategy session at the other end of the table. "*Gringo*, you can't go back the way you came. Immigration on the American side requires Gloria to have a passport."

"I know. When we left the States, I knew I would have to improvise to get back home."

"What will you do?"

"Don't have a clue. Somehow, I have to sneak back illegally. I have my U.S. passport and Gloria's birth certificate, but to come in without an actual passport could take days of red tape. It's probably easier to sneak across the border. You got any ideas?"

"I have a friend in Chihuahua, Rigoberto Casillas. Rigo owns a tequila distillery. He exports to the United States, and he travels there a lot. Flies his own plane. Chihuahua is a couple hundred kilometers from Texas."

"That sounds promising."

"There are lots of private airports in the Big Bend area of Texas.

Rigo flies you and Gloria into one, drops you, and gets back to Mexico before anyone is the wiser."

"Felix, that sounds like it would be illegal, and you are a respected Mexican Federal Police officer. I am shocked—absolutely shocked—that you would recommend that anyone break the law."

Felix smirked. "It's not against Mexican law to leave the country. And U.S. law is not my responsibility."

"Will Casillas help us?"

"Rigo and I were college roommates. I am godfather to his son."

"Thanks, Felix. Call him."

Gloria and I landed in Chihuahua after noon. I pushed her stroller through security. A tall, slender man in khakis and a red PGA Tour golf shirt extended his hand. "Carlos, I'm Rigoberto Casillas," he said in English. "Call me Rigo."

"*Mucho gusto*, Rigo." I shook his hand and continued in Spanish. "We appreciate your help."

"I would do anything for Felix." He squatted in front of Gloria. "And you must be the lovely Gloria." He took her right hand in his fingers and kissed it softly. "It is a pleasure to meet you, *señorita*."

He smiled at me. "Four months old, no? My little boy is the same age."

"She was born April 5."

"My Felix was born April 15."

"You named him Felix?"

Rigo grinned. "Didn't Felix tell you we're best friends?"

"Of course."

He grabbed Gloria's diaper bag off my shoulder. "Let's get your bags. You want lunch before we leave?"

"Good idea. We won't be able to eat again until tonight."

After lunch, I changed Gloria's diaper and we caught a shuttle to the general aviation terminal. "Rigo, I saw the Chihuahua desert as our flight from Mexico City descended. I expected it to be hotter in August."

"Fifteen hundred meters altitude. It's thirty degrees right now. That's eighty-five Fahrenheit."

"Yeah, I speak metric. Remember, I'm half Mexican."

The shuttle dropped us beside a shiny, white Cessna 182 Skylane with red and green stripes—the same colors as the Mexican flag. Rigo tipped the driver, unlocked the cabin door, and climbed into the back seat. "Hand up the bags."

He stowed our baggage behind the rear seat. "Now hand me Gloria."

Gloria was in a portable car seat I had detached from the stroller. Rigo fastened the rear safety harness through the car seat. "This is how I strap my son in. She'll be fine."

"Thanks."

He climbed into the front and patted the co-pilot seat beside him. "Let's go."

After five minutes of pre-flight checklists, talking with the tower, and reading dashboard gauges, we taxied to the runway.

"Rigo, is that rain over there?"

He gazed where I pointed. "Yeah. We don't get much rain, but this is our wettest month, such as it is. Don't worry; we'll dodge it."

Ten minutes later, we leveled out 2,000 feet above the desert. Rigo raised his voice above the engine's drone. "We have ninety minutes to Lajitas, Texas. Enjoy the view."

The land sloped gradually to a flat valley with miles of circular green irrigated fields. Rigo pointed ahead. "No towns here but lots of farms."

We left the irrigated circles behind. The only civilization we saw until we reached the Rio Grande was a dirt road that sliced across the desert.

Gloria slept peacefully.

Rigo raised his voice again. "It gets a little rougher as we descend, but don't worry, I've done this lots of times. I'll drop below the mountain tops in the radar shadow from El Paso."

We passed 500 feet over the Rio Grande. It didn't look very *grande* in this summer heat. Giant puddles marked the river course amid the brown sand of the riverbed. "That's Lajitas down there."

The American side held resort buildings and a large RV park. On the right, a lush green golf course spread along the riverbank. Rigo pointed. "Population about eighty-five residents. Most of them work at the resort and golf course."

A dozen houses sat on the Mexican side. I didn't see any paved streets.

Rigo pointed ahead. "We'll follow that road fifteen kilometers to the airport. You can already see the runway if you know where to look."

"You've done this before?"

Rigo laughed. "I come often to play golf, and twice I came to the Terlingua Chili Cook-off down the road a piece. I called ahead and arranged things with friends. People here are pretty informal about the border. Did you see those houses on the Mexican side back there? Those folks work at the resort."

"I didn't see a bridge across the river." I hadn't seen much river, either. Mostly mud flats.

"They row across the river if it's high and wade if it's low. Right now, it's low. The U.S. border patrol puts checkpoints about forty miles inland. Anybody leaving this area, U.S. citizens and illegals alike, has to take one of three highways to the rest of the United States. Easier to catch them on those three highways than at the border, which makes it pretty easy to fly in unnoticed."

Rigo pulled back on the throttle and the Skylane dropped toward the runway like an express elevator, leaving my stomach 300 feet in the air. Gloria cried out in her sleep, then quieted.

We taxied to an apron near the terminal. Rigo opened his cabin door. The outside air felt like a pizza oven, but it smelled like dust.

Gloria began to fuss. "Don't worry, *chiquita*," Rigo promised, "Soon we will have you in the air conditioning."

A Jeep stopped on the pilot side of the airplane. The driver hopped out and waited below the door. Rigo unfastened Gloria's car seat. "You get the baby. I'll have the driver get the bags."

"Right." I picked up Gloria, car seat and all, and popped the other door. The landing gear cowling served as a step down to the runway at the unlikely-named Lajitas International Airport. The pizza oven heat got hotter, edging closer to blast furnace temperature with the dry, gusty wind. Gritty dust stuck to my face as the sweat dried instantly in the low humidity. I draped a baby blanket over Gloria's car seat to keep out the blowing grit and blinding sunlight.

The driver transferred our bags to the Jeep.

I clasped hands with Rigo. "Amigo, I can never repay you for this, but at least you can let me fill your gas tank."

"Don't worry about it, Chuck. Buy me a steak dinner next time I'm in Port City. I usually come here legally, and I won't feel comfortable until I'm back to Mexico. I have enough fuel, so I had better not take the time."

He said his good-byes, and the Jeep ferried Gloria and me to the terminal. I left the bags and carried Gloria to the reception desk. I sighed with relief when we entered the air-conditioned interior. I think Gloria was pleased too.

A pretty girl in western attire goo-gooed at Gloria and shook my hand. "You must be Mr. McCrary. I'm Elizabetta Barilla. Your air taxi is on the way from Terlingua. He'll be here any minute."

"Pleased to meet you, Elizabetta. I'm Chuck." I held up my phone. "I have one bar of service."

"Nearest cell tower is in Lajitas, seven miles that way..." she pointed, "or Terlingua, eight miles the other way. Use this land line." She shoved a telephone across the counter.

"It's long distance."

She grinned. "Everything is long distance from here. Don't worry about it."

I touched base with Nancy at the office, played back my voicemail, and called Snoop. Nothing that couldn't wait until I got home.

I carried Gloria to a seating area and set her carrier on a chair. "Gloria, I'm sorry to drag you around like this. I know you would rather be home." She studied me with wide, innocent eyes and blew tiny spit bubbles through her lips. "You didn't ask for these complications, pretty girl. You didn't even ask to be born. But everyone is really glad you were."

She rewarded me with a toothless grin that made all the trouble worthwhile.

I heard propeller noise and a Cessna 206 six-seater taxied up to the terminal.

Elizabetta came over. "That's Marcos, your air taxi."

The high summer breath of West Texas sucked the cool air through the open door.

A tanned man with deep wrinkles entered the terminal. "Mr. McCrary?"

"Call me Chuck."

We shook hands.

"Marcos Sanchez," the pilot answered. "You're legal, right? I don't transport no illegals."

"Born and raised in a little town in East Texas."

"Oh? Where 'bouts?"

"You probably never heard of it—Adams Creek, land of the virgin pines and tall women."

He chuckled. "You're right; never heard of it. Those your bags in the Jeep?"

"Yeah, but I need to change Gloria's diaper before we leave."

"Sure. I see you have her diaper bag. I'll load your other stuff out of the Jeep."

The next morning Gloria and I were waiting to board our flight from El Paso when my phone played "When the Saints Go Marching In."

"Hey, Snoop. What's up?"

"I tailed Wallace like you said. Guess where I'm calling you from?"

"Rio de Janeiro."

"Guess again."

"Reynaldo Mateo's apartment."

"Nope. I'm in the Port City Marine Terminal. Wallace got on a seaplane flight to Nassau. Alone."

"Why didn't you get a ticket on the same flight?"

"I don't carry my passport with me. Sorry."

"Don't be. I don't carry mine either. It's okay. We'll figure out something when I get back."

SIXTEEN

I chauffeured Gloria to her nanny that afternoon. She liked the idea of staying in a guest room at Ramona's mansion, but come Monday she had to go back to class.

I had Sunday to arrange for a full-time nanny for a week or so until I could clear Ike to come home. I called Dennis Howley.

"Dennis, Chuck Calderone. There have been developments you need to know about."

I filled Dennis in on Ramona's arrest in Mexico and my adventures sneaking back to the United States. "Gloria needs a live-in nanny for a week or so. You have any connections in that field or anyone you could recommend?"

"Indeed I do, Mr. Calderone, my wife Margaret. I'm sure she'll fill in until Mr. Ike makes permanent arrangements."

"Thanks, Dennis."

"Maggie shall accompany me to work Monday morning. We shall come prepared to stay indefinitely."

"Of course, the estate will pay the customary fee for such work."

"I never doubted it, Mr. Calderone."

"Uh, Dennis, about that, Calderone is my mother's maiden name, which I use for my dual Mexican citizenship. I can tell you now that I'm a private investigator hired by Ike Simonetti."

"As you know, I already assumed that."

"What you probably didn't know was that my American name is Carlos McCrary."

"Very good, sir."

"You don't act surprised by any of this, Dennis."

"Mr. McCrary, a good butler is never surprised."

I called Simonetti's satellite phone. "Ike, Lorraine has left for Nassau. I need to access her personal computer while she's gone. I'll be back in Port City in a few hours."

"Why is she in Nassau?"

"I don't know. That's one reason I need to hack her. Does she leave her computer at home?"

"Just a damn minute. She's in Nassau? This is not like her. Don't you have any idea why she went?"

"Maybe when I access her computer, I'll find out. Does she leave her computer at home when she travels?"

"Probably. She uses a tablet when we travel."

"Does she use a password on her computer?"

"It's kissmekate lower case, no spaces."

"Thanks. How do I get into your house?"

"Call Tom; he has a key."

"You'll call him and okay it?"

"Sure, as soon as you and I hang up, but, Chuck, now you have me worried. What's she up to?"

At least now I wasn't the only one wondering about that.

An hour after I dropped Gloria with the nanny, Flamer and I sat at Wallace's computer. This was the second time I had met him in person.

Flamer shook his head. "It never ceases to amaze me how smart people can do such stupid things. See this?" He pointed at the screen. "She has a file named *passwords* and it's not even encrypted. I'll copy everything for you."

Ike had already given me access to his joint accounts with Lorraine. She also had separate property brokerage accounts, IRAs, credit cards, and a bank account. She had credit cards and a bank account for her dermatology practice, and I had the passwords to every account. I felt like a kid in a candy store.

Flamer made a mirror-image copy of her hard drive, and we were out in two hours.

First thing Monday I called Ramona's house and made sure Dennis and Margaret Howley had arrived.

I had Tom Collins send me the dates of Simonetti's wilderness trips for the last two years. He had taken twelve. Canada or Alaska in the summers and Mexico or Central America in winter. The Mexican and Central American resorts had cellphone and internet service.

I emailed the dates to Flamer and then called him. "Find out where Lorraine Wallace went during the dates in the email. Check her brokerage accounts, credit cards, debit cards, ATM cards, and bank accounts for those periods. Can do?"

"Do fish get wet when it rains?"

Within two hours, Flamer emailed Wallace's card charges and copies of her cleared checks. I printed and sorted the copies across my desk. I also got the monthly Wessington Club statements from Collins. Lorraine had tennis lessons with Mateo every Wednesday. That wasn't criminal. In fact, she told me she took lessons from him. Still...I began to feel bad for Ike Simonetti. I hoped that my suspicions were unfounded.

I checked the dates Simonetti was in Latin America. Those weeks, Wallace had two additional tennis lessons on Mondays and Fridays. I studied the periods Simonetti was incommunicado in Alaska or Canada. Six of seven periods Wallace had no charges at the Wessington. No tennis, lunches, cocktails, *nada*.

I referred to Wallace's personal checks, ATM, and credit card charges that I had arrayed across the desk. I selected the oldest hunting trip to Canada two summers ago.

Bingo. Lorraine Wallace had bought two tickets to Nassau on separate flights. She had stayed at the Bahamian Caribe, a five-star resort on Paradise Island. She also had charges at the Cracked Conch. I Googled for a Bahamian website with that name. It was a restaurant in downtown Nassau. Things were looking bad for Simonetti's marriage.

I checked the other days Simonetti had gone to Alaska or Canada. Three times Wallace went to Nassau and once to Bermuda. Once she charged a cruise from Miami to Jamaica and Grand Cayman. The cruise took ten days—too long for Wallace to stay gone. Then I saw she had charged air tickets from Jamaica to Port City. If she was with Mateo, they must have skipped Grand Cayman and gotten off the ship early so she could beat Simonetti home.

Wallace stayed at the Bahamian Caribe and visited the Cracked Conch every time she went to Nassau.

Time to go look for Mateo again. I suspected he had already left for Nassau. I wondered if he liked Bahamian food. I already knew he had a taste for Lorraine Wallace.

I got to the Wessington Club before lunch. I stopped at the reception desk. "I'm here for lunch with Reynaldo Mateo."

The receptionist picked up the telephone and punched a number. "A gentleman is here for a luncheon meeting with Reynaldo." She listened.

"Thanks, I'll tell him." She hung up. "Mr. Mateo had to leave town for a family emergency."

I called Wallace's office. "This is Chuck McCrary. I'm a friend of Lorraine's. Can I speak to her?"

"I'm sorry, Mr. McCrary. Dr. Wallace has taken a week off."

"That's funny. I met with her earlier this week, and she didn't mention a vacation."

"It was spur-of-the-moment. She called me this morning from Houston and told me Ike had gone fishing. She's visiting her sister. Would you like me to take a message?"

"No thanks. It'll wait until she gets back."

I sat there with the phone in my hand. I didn't want to call Houston. I feared that the call would confirm my suspicions. But postponing the call wouldn't change unwelcome facts, so I looked up the number of Wallace's mother in Houston.

She hadn't talked to Lorraine in a week. I asked her for her daughter Virginia's number.

I called Virginia Compostela, Wallace's sister, also living in Houston.

She said Lorraine was out shopping.

I called Simonetti's PA again. "Tom, do you know where Lorraine is?"

"Have you called her office?"

"Yes." I told him about my calls looking for Wallace.

"If she went to Houston, she would visit her mother. She and her mother have a close relationship."

"Not as close as the one with her sister."

"What do you mean?"

"I hate like hell to be the bearer of bad tidings. Ike didn't hire me for this, but I found something he needs to know. Ike told me he has no secrets from you."

"That's right."

I told him that Snoop had tailed Wallace to the seaplane flight to Nassau. I told him about the Wessington Club statements and Wallace's credit cards and checks. "I went by the club to see Mateo. He told the club that he was leaving town for a family emergency. I'll bet a buffalo burger to a biscuit that Lorraine is with Mateo, and her sister in Houston is in on the secret and she's Lorraine's alibi."

I disconnected and called Flamer.

"Login to Lorraine Wallace's American Express account. Tell me if she's charged any tickets in the last two days. I'll hold."

Flamer was back in two minutes. "Two tickets to Nassau on different flights Saturday, then a charge for a Nassau limousine service, then a credit card hold from the Bahamian Caribe hotel when she checked in. She's bunking in with her boyfriend."

"I'm afraid so. I drew the short straw. I have to tell her husband."

I hung up and called Terry. "You free for dinner, Queens?"

"Business or pleasure?"

"Does it matter?"

"I need to know what kind of panties to wear—if any."

"How about business *and* pleasure?"

"I prefer a little business and lots of pleasure."

"Tough negotiator. Okay, lots of pleasure. Even some heavy petting."

"And hanky-panky?"

"You drive a hard bargain."

"I'm counting on a hard bargain. When do we begin the festivities?"

"Seven-thirty. The business part we take care of at dinner; the heavy petting and hanky-panky come after."

"Come over here. I'll cook dinner for you. And breakfast."

"This is a business dinner, so I'll bill the client. We can have dessert at your place."

"Dessert involves whipped cream and gooey, sticky chocolate syrup."

"I love it when you talk sticky."

Terry and I were seated at Nine Dragons after eight. She toasted me with a nice Pinot Noir.

"So, lover, I don't mean to pry, but where were you last weekend?"

"Fighting for truth, justice, and the Mexican way."

"That's Superman. And isn't the phrase truth, justice, and the *American* way."

"In this case, it's the Mexican way. I delivered Ramona Elena Gomez Simonetti to Mexican justice last Thursday." I told her the story.

"…and the last thing I said was 'Surprise.'"

Terry guffawed. "I wish I could have seen her face."

"It was funny, but sad too."

"How was it sad?"

"Now Gloria will grow up without a mother."

We finished our first glass of wine. We had taken a taxi, so I had ordered a bottle. "Terry, I'm investigating a woman who's having an affair with her tennis pro."

"This the same woman and the same tennis pro you asked me about a month ago?"

"Different woman, same tennis pro."

"This guy gets around."

I related the important aspects of the case. "I thought you might have an insight I overlooked. My client is the husband. He's quite wealthy, but so is she. That's what I want your take on."

"Does either one travel for business?"

"He does. He hunts and fishes without his wife for a week or more at a time. But he phones home or Skypes his wife every night when he can."

Terry rubbed her chin. "That means she and her honey do their tummy rubs in the daytime. Does she work?"

"She's a dermatologist and sets her own schedule. That schedule includes weekly tennis lessons with the pro."

"What about emergencies?"

"Dermatologists don't have many emergencies."

"What if hubby calls during the day?"

"He never does. During the day, he hunts and fishes."

I refilled our wine glasses when the appetizers came. "There's something else too. Some trips are by float plane to the wild country in Alaska and Canada where there is no internet or cellphone service."

"Then she's home free. She could meet the guy in Bermuda or the Bahamas if she wanted."

"Funny you should say that. She flew to Nassau Saturday morning."

"With the guy?"

"He took a later flight. But she bought both tickets."

"Makes sense that they wouldn't travel together. Someone could recognize them."

"Why would she pay?"

"That depends on whether the man is rich too. Since she paid, I assume he was never a touring pro. I understand that touring pros have lots of money."

"He's a club professional. Rents a middle-class apartment and drives a Mustang, not a Ferrari."

"Does she have money?"

"Millions."

"Does she like to control things?"

"I have seen her with her husband. She controls the hell out of him. He didn't even want to hire me, but she insisted. She's quite forceful, but that could be because she wants to misdirect my investigation away from her."

"That leaves us with the fact she has money and boy toy doesn't. If they go anywhere expensive, like traveling, she'll pay. Her tennis pro will be a kept man. But you're overlooking the obvious."

"How so?"

"Her husband's trips to the outback? I'll bet he's getting a little strange also."

"I'll have someone look into it."

Two hours later, we lounged in Terry's apartment. She poured us Sambuca Molinari over coffee beans and set them on fire.

And then the evening got even hotter.

Lieutenant Weiner gazed at me from behind her desk. "We received the exhumation order from the Medical Examiner. We'll get the body this afternoon. The ME will do the autopsy this weekend."

"Okay. Lorraine Wallace is boinking her tennis pro in the Bahamas. Terry and I are off to Paradise Island this evening to investigate. I'm here to pick her up. I'll call you when I get back."

"Make sure she's on the job Monday morning."

"Yes, Mother."

As I left the LT's office, Renate Crowell stopped me in the hall.

Renate and I had crossed paths when I was a cop. She had cooked me a few dinners, but she liked to pump me for crime news. Well, she pumped me for other things too. She was a good cook, especially her breakfast omelets.

Her Facebook page showed that she had worked at the *Port City Press-Journal* for twenty years, the last twelve on the police beat. She didn't look that old, unless she had started at the *Pee-Jay* when she was thirteen. She had the body of a twenty-something.

Today, Renate wore designer jeans, purple running shoes, and an imitation man's dress shirt topped by a dark gray vest. Reading glasses hung on a gold chain around her neck. Somehow, she made the outfit work. She was smart and she was the pushiest woman I ever met, but I had always found her to be fair and honest. "Chuck, why the order to exhume Sam Simonetti's body?"

"What order?"

"Don't even think you can deny it, handsome. Our courthouse snitch gave me the heads up when the DA requested the order. I have been lurking in the background ever since."

"You always were a good lurker."

"You are such a sweet talker. Anyway, our courthouse nerd tells me the order was delivered to Lieutenant Weiner's office this morning, so I came to interview her. And here you are." She raised an eyebrow.

"And here I am."

"And you have come from Weiner's office."

"And I have come from Weiner's office."

She paused for me to say more.

When I didn't, she added, "The exhumation order means that they intend to get an autopsy. And I heard the cops view Sam's death as suspicious."

"Cops view every death as suspicious; it's what they do for a living."

"Ike Simonetti inherited a lot of money from Sam." She paused again.

She was using an old reporter's trick to get me to fill the silence. I decided to go for it. "So?"

"A few days ago, I saw you in the Simonetti Towers."

"Lots of people go to the Simonetti Towers."

"On Saturday? Ike Simonetti offices in that building, sweetie. Is he under suspicion? Do you represent him?"

"Oh? Does Ike Simonetti office in that building? Renate, the Simonetti Towers has thirty-nine floors."

I tried to walk around her, but she stepped in front and stopped me.

"Slick, I watched you get on the elevator. Alone. I watched the floor indicators; it went straight to the thirty-eighth floor. Ike Simonetti occupies the entire thirty-eighth floor. Don't bullshit a bullshitter. Ike Simonetti is your client."

"You know that I would never confirm or deny a client's identity. I have a confidential relationship with all my clients."

I tried to walk around her again. Again, she stepped in front.

"Sam Simonetti was a billionaire and one of the wealthiest men in the whole state. His death was big news, handsome. Exhuming his body is even bigger news. If you cooperate, you could spin the story to your client's benefit."

"Until the ME does the autopsy, there is no story, Renate, and you wouldn't publish mere speculation."

She smirked. "You don't know much about the news biz, do you, sport? We speculate all the time."

"If you'll allow me to pass, I'm here to pick up my girlfriend. She's a cop in this precinct, and I paid a courtesy visit to Lieutenant Weiner, who is my old boss. My girlfriend and I have a date for the weekend." This time I managed to get around her.

She called after me. "Remember, handsome, I'll get the story one way or another."

I didn't want Renate Crowell blundering around muddying the waters…yet. I baited the hook. "Wait for the autopsy. It'll be worth it." I winked.

Terry and I strolled hand-in-hand to the hostess desk at the Sand Dollar restaurant in the Bahamian Caribe. Just two young lovers on a romantic idyll. A smiling young woman in an island-style dress picked up two menus as we approached. "Enjoy your day in Paradise. Table for two, sir?"

"No, thanks. We're meeting another couple for breakfast and they're probably waiting at a table for us." I peered over her shoulder. "In fact, I see them now." I took the menus from her hand and thanked her.

Both Mateo and Wallace knew me, so I had worn a Panama hat and sunglasses as a simple disguise. Terry and I sauntered across the coffee shop to look for them. It was a big place. After five minutes, we returned to the hostess. "I can't find our friends. Are there other places to get breakfast in the hotel?"

"Yes, sir. We have eight restaurants, and four of them serve breakfast."

"Which is the most exclusive?"

"The Café Manta Ray."

"That must be where we're supposed to meet. How would I find that?"

The hostess pulled out a small map and marked directions on it. "Take this with you, sir. Enjoy your day in Paradise."

We pulled the same looking-for-friends routine at the three other restaurants. It was now ten o'clock. I winked at Terry. "Time for Plan B." I found a house phone in a quiet spot behind the elevator bank.

I dialed the operator.

"Enjoy your day in Paradise. How may I direct your call?"

"Ms. Wallace's room please."

"Do you have a first name?"

"Yes, Lorraine."

"Hold please."

The phone rang four times. A man answered. "Hello."

I put on my best fake Bahamian accent. "Enjoy your day in Paradise, Mr. Wallace. This is the room service kitchen here. We have your order ready, sir, but the clerk who took your order—I'm sorry, sir, but I can't make out his handwriting for your room number. I can make out the first two digits: 1-7." I had figured they were staying on the concierge floor, the seventeenth.

"We already had breakfast."

This time he said enough for me to recognize Mateo's accent. "Really? Let me see. Oh, I see. It's a complementary fruit and wine basket from management."

"That's nice. It's suite 1762."

"Thank you, sir. We'll have it there in less than thirty minutes. Enjoy your day in Paradise."

Terry and I boarded the private elevator to the concierge floor. We went to our suite, number 1715. I didn't linger in the hall because both Wallace and Mateo might see me, although Mateo knew me as Charles Andrews. I ordered a fruit and wine basket for suite 1762.

I hung up. "Mateo answered when I rang Wallace's room."

I dialed the front desk.

"Enjoy your day in Paradise. How may I help you, Mr. Andrews?"

"I would like to change to a room across the hall."

"Is there something wrong with your suite, Mr. Andrews?"

"Oh, no. The suite is beautiful, but the balcony is on the east side. My fiancée would rather watch the sunset than the sunrise. Could we change to a room with the balcony on the west?"

"I have suite 1724 available. It will have a lovely sunset view from the balcony."

"Great. I'll come get the keys."

"Oh no, Mr. Andrews. A porter will bring you two keys and help you move your luggage. Would you like to do it right now?"

I gawked at Terry, who was applying skin moisturizer to her nude body. She stood and pirouetted for me. "I think you need to rub it in for me."

"Give us an hour," I answered the desk clerk. "In fact, I'll call you when we're ready."

The *you are here* diagram in our new suite showed fire escapes and room layouts for the entire floor. Eight even-numbered suites lay between us and Wallace and Mateo's suite. I paced our room—sixteen feet wide. I could tell from the diagram that the intervening suites were either thirty-two or forty-eight feet wide. Ours was one of the four smallest. I estimated Wallace's balcony at 300 feet away. Good thing I brought a telephoto lens.

Eight balconies separated us from Wallace. This was off season, so we had a good chance the suites between us and the target would be empty. I wouldn't have to shoot around a bunch of people on the other balconies.

I looked up local sunset time on the internet. Wallace and Mateo could be on their balcony from, say, 7:30 to 8:00 p.m. Or they could be at the Tiki bar. Or at one of eight restaurants on the property. Or the Cracked Conch in downtown Nassau. I asked Terry, "If you were on a tryst with your lover, wouldn't you watch the sunset from your own balcony?"

"As it happens, I am on a tryst with my lover, and I do want to watch the sunset from our own balcony. Let's take our chances up here. If we miss them, we can have dinner at the Cracked Conch."

"I can't take a chance that either one will recognize me."

Terry shrugged. "No guts, no blue chips. Now we have the rest of the day to ourselves. I move we go to the beach. I heard it's topless."

"Motion carried."

We got back to our suite at 6:30.

Terry grabbed my hand and dragged me into the bathroom. She opened the glass door to a shower that was large enough for a small dance party, and pulled me in for a little good, clean fun.

We put on terrycloth robes and I poured glasses of Pinot Grigio. The clock beside the bed said *7:24*. "Let's check out the balcony." We were

300 feet from our targets. They couldn't make out my face at that distance.

Two balconies between us and Mateo's suite were occupied. I sighted through the telephoto lens and could recognize Wallace and Mateo in the distance. Terry went to the side of the balcony closest to the target and faced me. I stood on the other side with the camera. If anyone noticed, they would think I was photographing Terry. I aimed over her shoulder. I murmured to Terry. "I'll wait for the others to move away. Can you stand there and look gorgeous for a while?"

"How's this?" She opened her robe and flashed me. Her tan skin framed the thin white triangle where her bikini bottom had covered barely enough to meet the legal requirements.

I peeked over my shoulder to see if the balconies behind us were occupied. One was, but the couple was sunset watching. "You're gorgeous, Queens." I almost took a picture, but embarrassing things often surface on the internet. Better keep the picture in my mind. What a picture. She shimmied and the queens danced back and forth.

The sight line between Wallace and me cleared. "Show time; close the robe." She did.

I snapped the picture.

I would crop Terry out of it before I showed it to Ike. I didn't look forward to telling him that his marriage was toast. Or at least headed for a round of marriage counseling. It was no consolation that the marriage would be history anyway when I proved she was a triple-murderer. Actually, if she had arranged for the gunmen who invaded my townhouse, she was guilty of felony murder for the death of the one I had shot. I shook my head.

Mateo and Wallace leaned against their balcony railing, arms around each other, admiring the sunset. I began to video and got another good shot of their kiss. Then I panned the same take to include the beach view and the hotel to establish the location. I snapped off another half dozen photos.

I put the camera down. "Now we can relax and enjoy our vacation, Terry. Back to the real world tomorrow afternoon."

It was late afternoon when I carried Terry's bag to her apartment. She closed the front door behind us and wrapped her arms around my neck. "Chuck, I had a wonderful time, even if it was business. Would you like to stay the night?"

I figured Terry had had enough of me for one weekend. Better to leave her wanting more instead of overstaying my welcome. I kissed her forehead. "The offer is tempting, Queens, but we both have early days tomorrow. However, I might be convinced to stay another half hour."

She kissed me slowly and thoroughly.

"Okay, make that an hour."

SEVENTEEN

After the car bomb, I had installed better locks on my townhouse and garage. I felt reasonably safe as I unlocked my front door and stepped inside.

Big mistake.

I closed the door behind me and threw the deadbolt, dropped the keys in my pocket, and lugged my suitcase down the hall. I didn't need a light because I knew my townhouse like my tongue knows my teeth. Too bad the landlady had told me to move.

The rear glass sliders admitted the waning daylight. Reflections off Seeti Bay shimmered through the living and dining rooms.

I saw movement between me and the back of the house. The intruder had waited in the dining room at the end of the hall.

I threw the suitcase at him, drew my Glock, and dived forward. The shooter's first two rounds went over my head. I put two of my own into him while sliding the length of the marble floor on my belly.

I didn't wait to see him drop in case he wasn't alone. If I had the assignment, I would post a second shooter near the front door to trap me in the entry hall. I rolled onto my back, sighting down above my feet, and waited for another shooter to come through the door off the hallway.

I heard glass break. It had to be the window in the downstairs guest room.

I ran to the front door and peeped through the narrow window beside it. The other shooter sprinted across the parking lot. The Santorini gang had sent three gunmen before. Was there another one in my house? I listened and heard only the groans of the one I had shot.

I threw open the door and galloped after the second man.

A neighbor was exiting his car.

"Jim, call 9-1-1. I shot a burglar in my apartment. He'll need an ambulance. Get the cops too. Then wait inside."

Jim pulled out his cellphone.

I hot-footed it around the garage and spotted the second man 100 yards ahead. *Here we go again.*

Since I had come from Nassau, I wore New Balances instead of dress shoes. I can run okay in my Rockport dress shoes, but with New Balances, I can run all day. I settled into an energy-saving stride and fell into pursuit mode. As he ran around the first corner, I had gained ten yards.

The next block was shorter, and I didn't want him out of my sight. I kicked it up a notch and closed to seventy-five yards as he crossed the canal bridge and headed for Seeti Bay Park. The park is full of tall palms and low flower beds. There are no bushes big enough to hide anyone.

The bad guy peeked over his shoulder and saw me rolling toward him like a tank. He was mine, as inevitable as nightfall, and he knew it.

He sprinted through the lengthening shadows into the park, dodging families and couples walking hand-in-hand. He left the pavement for the grassy lawn, which slowed him more than it did me. I had closed to forty yards by the time he hit the parking lot.

Families were returning to their cars in the fading light. He sidestepped a car leaving the lot, and I pulled closer. He slowed as he saw a young couple with two children loading an ice chest.

The gunman slammed the father on the side of the head with his pistol and knocked him to the ground. He grabbed the woman around the neck with his left arm. The children screamed as he jerked their mother around to shield himself from me. He jammed his pistol into her ribs and yelled, "Stop right there."

I pulled up five yards away with my Glock pointed between his eyes, two-handed Weaver shooting stance. I checked the field of fire behind him. It was clear.

I caught my breath. "Fellow, you don't want to do this. Drop your gun and let the lady go. It's over."

"You come any closer, and I'll kill her."

"If you shoot her, you die a hundredth of a second later. Look at me. You know me from your last attempt. I won't miss. Your buddy's already dead. If you want to live, drop your gun and let her go. You can make a deal with the DA to tell her who hired you. Prison is a lot better than a grave."

He jammed the gun harder into the woman's ribs. "No. I'm not kidding, McCrary; I'll kill her. Don't think I won't."

"Last chance, Bonano. Or are you Scarpetta? Which name do you want on your tombstone?"

His eyes widened when I called his name. He loosened his grip on the pistol as he started to say something, and I shot him in the bridge of his nose. He fell like the sack of shit that he was.

I holstered my gun and started to kick the pistol away from the dead man's hand. Then I thought of all the families and kids around and put the pistol in my pocket instead.

I faced the couple. "You all okay? What about your children? They look a little shook up."

Mother Weiner taught me that you should give people who've been through a trauma someone else to look after. They don't get so worried about what just happened. It worked. Each of them picked a kid to hug.

I called 9-1-1. "Dispatch, this is Carlos McCrary. I have a 419 in Seeti Bay Park Parking Lot…" I scanned around and found the sign, "…North 2A. I shot another guy back in my townhouse so I'm leaving the scene to see to him." I gave dispatch my home address. "He may be alive. My neighbor was supposed to call in that incident."

As I spoke, I pulled out my business card case. I handed the young couple each a card. "I'm sorry I can't stay, but this guy and another guy tried to kill me. The other one is wounded in my house. I have to go back so I can help him. Will you folks please stay here and tell the police what happened? Here is my license."

The man viewed my license and took my card. "You saved my wife's life. Thanks. We'll tell the cops what happened."

I jogged back home. I was tired. The ambulance and cops weren't there yet.

My neighbor Jim stood in the parking lot. I had warned him to go inside, but there you go. People are people.

"You don't need to wait for them, Jim. You better go inside; it's safer." I hurried into my house, broken glass from my guest room window crunching under my shoes.

I switched on the hall light, walked to the dining room, and switched on the chandelier, turning the dimmer to full bright. The crystals cast multi-colored light prisms all around the room. The gunman's blood had pooled on the white marble floor, a red so dark it was nearly purple.

I kicked his pistol into the living room, patted him down, and found a Texas driver's license with his picture.

He was gut shot. I saw abdominal wounds in Afghanistan—mostly on the bad guys, thank God. He was a goner, even if he had been *en route* to the hospital in an ambulance. This guy would be lucky to last ten more minutes. Or unlucky. He was in that much pain.

I felt nauseous again, but not as bad as the last time I shot someone. I hoped I was not getting used to shooting people.

I squatted out of reach. "Well, if it isn't Bones Bonano. How you doing, Bones? That must be Scrambles Scarpetta I killed in the park."

Bonano groaned. "Call me an ambulance."

"Okay, you're an ambulance. Bones, who hired you?"

"I'm dying. Call an ambulance."

"All in good time. First, tell me who hired you."

Bonano stared at the blood flowing between the fingers he clasped over his stomach. "Am I going to die?"

"Bones, you haven't got much time. I'll call the ambulance after you tell me who wants me dead."

"Charlie Chops."

"What's his real name?"

"Charlie...Civitis."

"Why?"

"He...don't pay me...to ask questions." He passed out as I heard the sirens outside.

I called Flamer. "I have another name for you to research."

Vicky met me for breakfast. "I watched the excitement on the eleven o'clock news last night. I didn't call because you seemed okay when that reporter interviewed you, and I knew I would see you this morning."

She waved at the server, who approached with a coffee pot. After the server left, she put her hand on mine. "I'm glad you're okay. Does that account for everyone who wants you dead?"

"Until they send more."

"Until who sends more? You told the reporter you didn't know who sent the gunmen. And you claimed they died without saying anything."

"I did say that, didn't I? They worked for Charlie Civitis, a boss in the Houston mob."

Vicky seemed concerned. "What does a Houston mob boss have against you?"

"Haven't got a clue...yet. But Civitis is a lieutenant for the Santorini crime family in Houston."

"Mafia?"

"Beats me. Are they Mafia when they're Greek-American? They're still hoods," I said. "There may be a connection between them and Lorraine Wallace."

"What kind of connection?"

"Albert Compostela is a boss in the Houston mob. The Compostela and Santorini families have divided Houston between them. Big Al Compostela has four sons. One is married to Lorraine's sister."

"You think Lorraine used her sister to gain access to a hit man?"

"Someone did. Do the math. So far, she's the top of my list."

"Geez," Vicky said. "What will you do?"

"My usual approach is to blunder around, annoy people, and ask embarrassing questions. If I turn over enough rocks, eventually I'll find a snake."

"It would be a bad idea to ask a Houston mob boss on his home turf why he keeps sending hit men after you. You need another approach."

I took another slug of coffee while I thought about Vicky's advice. "I'll be extra alert and hope for the best."

The server approached and took our order. While we waited, I told her how I took Ramona and Gloria to Mexico. "Gloria is safe at home with a new nanny until we can get this thing with Lorraine sorted out. I have three off-duty cops on shifts to guard her 24/7."

"I'm glad she's okay."

"It's all part of the expenses I charge to Sam's estate."

"Still, not everyone would have done what you did to protect Gloria."

I flipped my tablet computer around and showed the video and photos from the Bahamian Caribe that I had taken the previous weekend.

"Is that your girlfriend in the foreground?"

"Teresa Kovacs. She's a cop."

Vicky narrowed her eyes. "Under cover I suppose?"

I shrugged. "It is what it is. Remember, you and I have no commitments."

"She's nice enough looking I suppose, if you like your women young, sexy, and blonde." Then she grinned. "I'm sorry. I'm being a bitch."

"You can't help it. You're a female attorney."

She shot me the bird again. "I had to check out the competition." At least she smiled as she said it. "Okay, Chuck, down to business. Now that you have proof Lorraine is involved, what do you do next?"

I shook my head. "I proved that she is a client of Franklin Turbot's. That's not a crime. I haven't proved that she hired him to find an arsonist. Her connection to Turbot is legitimate on the surface. I have missed something."

"What did you miss?"

"If I knew what it was, I wouldn't be missing it."

The LT was in the autopsy suite with a woman in her early forties who wore a blue lab coat. Weiner waved me over. "Doc, have you met Chuck McCrary?"

The woman shook my hand. "I'm Anandi Mahajan. Please call me Annie." She pushed a wayward wisp of thick, dark hair behind her ear.

"Nice to meet you, Annie."

Lieutenant Weiner gestured at the stainless-steel door. "Annie, show Chuck what you showed me on Sam Simonetti's body."

Mahajan slipped on a fresh pair of nitrile gloves and pulled the cadaver drawer open. She lifted the drape and pointed to the cadaver's left foot. "Look between the second and third metatarsal." She parted the two toes and showed me a small indentation.

"See that, Chuck? That's a puncture wound where someone gave him an injection. If the lieutenant hadn't told me this was a possible homicide, I wouldn't have examined there."

"What was injected?"

She replaced the drape and pushed the drawer closed. "We found Fentanyl in a tissue sample."

I knew about Fentanyl. "Whoever injected the Fentanyl induced a heart attack?"

"A fatal one," Mahajan said. "This is now officially a homicide." She stripped her gloves off and tossed them in a waste bin. "It'll be in my report. Any more questions for now, Lieutenant?"

"No, thanks, Annie," Weiner said. "Now we have to find out who gave the injection."

"Annie," I asked, "did it require any particular skill to inject the Fentanyl?"

"Anyone who's ever seen a medical drama on television can give an injection. All you need is the drug and a hypodermic."

"My vote is for Lorraine," I said.

Mother frowned at me. "You know better than to jump to conclusions, Chuck. Follow the evidence. We don't have enough to point fingers yet."

The LT and I walked out the door and nearly bumped into Renate Crowell. She stuck a microphone in the lieutenant's face. "Lieutenant Weiner, was Sam Simonetti murdered?"

"The autopsy report hasn't been released yet."

"That wasn't my question, Lieutenant. Was Sam Simonetti murdered?"

Weiner paused.

Renate was a shark that smelled blood in the water. "Lieutenant, Medical Examiner cases are public record. Anyone can copy the ME's Report. I know the report isn't final, but it will be soon, and the public has a right to know if Sam Simonetti was murdered."

Weiner hesitated.

Renate put her microphone away. "Lieutenant, we can go off the record. You could be 'an unnamed source close to the investigation.' This is a big story."

Weiner waved at me. "You tell her, Chuck. I have work to do." The lieutenant left without saying good-bye.

Renate stuck the microphone in my face. "So, was Sam Simonetti murdered?"

"Yes."

"How?"

"Someone injected Fentanyl between his toes."

"Isn't that a recreational drug?"

"That's not all it is."

"What else does it do?" she asked.

"It mimics a heart attack."

"Who injected it?"

I shrugged. "I don't know yet."

"Are there any suspects?"

"You should ask Lieutenant Weiner."

"Well, do you, personally, have any suspects?" she asked.

"None I can discuss."

"Is Ike Simonetti a suspect?"

I frowned at her. "Not as far as I know."

"What about Ramona Simonetti?"

"Again, not as far as I know."

"You'll tell me when you're ready." She put away her microphone.

I had baited the hook a few days before. Now I dangled it in front of her. "It won't be long, Renate."

Tropical Storm George had popped up in the Gulf of Mexico two days before. The weather gurus expected George to make landfall on the west coast of Florida sometime that night. George's outer bands alternated between periods of sunshine and buckets of rain and gusty winds and calm. Thirty minutes before, the sun had beamed down like the Port City Tourist Bureau had it on the payroll. Then another band of George joined our regular sea breeze. The humid air over the Everglades multiplied the thunderheads, and they bloomed like mushrooms in the spring.

Thunder crashed like pins in a distant bowling alley as Snoop drove my Dodge Grand Caravan to Wallace's medical building. The lower floors of the parking garage were full. We snaked our way back and forth up to the roof and didn't find a spot.

Snoop braked by the elevator lobby that perched like an island on the roof deck. "Get out here, bud. I'll find a spot and meet you in the lobby later."

It would be raining buckets when I came out. I grabbed my folding umbrella as I left the van. The storm blustered and lightning flashed to my left. Before I could say one-thousand-one the ear-splitting *cr-a-a-ck* shook the building. It had struck less than half a mile away. There would be gusty winds and flying debris later, and I was glad we hadn't come in the Silver Ghost. The Avanti's fiberglass body was a perfect insulator against lightning, but it wouldn't care much for flying branches.

Port City Dermatology Associates was on the third floor. I rang the bell beside the frosted sliding window.

"Good afternoon, Mr. McCrary. I'm Sylvia Chang," the nurse said. "Has the storm hit yet? I heard thunder, but we don't have any windows in this area."

"No, but I expect it any minute, and it's gonna be a big one."

"Thanks for the weather report." She handed me a clipboard and a ballpoint pen. "Please fill out this medical history form and sign the notices and bring it back when you're finished."

I filled out the medical history; I had no reason to lie. Under *sex* I resisted the temptation to write "you bet." Under *reason for visit*, I wrote "scar tissue."

In minutes, the glass window slid open again. Nurse Chang stuck her head out the opening. "Dr. Wallace will see you now, Mr. McCrary. Exam room three, second door on your left."

"If you have a room free on the south side, I would like to watch the storm."

Chang surveyed her schedule board. "Exam four, second door on your right."

"Thanks."

I opened the blinds in exam room four. The storm arrived with a crash as sudden as turning on a garden hose. Rain cascaded down the glass in rivulets. I raised the blinds all the way. The deluge traced braided streams down the window.

A different nurse came in to take my vitals. Her hair was shellacked into a salt-and-pepper helmet, no makeup, no smile. "Please remove your shoes and step on the scale." Her lips didn't move so I figured she was a robot.

Before I stepped on the scale, I unclipped my belt holster and laid the Glock 17 on the examining table. I slid up my right pants leg and unfastened the ankle holster. I placed my Browning .380 beside the Glock. No point in adding three unnecessary pounds to my weight.

If robo-nurse noticed the guns, she gave no sign. Maybe she had lots of patients who wore guns. "Dr. Wallace will see you soon."

The storm gathered intensity. The lightning seemed like God was taking flash pictures of the landscape.

Wallace knocked twice on the door and entered. "Sorry to keep you waiting, Chuck. It's nice to see you." We shook hands and sat down. "You have a problem with scar tissue?"

"I said that, Lorraine, but I lied. My real problem is with the people you sent to kill me."

Wallace's eyes widened and her mouth formed an O. "What did you say?"

I handed two mug shots to her. "Charlie 'Bones' Bonano and Hector 'Scrambles' Scarpetta, two soldiers from the Santorini crime family in Houston that you hired to put a hit on me." Her eyes widened again and I added, "Also, Vittorio Martinelli, a/k/a Victor Martin, a local driver originally from New Jersey who Bones and Scambles hired to drive for them." I handed her Martinelli's mug shot.

She acted flustered. "You're saying I hired these men to kill you? That's ridiculous." She dropped the photos on the counter. "I feel like I'm in a nightmare here. This can't be Candid Camera because this isn't funny."

She jammed her hands on her hips. "Why on earth would I want you dead?"

"So I wouldn't find out that you arranged the fire that killed Ike's half-sisters."

She paused a second. "Now you're saying I'm responsible for the fire?"

"You hired Frank Turbot to have Ike's half-sisters killed."

"Frank Turbot?" She scoffed. "This is like *Through the Looking Glass* or maybe *The Twilight Zone*. Frank Turbot is a family law attorney, not a mob lawyer. He wouldn't know the first thing about having someone killed, any more than I would. I didn't want Ike's half-sisters dead. I have no motive."

"Sure you do. You wanted Ike to inherit all of his father's estate instead of one-third. Last Labor Day week, when you were in Houston, you arranged to have Ike's half-sisters killed. Then at Thanksgiving, you found out Ramona was pregnant and realized that Ike would get only half."

"That's absurd."

"I would bet that you intend to kill Ramona and Gloria too, eventually. That would leave Ike as sole heir. Then you kill him like you did your first husband and you inherit $400,000,000 plus whatever money Ike's made on his own. You inherit $80,000,000 per murder. People have killed their whole family for less."

"That's ridiculous. My first husband Walter had a heart attack. And I have plenty of money of my own. So does Ike. We don't need more."

"For some people that might be true, Lorraine. But for you, not so much. A jury can decide." I leaned back in the chair. "Lorraine, I know everything. I know about your sister, Virginia. I know that her father-in-law is Big Al Compostela."

She flinched. "Virginia has nothing to do with that aspect of Norberto's family. Ginny married Norberto in college when she got pregnant. We're Catholic." She said it as if that explained everything.

"Ginny didn't know about Norberto's family when they were dating. She knew he was smart, handsome, and charming. Charming enough that he got her pregnant." Tears welled in her eyes. "They eloped that weekend. She's made the best of a bad situation ever since...for the children's sake."

I waved her remark off. "I know about your deal with Frank Turbot too."

"I don't have any deal with Frank Turbot. Last September I was in Houston to visit family, and I had Frank set up a foundation to help children of drug-addicted parents. He revised my will to include the foundation."

I waited to see if she would admit anything.

Wallace added, "That trip to see Frank Turbot was purely professional."

"Lorraine, I hacked your bank account." She said nothing so I continued. "A couple days after you met with Turbot, you wrote him a check for $20,000. I have a picture of the check. Right after he got the money, he approached a local criminal defense lawyer named Lenny Lucas. Did he tell you about Lucas?"

"Frank Turbot didn't tell me anything! That $20,000 was his fee to set up the foundation and to revise my will."

"Lenny Lucas is a former public defender who knows lots of scumbags. Turbot paid Lucas to hire someone to kill Ike's half-sisters. Lucas subcontracted the hit to an arsonist named Howard Hopper. Hopper torched the Montrose mansion in Cleveland. I haven't hacked Turbot's escrow account...yet. But I would bet a subpoena of his account will reveal that he paid off Lenny Lucas with the money you gave him. You hit the jackpot with the fire, Lorraine. You killed your husband's half-sisters, and you got their mother too."

I waited for a reaction.

Thunder rumbled through the room while the tropical storm beat white noise on the window. I counted seconds to myself to resist the temptation to fill the silence. When I got to nine-thousand-nine, Wallace spoke. "I am innocent. I explained everything. What more do you expect me to say?"

"How about, 'You can't prove any of this'?"

"Well, you can't," she said, "because it never happened. The $20,000 was to set up the foundation. I told you that."

"How do you explain Turbot hiring Lenny Lucas?"

She sat on the stool again. "All I have is your word that he did."

"I can prove it. The Houston police can prove it too."

Her shoulders slumped. "Then I can't explain it."

"Lorraine, I connected the dots, and they lead straight to you. The police can connect dots too."

I ticked my fingers as I reeled off the facts. "Dot one: The Cleveland crime scene investigators found Hopper's fingerprint on the electrical box at the Montrose mansion. The Cleveland police know that. They will look for Hopper in Houston. He's not hard to find. I found him in two hours.

"Dot two: Hopper told me Lenny Lucas hired him to kill Ike's half-sisters. He'll rat on Lucas to the cops to get a lesser sentence.

"Dot three: Lucas told me that Turbot paid him $20,000 to find someone to kill the sisters. He will testify against Turbot to get a lesser sentence too.

"Dot four: Frank Turbot confirmed that you came to see him after Labor Day and he did legal work for you."

I spread all the fingers on my left hand. "Dot five: You paid Turbot $20,000 three weeks before the fire."

I leaned back in my chair and spread my hands. "Ta-da."

This time I counted to seven-thousand-seven before she reacted.

"This can't be happening. I'm innocent. I hired Frank Turbot to revise my will."

It was time for the *coup de grace*. "And there's a sixth dot: Sam Simonetti was murdered."

"Pop was murdered? How?"

"It was pretty clever, Lorraine. You injected Fentanyl between his toes, where no one was supposed to notice."

"Fentanyl? That's a controlled substance. Is that what the autopsy showed?"

"It's a controlled substance, but it's easy to get for a physician on staff at the hospital. A physician like you."

She gawped at me, eyes red. "There has to be a logical explanation. I had nothing to do with that fire or with Pop's death."

Wallace strode toward the door, tears in her eyes. "I'm...I'm...I'm hiring an attorney." The tears spilled over. "If you make these ridiculous accusations public, I'll sue you for every penny you have or ever hope to have."

She jerked the door open and whirled back toward me. "I had

nothing to do with that fire. And nothing to do with Pop's death. Nothing. Now get the hell out."

Snoop leaned against a marble column in the lobby. When I unfurled my umbrella, he sneered. "Real men don't use umbrellas."

"In this case, I think they would." I clutched the umbrella with both hands as we stepped into a tropical storm that whipped the downpour horizontally. We jogged straight across the street, dodging the traffic and the puddles. The rain soaked me from the waist down, but that's life in Port City. Snoop looked like he had gone swimming in his suit.

The building lobby across the street offered shelter. I shook off my umbrella and we took the elevator to the fourth floor, where we entered the door marked 416 without knocking.

Special Agent Eugenio Lopez from the FBI stood at the window.

Lieutenant Weiner stood by the monitor she had been watching with Sergeant Ernesto Donatello. Weiner smiled at Snoop. "Snoop, you're wet."

Snoop stood in a growing puddle on the linoleum floor. "Thanks for telling me, Mother. I never would have noticed." Snoop stripped off his wet jacket.

"Snoop says real men don't use umbrellas." I took off my shirt and removed the microphone and transmitter taped to my torso. The tape stung like hell as it ripped off the hair on my stomach. "Did you get everything?"

Weiner smiled. "Picture and sound, clear as a bell. That was a good idea to raise the blinds. Unfortunately, what we got is *bupkis*."

"You think Lorraine's innocent, Mother?"

Weiner sighed. "*Bubalah*, no one is innocent, not even me. If you're asking 'did she do it?' I answer what I always answer: Follow the evidence."

"Our evidence leads to Turbot, but we have no proof Wallace hired him to hit the Simonetti sisters and we have nothing that says she injected the Fentanyl."

"I've had people working the hospital drug records since Tuesday," Mother said. "A Fentanyl vial went missing a couple days before Sam's death, but we can't nail down who took it. Could be anybody from a maintenance man to a doctor with access to the controlled substances."

"So, it could be Wallace?"

"Sure it could, Chuck, but it could be a nurse or even a janitor with a key. Anyone could have bribed a hospital employee."

She jerked her chin at Donatello and Lopez. "We gotta do this the hard way, guys. Ernie, take your team and execute the search warrant for Lorraine Wallace's house, office, car, and all bank and brokerage accounts. Gene, I guess your FBI people and the Houston cops will execute on Frank Turbot, Lenny Lucas, and Howard Hopper?"

"Yeah, Mother. I'll text them the go-ahead."

I buttoned my shirt. "So, if Wallace didn't arrange the fire, who did?"

Renate Crowell texted me:

Will run story that cops executed search warrant on Lorraine Wallace in connection with investigation of Sam's death. Care to comment first?

I called her.

"I thought you would call, Chuck. Buy you lunch?"

"Meet me at the Rusty Pelican."

"That's the high rent district. Do you know how much this lunch will cost me?"

"Put it on your expense report, Renate. I guarantee it'll be worth it to the *Press-Journal*."

Tropical Storm George had blown into the Atlantic and was on its way to menace Bermuda. The air in Port City hung like wet clothes on an old-fashioned clothesline, more oppressive than usual. The sun burned hotter on my arms, and the cooling coastal trade winds were notable by their absence.

I took a table overlooking Seeti Bay. The air stirred without any conviction. If the ceiling fans hadn't been spinning beneath the thatched roof, I would have worked up a sweat lifting my drink. But the skyline view across Seeti Bay took your breath away, and the ceiling fans made the humidity bearable. I hung my jacket on the back of an empty chair, rolled up my sleeves, and removed my tie.

Every time I had seen Renate, she had dressed pretty informally, but today she wore a pin-striped pants suit that was a knockoff of one of Hillary Clinton's outfits back when she was Secretary of State. I whistled as I stood. "You clean up really well, Renate."

Then I kicked myself. I really needed to work on my social skills with women.

She did a mock curtsy. "I figured my usual uniform wasn't classy enough for the Rusty Pelican." She appraised the other well-dressed women nearby. "Looks like I made the right decision." She sat and gestured at my glass as the server came over. "What're you drinking?"

"Iced coffee; I have to work this afternoon."

"What a waste of a good waterfront table—and expense account." She smiled at the server. "Bring me a rum drink in a coconut with a paper umbrella in it. Or maybe something decorated with a flower."

"We have several drinks that fit that description, ma'am."

"Surprise me."

The server laughed and left.

"Okay, handsome. Is this for attribution or deep background?"

"Deep background. Can't use my name yet."

She set her tablet computer on the table.

"Hold on, Renate. What do you already know?"

"The autopsy report shows someone killed Sam Simonetti by injecting Fentanyl between his toes to induce a heart attack, like you told me. The heart attack occurred after he was visited in the hospital by Ike Simonetti, Lorraine Wallace, and Ramona Simonetti. Dr. Wallace is on staff at the hospital where Sam died, and she had access to Fentanyl. The cops executed a search warrant yesterday afternoon at Wallace's house and office. This is front-page juicy."

"You didn't hear it from me," I said, "but the warrant also covered Wallace's cars, computers, and bank records."

"I didn't know that. What did they find?"

"Nothing yet, and that makes me wonder if they have the right suspect. They're still digging, but nothing incriminating has shown up so far."

"The public will put two and two together, Chuck."

"If they do, they may get five."

"How so?"

"Something's not right."

"Not right how?"

"I don't know yet; that's why I agreed to talk to you. Don't let the dogs out on Lorraine Wallace yet. I once thought she was involved; now I'm not so sure. I don't want to ruin her life with false accusations and innuendo."

"What other suspects do you have?"

The server arrived with an alcoholic coconut with a pink paper umbrella stuck jauntily in the top. "How does this look?"

Renate grinned. "It looks perfect. Thanks."

"You ready to order now?"

"Give us five more minutes?"

"Of course." She left.

Renate took a long pull on the biodegradable paper straw. "Zowie, that's good." She took another long pull. "Okay, where was I? Oh, yeah, you have any suspects other than Lorraine Wallace?"

I had baited the hook and dangled it in front of her. Now I set it. "Ramona Simonetti."

"The widow?"

I dropped my bombshell. "Ramona Simonetti was arrested for murdering one of her three previous husbands in Mexico. She's now in a Mexican prison awaiting trial."

"Holy crap."

"That's not all. All three of her previous husbands died under suspicious circumstances."

"What suspicious circumstances?" she asked.

"I'm not going to do all your work for you. You'll have to dig that up for yourself. I'm sure you have researchers in Mexico."

Renate stuck her tongue out at me. "Kill joy. Okay, I'll do the research. By the way, what's your source for her arrest?"

"I'm the guy who delivered her like a Christmas present to the *Federales*." I told her how I enticed Ramona to Mexico. "You can use my name as the source for that story."

I didn't tell her how I smuggled Gloria back to the United States. She was smart enough not to ask.

I didn't want the media sniffing around either Lorraine Wallace or Ike Simonetti yet, so I had served up Ramona on a silver platter. Once the news hit the *Pee-Jay*, the TV and radio news programs would take the bait too.

She smiled up from her tablet. "This will get my byline on the front page. I can see the headline—*Did Black Widow Make Sam Simonetti Her Fourth Victim?*"

Renate Crowell had her front-page headline and byline the next morning. I switched off my McCrary Investigations cellphone to avoid the media sharks circling for more blood. My receptionist would screen calls and take messages on the land line. The publicity would have been good for business, but I had more pressing obligations that weekend.

I had to move into my new apartment.

Vicky had been right—the Simonetti case was paying off like a broken slot machine. Of course, I was earning every penny of it by dodging assassination attempts. Maybe I should have made a deal to charge Simonetti by the bullet. With my improved finances, I had leased a waterfront high-rise with 24/7 security and a marina. It was smaller than the townhouse but no gunmen could surprise me behind the front door. The balcony was larger than my townhouse deck and wrapped around two sides of the building. The view was spectacular. So was the monthly rent. I stood at the rail and admired the *Gator Raider* at my personal dock fourteen floors below.

Terry helped me unpack. We spent the weekend on the *Gator Raider*. Since I had proved Sam was not Gloria's father, I stood to collect a bonus of a cool $1,000,000.

Naturally, like any true Floridian, I was shopping for a bigger boat.

EIGHTEEN

Monday dragged like a snail in molasses. I killed time by returning messages from Fox News, CNN, and Telemundo.

At five o'clock my phone played the Dragnet theme. "Good afternoon, Mother. Any news to brighten a boring day?"

"Bad news, I'm afraid. The Feds searched Howard Hopper's apartment and found nothing."

"What does Howie have to say?"

"That's the other bad news. Haven't found him yet. He's disappeared."

I had a bad feeling about Howie. "Somebody must have put out a hit on him. He's too broke to run. He burned through the $20,000 that Lucas paid him in about four weeks. His girlfriend Darshonnay put most of his money up her nose. What about Lenny Lucas?"

"The Houston cops searched Lenny Lucas's office, car, and apartment. The office and car were clean. Lucas was found dead in his apartment."

"How?"

"The autopsy isn't finished, but it looks like an overdose two to five days ago. His air conditioner was set on *meat locker*."

"And his computer and cellphone?"

"Missing. Not in his office, his apartment, or his car."

"How convenient. What about Turbot?"

"Missing also."

"What about Turbot's wife?" I was worried about the forty-something lady who had been so polite to me.

"As far as I know, she's okay, *bubalah*. I have no report on her."

"If she's still around, it means that the cops haven't found his body yet. She's a sweetheart; I don't think he would run without her. That leaves us with Wallace. I'll bet you're going to make my day with the news on her."

"Yeah. We gave her stuff a colonoscopy. There's nothing incriminating anywhere: computer, files, brokerage accounts, the whole *megillah*. She doesn't even cheat on her taxes. She's either clean, or she's a freaking genius at covering her tracks. Plus, she's lawyered up. Won't give us the time of day."

Clicks and buzzes as the satellite phone system found Simonetti. Then four rings. "Hello."

"Ike, Chuck McCrary here."

"You have news?"

"Yeah, and it's all bad, but you weren't expecting good news." I told him about my return from Mexico City with Gloria, my encounter with Wallace in her office, and the search warrant results.

"So, the arsonist is missing, and the attorney who hired him is dead?"

"Yeah."

"Do the police know what happened to that arsonist—what's his name?"

"Hopper," I answered.

"Hopper."

"They're investigating."

"Any leads?"

"Don't know, Ike. They're in Houston and I'm in Port City. I told them everything I know, so they don't need to talk to me anymore."

"And Turbot is missing too?" Simonetti asked.

"I think he's dead and they haven't found his body."

"You know Lorraine invited him to our wedding."

"Yeah, you told me."

"Frank was a nice guy—not the sort to have mob contacts. Of course, people can change in ten years."

"Lawyers meet all kinds in their practice," I said.

"Lorraine denies she hired Turbot to find an arsonist?"

"She insists she had nothing to do with the arson. She says there must be another explanation for Turbot's involvement. And she's retained an attorney and threatened to sue me if I make the accusations public, which I had no intention of doing anyway. And there's more bad news, Ike."

"How much worse can it be?"

"Listen…I'm really sorry to have to tell you this…As soon as you left for Alaska, Lorraine met Reynaldo Mateo at a resort in the Bahamas. She's been seeing him every time you leave for the Great White North."

"How long has this been going on?"

"I went back two years. I don't know when it started."

I waited. I heard a sound on the phone. Maybe it was a sigh. Maybe a sob.

"How you holding up, Ike?"

"Not so good."

I waited again.

"Any more bad news?"

"Yeah."

"Oh geez…Okay, I'm ready. Hit me."

"We got the autopsy results on your father." I waited. I hoped that my hesitation would help break the news gently.

"What were the results?"

I paused. "Someone injected him with Fentanyl, which caused the final heart attack."

There was a long silence on the line.

"So, it was murder."

"Yes."

"Who did it?"

"Lots of people were in and out of your Dad's room, including Ramona and Lorraine."

"Who do you think did it?"

"Lorraine would know how to find Fentanyl and how to use it. And Ramona has a history of husbands dying."

"At least the cat's out of the bag. Lorraine knows we're onto her. So, no more secrecy."

"Yeah, you can come home and take care of Gloria."

"My marriage is toast, of course."

"Yeah."

"I can't go back to our house; Lorraine will be there. I need another place to live."

"Doesn't Ramona's house belong to your dad's estate?" I asked.

"I forgot about that. I can move there. The silver lining in this whole shitty mess is that I get to be Gloria's guardian. That reminds me—have you told Howley and the nanny what's going on?"

"Not yet. I told you first. What should I tell them?"

"Tell them everything. Tell them I'll be back in a couple of days to take custody of Gloria. Ask Vicky if we need to do anything legally to make that happen. Then get someone to pack up Ramona's personal stuff and donate it to charity."

"Her stuff could contain evidence the Mexican police can use."

"Okay. You look through it and send them anything that helps their case," he said.

"I planned to invite my contact with the Mexican Police to come up here and look though her stuff personally."

"Whatever."

"What about your personal stuff at your house?"

"Forget it. I'll buy new clothes. I don't want to talk to Lorraine about getting it."

"Including your hunting and fishing gear?"

"I call always buy more gear. The gear will wait until the Lorraine situation is resolved, one way or another."

"What about your guns?" I asked.

"They're in the gun safe, and Tom and I are the only ones with the combination. And Lorraine has no interest in my fishing gear. Look, it's getting late, but it'll be light until ten p.m. I'll have my guide fly me back to Anchorage today, but we might not arrive in time to catch tonight's flight. A flight at 8:42 p.m. connects in Houston and gets into Port City around noon tomorrow, if I make it. If not, I'll be back the next day."

"Okay. I'll see you when you get here."

I was halfway across the parking lot on my way to the Silver Ghost when the bullet hissed past my head, followed a split second later by the bang. I vaulted sideways and sprinted to the dumpster enclosure at the far end of the lot. The wind from another round passed near my neck. Concrete chips exploded where it shattered against the wall of my building.

The shots came at a downward angle and hit the wall a foot above the pavement. Only one place the shooter could be—the parking garage across the street. I dived behind the dumpster corral. A rifle bullet would blast through its concrete block walls, but the shooter couldn't see where I was. I peeked out from near the bottom of the wall. If the garage was as empty as my own lot, there would be few places for the shooter to hide. I glimpsed a rifle barrel and a faint reflection from a telescopic sight on the top floor. I pulled my head back as another shot rang out, and a bullet *whanged* off the asphalt where my head had been.

Accuracy from that distance meant his rifle was probably bolt-action. That worked to my advantage. He had to work the bolt between shots, at least one second. No more than five rounds plus one in the chamber, say six shots before he reloaded, maybe four. He had either one or three rounds left.

He was 100 yards away—too far to hit with my Glock 17. I bounded around the trash enclosure and sprinted across the lot. He didn't shoot, which meant that he was conserving his final round until he had a better shot. Forty-foot Royal Palms lined the median and both sides of Bayfront Boulevard. They would disrupt his line of sight. So would the shadows from the sun setting behind me. He was shooting into that sun.

I counted the time it would take him to draw a bead on a moving target and lead me by the right amount. I juked at a forty-five-degree angle as a fourth shot sprayed dirt and grass in the direction where I had been running.

I zigzagged across the boulevard to the garage, but heard no more shots. The gun barrel I spotted had disappeared. Four shots and he had to reload. Reload takes thirty seconds.

The shots had come from the northwest corner, but that didn't mean he had stayed there. Still, that was the first place to look.

I made a beeline for the garage entrance at the southwest corner. I hit the exit door and pounded full speed up the fire stairs to the top.

There were fire escapes and elevators in the northeast and southwest corners of the building. I ended up at the southwest corner, sixty yards from where the shooter had been. The shooter had picked a nest where he had the best angle at my parking lot. If it had been me, I would have picked a spot near one of the fire stairs for easy exit in case things went wrong. In the Special Forces, we learned to plan for contingencies. This shooter had to be overconfident of his aim or he was an amateur. Not likely. So far, the guys sent to kill me had been professionals.

I eased open the steel door at the top of the stairs and peered across the darkening parking area. A bullet ricocheted off the door at head height. I dropped to the floor and crawled out into the twilight. I lay in the shadows behind the car parked there. I studied the length of the garage from under the car. The parking spots between the shooter and me were empty. The shooter squatted behind a dark SUV backed into the northwest corner space.

Another shot hit the pavement under the car. I closed my eyes against the concrete dust. Smart shooter. He had figured out I was behind the car and tried to hit me with a ricochet. I crabbed back behind the front wheels and squatted behind the hood. I sneaked a quick look over the hood and dropped as I saw the muzzle flash. The bullet smashed into the wall behind me. I used a hand mirror from my jacket and peeked around the front of car. The sniper raised his rifle and disappeared behind the SUV. He was down to one bullet. He didn't like the odds.

The SUV rocked as someone got in on the driver side. The engine roared to life. Wheels screamed. The SUV sprang from its parking spot. The shooter was trying to escape.

I rose from behind the car and steadied my Glock on the hood. I squeezed off four rounds before the SUV reached the exit ramp. My rounds shattered all four rear windows. The SUV hurtled down the ramp without pause.

I jerked open the fire door and raced down two flights to the fifth floor. I hit the crash bar on the stair door and ran out onto the parking deck. The SUV's tires squealed above me. I was fast enough to intercept the SUV on the sixth floor, but I wanted time to prepare.

The floor shook as the concrete flexed from the two-ton vehicle dashing down the ramp. I heard it hit bottom on the sixth floor and the building shivered. I jogged to the bottom of the ramp and picked a spot behind the last pillar on the east side. I watched the ramp, took a deep breath, and slowed my breathing.

I braced my forearm against the pillar and aimed up the ramp, slowing my breathing further. *Easy squeezy, nice and easy.*

After making the next turn he would be heading straight for me. I had thirteen rounds left—plenty to put this guy away, even if he wasn't alone.

The deck shook harder, the SUV pounding the length of the sixth floor to the top of the next ramp. It screeched around the left turn and raced toward where I stood in the shadows. Focused on his breakneck race, the driver would be unlikely to see me behind the pillar. But I couldn't see his face either. The garage lights reflected off his tinted windshield and he moved too fast.

I put three rounds into the windshield as the SUV approached. Spider webs streaked the safety glass. Ten rounds left. If the driver noticed my muzzle flashes, he knew where the shots came from. I had chosen my spot well; he had no choice but to keep coming toward me.

The SUV braked hard and fish-tailed around the pillar where I stood. I saw the driver's outline in the dim light, but I couldn't see his face. I aimed with two hands and rapid-fired three rounds at his head and three more through the driver door. The SUV swerved right, bounced off a parked car and accelerated north toward the next down ramp.

He swerved and jerked the SUV like I had hit him.

Four rounds left.

I raced to the stairs and pounded down three flights to the ground floor. Bolting out the exit, I ran toward the empty cashier booths. I switched out the magazine for the spare in my jacket.

No way he was going to get past me. His ass was mine.

I listened at the bottom of the ramp. An engine raced up above, but I heard no squealing tires and felt no shaking floor. The SUV wasn't moving.

Sirens wailed in the distance. Someone had called the cops.

There were five ways to leave the garage on foot, and I covered three: the ramp, the southwest elevator, and the southwest fire stairs. No way I could cover the northeast elevator and stairs. Nothing I could do about that, so I held my ground where I was.

I jogged back to the southwest elevator lobby and punched the call button. I watched the ramp as I waited. The elevator doors opened. I scanned the exit ramp again, leaned into the elevator, and pushed the emergency stop button. Then I opened the door to the stairway and listened.

The shooter's rifle was accurate to hundreds of yards. My Glock was accurate to forty yards, fifty under ideal conditions. Even with a full magazine, I didn't like the odds. Besides, the sirens meant help was on the way. Glancing back at the deserted ramp, I stood in the open fire door and waited for the cavalry. No need to be a hero.

With the pause in the action, I felt sick to my stomach. I fought the urge to vomit.

The sirens got louder, then stopped in mid-wail as the cars arrived. Red and blue lights swirled across the walls and ramp. It was the SWAT truck and two black-and-whites.

The first two cops approached the garage with guns drawn. I held up my hands, my Glock in one and my open wallet with my PI license in the other. I called out, "Over here in the stairway door. I'm Carlos McCrary. I'm a PI."

I held the Glock by the barrel so they could see it. "I'm placing this on the ground so you can search me." I placed the pistol on the floor with the barrel pointed to the wall and stepped back. "There's at least one shooter on the floor above me. I got off several rounds into the SUV's windshield. I must have hit the driver. The northeast elevator and fire stairs are not covered. If I were you, I would send a team over there."

Four SWAT cops approached behind shields, followed by four more uniforms. I recognized one of the uniforms. "Gracie, good to see you."

Sergeant Graciela Garcia waved the SWAT team to a halt. "You two cover the northeast elevator and stairs." She nodded to her partner. "He's okay." She pointed at my pistol. "You can pick that up, Chuck. What do we have?"

When I bent over to retrieve my pistol, my seasick stomach nearly betrayed me. I shook like a tambourine at a holy-roller revival. I leaned against a wall and slid down to sit on the concrete fire stairs.

Gracie put a hand on my shoulder. "You all right?"

"I ran up and down six flights of stairs in the middle of a gunfight. Let me catch my breath." I breathed slowly until I could talk without throwing up. It would be bad form to pitch my cookies in front of Gracie. Bad for my tough-guy image.

"The SUV stopped moving, but I hear the engine still racing." I pointed up the ramp. "I think they crashed. I spotted one guy in the front seat. I couldn't see the other seats. Last time they came after me with three shooters."

Gracie surveyed the scene. "Okay, Chuck. We'll take it from here." She waved at two more uniforms that had arrived. "You two make sure no one comes down these stairs. You two go with the SWAT guys to the northeast corner." She motioned the remaining SWAT team members to proceed and then faced her partner. "You come with me."

I felt a little better, so I started after the SWAT team. Gracie scowled at me. "This is a crime scene; civilians aren't supposed to be here."

"Gracie, the only way to keep me out of there is to shoot me." I kept walking after the SWAT team.

She shrugged, but she didn't say anything. The six cops advanced up the ramp to the second floor with me behind them. From the top of the ramp, we gazed south where the SUV had crashed against a pillar. Smoke escaped from under the hood as the engine screamed.

The SWAT team took point down the east side. Gracie motioned to her partner. "You and I go up the other side."

I let the SWAT team walk ahead and then followed across the deserted deck. They had body armor. I didn't.

The engine back-fired twice, clattered, and stopped. The silence sounded ominous after the shriek of the racing motor. The loudest noise was the garble of police radios from the vehicles on the deck below.

Gracie and her partner reached the SUV right after the SWAT team. The SWAT team formed a semicircle around the wrecked vehicle. A wisp of steam leaked from the crumpled hood.

A man dressed in black lay motionless on the concrete, right foot still inside the driver's footwell. A dark smear of blood streaked the side of his neck. The collapsed airbag showed a bloody smear that appeared purple in the dim light. My gorge rose again.

As Gracie approached the body, I took a Weaver stance opposite the open door and covered the shooter.

"Doesn't look like any survivors," Gracie said.

A rifle lay on the deck near the driver's outstretched left hand. Gracie shoved the firearm aside with her foot. It was a Ruger Model 77 Standard Hawkeye 7 mm rifle with a Leupold 3x9 telescopic sight. My stomach churned as I remembered a similar weapon displayed in a gun case in Ike Simonetti's office.

Gracie frisked the driver. *Nada.* She felt his pulse and shook her head. She rolled him onto his back. The dim light revealed a large blood stain on his chest that had made the red mark on the airbag. "You know him?"

"Too dark to see his face," I answered. "Use the flashlight."

She pulled a Maglite off her belt and shined it on the dead man's face.

In the stark bluish light, I recognized the face of the man I killed. My queasy stomach caught up with me, I stepped away from the crime scene and threw up on the parking deck. *So much for my tough-guy image.*

When I finished tossing my cookies, I walked back to the SUV. Gracie had pulled on crime-scene gloves and was holding the dead man's wallet and cellphone.

I stared down at the corpse. "Yeah, I know him. It's Tom Collins, Ike Simonetti's personal assistant."

As I stood over Collins's body, thoughts surged through my mind like stampeding buffalo. Clues I had seen but not noticed. Stray thoughts I had pushed aside because they didn't fit my preconceived theories. Hindsight is always 20/20.

Snoop would have said I was wearing blinders—so intent on Wallace that I had not considered other possibilities. He would have been right.

I mentally head-slapped myself for not running a background check on Tom Collins. It had not occurred to me to run a background check on a personal assistant, any more than I would have done a background on a secretary. A personal assistant often has a closer relationship to his or her boss than a secretary, and Simonetti had told me he had no secrets from Collins. *No secrets.* That should have been a clue.

Learn from your mistakes and don't repeat them, dummy.

I pulled Gracie to one side. "Whoever hired Collins will expect him to call to confirm the kill, wouldn't you think?"

"That's logical."

"And when Collins doesn't call, the guy that wants me dead will call his cellphone, wouldn't you think?"

She eyed the phone in her hand. "Again, that's logical. Where you going with this, Chuck?"

"I suggest that you keep the phone handy, so you can read the caller ID, but not answer it. Collins's boss might leave a voicemail."

Gracie studied the screen and smiled. "Since the phone is on and the battery has a ninety percent charge, I see no reason to turn it off. I'll keep an eye on it until CSU asks for it. If anyone calls, I'll send you a text."

"Thanks. Now can you open his wallet to his driver's license for me?"

She did. I took a picture of it with my cellphone.

"Thanks, Gracie. I owe you one."

"You owe me a lot more than one."

Walking back toward my own parking spot, I called Vicky to tell her what had happened, what my new theory was, and what evidence I needed to prove it.

Then I called Flamer. "This is Chuck McCrary."

"Yeah, yeah, yeah, caller ID *et cetera*. Whaddya need?"

"I sent you a photo of a driver's license. I want everything on Thomas Collins, including who his nanny was when he was a kid. And I want it tonight. Can do?"

"Does a bear eat berries?"

I called Sharon Farragut at the DNA lab and left a voicemail. I phoned Bettina Simpson in Houston with a heads-up. I called Terry last. "Queens, I have news."

"Just news? You're supposed to say you have good news and bad news, and ask which I want to hear first."

"Okay. I have good news and bad news. Which do you want first?"

"The good news."

"I survived."

"That sounds ominous. What's the bad news?"

"A sniper tried to kill me."

"What happened?"

"I killed him first." I recounted the events of the last few minutes. I consulted my watch. Only twenty-five minutes? It felt longer while it was happening, but the sunset still lingered, faintly golden on the western horizon. "The sniper was Tom Collins, my client's personal assistant."

"Oh, geez. That can't be good."

"Flamer's doing a deep dive on Collins's background now. But to prove my theory, I gotta go to Houston tonight."

"How long will you be gone?"

"A day or two."

"Okay. Be careful, King."

"Always, Queens. That's why I'm still alive."

NINETEEN

Bettina Simpson met my flight at George Bush Intercontinental Airport. She eyed my empty hands. "Did you check your bag?"

"Don't have one. I had to hustle to make the last flight to Houston. And I had to leave my Glock and my computer in my car so I could get through security faster."

"Don't worry, big fellow, I'll protect you."

"I'm counting on it, at least until we can stop by a gun store. Could we stop by a Walmart on the way to your place so I can pick up a few things?"

"Are you sleeping in my guest room or my bedroom?"

"Guest room."

"Good enough. And I've taken two days' vacation."

"Was your lieutenant okay with you helping me?"

Bettina smirked. "It's better to beg forgiveness than to ask permission."

"You didn't tell him."

"Her. Let's go to my place. Have you eaten?"

"No, they didn't have any seats in first class."

"I'll fix you something when we get home."

"Great. I have research to do tonight if you'll let me use your computer."

Bettina stopped walking. "Of course. But this trip won't be all business, will it?"

"God, no. I'll may be sleeping in your guest room instead of your bedroom, but I'll take you out to dinner at your favorite restaurant."

I managed four hours' sleep before Bettina and I left her apartment the next morning. Our first stop was the Harris County Institute of Forensic Science on Old Spanish Trail, where I picked up the two autopsy reports I needed. Bettina's gold shield reduced the normal wait time. I was glad I had asked for her help.

I called Gracie to see if anyone had called Collins's cellphone while she had it. No one had.

At Turbot's office, Bettina's shield again greased the skids. She was in street clothes so she looked like a detective instead of a patrol cop. The managing partner was out, but the firm's accountant agreed to see us without an appointment. The accountant's office looked like a garage sale at a paper recycling center. He had stacked paper piles on every horizontal surface.

After Bettina asked the accountant a few questions, a bead of sweat glistened on his upper lip. He tugged at his tightly-buttoned white collar. He had been hanging around lawyers too long because he tried to intimidate Bettina. He asked her about probable cause and wanted to see a warrant. Bettina countered with veiled threats about hired killings, obstruction of justice, and him being an accessory-after-the-fact to multiple murders.

The accountant bowed to the superior force, lowered his battle flag, and we had a worthwhile meeting. His information sent us on a voyage to the Harris County Property Appraiser's District Office, followed by a visit to the County Clerk.

As Bettina and I sat down to lunch at her favorite barbeque joint, my cellphone rang. I read the caller ID and ignored it.

After lunch, I retrieved the voice mail. "This is Ike Simonetti. I missed the earlier flight. I spent the night in Anchorage. At least my cellphone is working again. I didn't call you last night because of the time difference and I didn't want to wake you. It's eight in the morning here. The next flight to Seattle is 2:15 this afternoon, local time. I have a four-hour layover in Seattle and then take a red-eye that gets into Port City about noon tomorrow. I wanted to see what news you had. Call me when you can." I saved the message.

Bettina and I met with a reporter at the *Houston Tribune* who Bettina had called the evening before. It was good to have access to her local connections. It's amazing the information sources reporters have, and what they'll do for a story.

Then we went to the Harris County Clerk's office and found a fascinating piece of information.

Everything was falling into place like the last few pieces of a jigsaw puzzle. I felt the excitement build in my gut as we neared the finish line. My ears practically buzzed with the adrenaline.

Simonetti called again. I let it go to voicemail.

I caught a late afternoon flight to Port City and drove to Terry's apartment to hide out, and not merely from more assassins. At my apartment, I still got occasional personal visits from reporters about Sam Simonetti's murder. I had dozed a little on the plane, but, God, did I need to unwind and relax. The biggest case of my young life and young career was coming to a head.

As I expected, Simonetti called again while Terry and I were having dinner at her place. I let it go to voice mail, then retrieved the message. "This is Ike again. I'm laying over in Seattle and I wanted any news you have. What's going on? Why haven't you called me back, buddy? I'm the customer, remember? It's not like you to be out of touch. Are you okay? Please call me as soon as you get this."

I saved the message. "He'll call again about eleven before he boards the plane. I'll turn the phone off."

Terry agreed to let me get to bed early. Sleep is a weapon, and I needed about nine hours' worth.

I was asleep by eight o'clock.

I eased in crosswise across two slots in the parking lot at Jerry's Gym. I nosed the Avanti to the privet hedge border. The sun was still below the horizon, lightening the sky in the east.

I felt like a million bucks. Sleep will do that for you. Now I needed a good workout to get my blood flowing.

In the still dark sky, three bats made a last insect sweep before they returned to their roost.

I had covered ten paces toward the entrance to Jerry's Gym when I heard the gunshot and saw the muzzle flash in my peripheral vision. The bullet tore through my sweatshirt and raked my ribs on the left side.

I had locked my Glock 17 in the glove compartment. *Murphy's Law strikes again.*

I rolled to my right, came up in a crouch, and sprinted toward my car. The shot had come from the north end of the privet hedge between the parking lot and the building. I scampered around the back of the Avanti and dived behind the passenger's side as another bullet shattered the rear window. I fished in my sweat pants for the car key.

It ain't easy to open a car door and a glove compartment from a crouch, even with the extra motivation of a hit man shooting at you. I got the passenger door open. As I opened the glove compartment, another bullet *spanged* off the pavement near my feet. That made three.

I grabbed the Glock and dropped the holster on the floorboard. I belly-crawled under the four-foot privet hedge. My sweats were dark gray, the hedge was dark green, and the sun was below the horizon. All that worked in my favor. I crouched on the opposite side of the hedge from the shooter. With any luck, he thought I was hiding on the passenger side of my car.

I scurried on my hands and knees up the east side of the hedge, rounded the corner, and crabbed along the north side toward the shooter. Another shot rang out. I heard the double *crun-unch* as the bullet passed through both sides of my car. Then a fifth shot shattered another window. *Good. He thinks I'm still behind the Avanti.*

Grandpa would not be thrilled at the damage to the Avanti.

The next two shots sounded so loud that I knew he was behind the hedge by the building's north wall. That made seven shots. If he was firing an automatic, he could have ten bullets left, depending on the model. If he had a revolver, he was nearly out.

Focused on the Avanti, he didn't see me until I stood up from behind the hedge, taking a two-hand Weaver stance. "Freeze. Drop the gun and raise your hands."

The shooter whirled my way and raised his pistol.

I started to put a double tap into his chest, but I hesitated. He was the last person I expected to see.

We fired at the same time.

I tried to squeeze off a second round, but I didn't feel any recoil. I stared at my Glock and wondered why it didn't fire and how its weight had increased to fifty pounds. Then it weighed nothing as my fingers lost feeling. I felt out of my body, watching from above as the barrel of the Glock pointed toward the ground. It fell in slow motion from my useless fingers. Then my arm fell in slow motion. My body collapsed like a puppet with its strings cut.

The last thing I remembered was privet leaves scratching my face as I pitched into the hedge.

I recognized the smell before I opened my eyes. I had not set foot in a hospital in about a month, but that odor is like riding a bicycle; you don't forget it. Being in a hospital meant I must be alive.

Another subtler smell lingered in the background, nearly overpowered by the hospital smell. A delicate but familiar fragrance. I took a deep breath and smiled.

"Hello, Terry." I opened my eyes to find her by the bed.

"How did you know I was here before you opened your eyes?" She leaned over and grasped my hand. It felt good.

"I have magical powers." Then I saw Snoop. "Good to see you."

Snoop came to the other side of the bed. "How're you feeling?"

"Like hell." I tried to look down at my right shoulder but my head wouldn't move that far. "Where did he hit me?"

"Right side of the chest, near the shoulder. Through and through. Missed the lung but nicked an artery. Ken and Terry found you quick, or we'd be drinking and telling funny stories about you at your wake right now."

"Sorry to disappoint you, Snoop. I know you like a good party. I'll buy you a drink anyway."

He squeezed my arm—the left one. "I'll hold you to that."

A smiling nurse entered. "Good, you're awake. I'm Gena Valle, your nurse. I monitor your vitals from the nurses' station. I called the doctor. She'll be here soon. Do you need anything right now?"

"Nothing, thanks, nurse. How long have I been out?"

Nurse Valle eyed the clock on the wall. "Fifty hours, more or less. I predict you'll be famished in twenty minutes. I'll order a meal." She clucked at my bandaged shoulder. "You'll have to eat with your left hand for a while."

"It's not the first time."

"I know. We have your medical records from the Army. I'm honored to treat a hero."

"Please, don't start that stuff. I was in the wrong place at the right time."

Nurse Valle smiled and left me with Terry and Snoop.

Terry squeezed my hand. "After you left my place day before yesterday, I cleaned up the breakfast dishes and headed for the gym too. I was pulling into the parking lot when I heard shots and called it in. Ken ran out the door of the gym with a .45 in his hand. We split up and I found you first. I rode in the ambulance with you."

"Thanks, Queens. And tell Ken too."

"I texted him. He's coming over. You can tell him yourself."

I waved at Snoop. "Okay, catch me up."

Snoop pulled a chair over. "First, tell me who shot you."

"You didn't find his body at the gym?"

"Nope, and it wasn't easy to find you, either. When Ken ran out, he saw your car with the windows shot out, but he didn't see anyone in the lot. He and Terry searched the whole lot before she found you in the hedge. You were the only one there."

"The shooter hid behind that same hedge at the northeast corner of the building. He was used to shooting a rifle so he didn't realize a handgun's range. He shot at me from too far away. That's why he missed the first time. Saved my life."

"Who was it?"

"Ike Simonetti."

Renate Crowell sauntered in with a flower arrangement. She placed it on the cabinet with the others. "I'm glad you're well enough to receive visitors."

I waved my left hand, the one I could move. "It's always nice to see a smiling face."

"How much longer they gonna keep you?"

"I go home tomorrow."

"That's good news." She pulled a chair to the bedside and sat down. "It's time to go on the record."

"No, but I'll tell you the story. You can use whatever you see fit, if you don't reveal me as the source."

"Okay. Shoot."

"Don't say 'shoot.' I have already been shot."

"Oops. Sorry." She pulled out her laptop. "Can I say 'fire away'?"

"It hurts when I laugh."

"What about client confidentiality, Chuck?"

"Ike Simonetti tried to kill me at least four times. I have a strict rule about clients who try to kill me—they don't get confidentiality. Most of the facts are public record or will be soon. You need someone to tie the public records together and give them context. I'll tell you what happened."

She poised her fingers over the laptop and I began.

I told her about Wallace's engaging Turbot to set up her charitable foundation. About Turbot employing Lucas to murder Simonetti's half-sisters. About Lucas's connection with Hopper and Hopper setting the fire.

Then I told her about Snoop and my trip to Cleveland and how I discovered Lucas's role in hiring the arsonist and then Turbot's connection.

"When I learned that Turbot was Wallace's attorney, I thought she ordered the Cleveland killings."

"What was her motive?"

"I thought she was a black widow. Wallace's first husband died of a heart attack, and she inherited a fortune from him. I thought she planned to murder him for his money, then murdered Sam to make Ike even richer. Both her first husband and Sam Simonetti died from heart attacks. Do the math. Then I figured she planned to murder Ike and inherit $400,000,000."

Renate whistled. "Plenty of motive."

"Yeah. Except none of it was true."

"How so?"

"When Ike's personal assistant Tom Collins tried to kill me with Ike Simonetti's personal hunting rifle, I rethought my whole theory about the Cleveland murders. I ran a background check on Collins and discovered he was a bad guy."

"How bad?"

"When he was in the Army in Iraq, he sold guns and ammo out the back door to Iraqi Islamist militias. The same guys that were killing American soldiers."

"So, he was crooked?"

"As a dog's hind leg. That could be why Simonetti hired him originally—because he was already bent."

Minutes passed as she tapped on her keyboard. "Okay, so you discovered Collins was a bad guy and he worked for Simonetti."

"Right."

"Go on."

"I went to Houston to check out both Simonetti and Collins with the Houston cops and the Texas Rangers. Unofficially, the Rangers suspected both men of dirty dealings when Collins worked for Simonetti's oil and gas operations. But neither the Houston cops nor the Rangers could make a case. Not enough proof for the DA."

"If Wallace didn't kill Sam Simonetti, then who did?"

"All in good time. Go with me here."

"Okay."

"I knew Ike and Turbot were both dirty, but I had no connection between them other than Wallace. I got autopsy reports on Wallace's first husband, Dr. Walter Wallace, and his father, Dr. Isaiah Wallace."

"So?"

"They both died naturally of heart attacks. It was apparently an inherited genetic disposition to heart failure. Walter Wallace's grandfather died at forty-three of heart failure. Walter's father, Isaiah, died at forty-five and Walter died at forty-one. Lorraine Wallace didn't kill her husband; he was born with bad genes."

"So, then you suspected Simonetti instead of Lorraine Wallace?"

"Right. But I hadn't found the connection between Simonetti and Turbot. When I ran a deep background check on Turbot, I learned he was flat broke—his whole law firm was."

More tapping. "What's your source on the firm's insolvency?"

"When I first visited the firm's offices, I noticed lots of empty offices. When I flew back to Houston later, I corroborated their problems with the firm's accountant and with Will Meacham, a business reporter at the *Houston Tribune*. Do you know him?"

"No, but I'll call him to get background if I need it. Spell his name."

I did. She tapped her keyboard again. "Go on."

"Then I discovered from Simonetti and Turbot's cellphone records that Simonetti had contacted Turbot directly while he and Lorraine were in Houston."

"How did you get the cellphone records?"

I winked at her. "Let's say that the NSA isn't the only one who can scoop up cellphone metadata."

In fact, I got the cellphone records from the Houston cops with Bettina Simpson's help. The Houston cops ran Turbot's cellphone records when they executed a search warrant. It wouldn't hurt my reputation for Renate to think I was a super-sleuth.

She laughed. "So, Ike Simonetti contacted Turbot..."

"To get him to find someone to kill Simonetti's half-sisters."

"Why would Turbot do that?"

"I searched county records on Turbot and discovered that the big mortgage on his River Oaks mansion was seriously delinquent. His house was so far underwater that a snorkel wouldn't help."

"So, Turbot was hanging by his fingernails when Simonetti approached him."

"Right. Plus, Simonetti's real estate company had acquired Turbot's mortgage from the original lender."

Renate paused from pounding her laptop. "Let me guess: Ike threatened to foreclose the mortgage unless Turbot helped him kill the sisters."

"I can't know for sure, but do the math and it seems likely."

More tapping. "This is great stuff. Let's hear more."

"Simonetti's real estate company deposited a large check into Turbot's escrow account at his law firm the day after he and his wife returned to Port City."

"How large a check?"

When I told her, she whistled. "That's got to be too much to be legal."

"Tell me about it. The next day, Turbot writes a check on his escrow account for $50,000 to Leonard J. Lucas, attorney-at-law. Turbot used the rest of the money to bring his mortgage payments current."

"How did you uncover the deposit into Turbot's account?"

"I have magical powers."

Again, Bettina Simpson gave me the information from the search warrant results. The Houston cops had cooperated fully in my investigation.

Renate chuckled. "Okay, how did you uncover the check Turbot wrote to Lucas?"

"Lucas told me. And I confirmed the check independently."

"And how did you confirm it?"

I waved my left hand in a magician's gesture. "*Abracadabra.*"

The Houston cops were making me look like a genius. I made a mental note to send Bettina a dozen roses. In fact, I would add her to my yearly Valentine's Day flower list.

"Okay," Renate said, "we'll leave out that part. Go on."

"As I said, Lucas was a criminal lawyer in Houston."

"Was?"

"He's now conveniently dead—convenient for Simonetti."

"Any previous connection between Turbot and Lucas?"

I sipped my water. "The police are looking. Turbot's law firm has connections all over Texas."

I waited while she entered that information, then continued. "Lucas took the check straight to Turbot's bank and cashed it—$50,000 in good old U.S. greenbacks. Normally, an attorney deposits a check like that into his escrow account."

"How do you know he cashed it?"

"The bank's policy requires the cashier to write a driver's license number on the check when someone cashes a check in person. That gives proof the payee showed identification. I have a copy of the check."

"I know you won't answer, but I have to ask: How did you get the check copy?"

I smiled. "*Abracadabra.*" Bettina again. *Maybe I should send her two dozen roses.*

"Okay, better left unsaid. Why did Turbot agree to arrange the murders?"

"The obvious answer is to avoid foreclosure. We'll never know unless Turbot turns up alive and tells us."

"Turbot's missing too?"

"Like you guessed, Simonetti could threaten to foreclose unless Turbot helped him kill his half-sisters. Turbot could have sold out to save his own skin. I do know that the week after the sisters died,

269

Simonetti's real estate company filed a Release of Lien form for Turbot's home mortgage."

"What's that mean?"

"In effect, Simonetti marked Turbot's mortgage 'paid in full' as his final payment for murdering the half-sisters."

Renate tapped her keyboard some more. "Go on."

"Six weeks after the sisters died, someone injected Sam Simonetti with Fentanyl, causing a fatal heart attack."

"Was it Ike?"

I started to shrug, then winced as my right shoulder reminded me I had been shot. "We may never know. A Fentanyl vial went missing from the hospital a couple of days before Sam died. Lots of people had access to the drugs."

"Did Ike steal it?"

"Not personally, but he could have hired a janitor to steal it. A hospital janitor did disappear the day after the Fentanyl went missing."

"Did Ike have the janitor killed?"

"Who knows? The janitor walked out the door one morning on his way to work. No one's seen him since."

"What about Sam's widow, Ramona? Originally, you pointed to her as a suspect. Could she have injected the Fentanyl?"

"Yes, but after her previous husbands died, she cremated them to destroy evidence. She buried Sam. That's what we professional sleuths call a clue."

"I get it. It means she didn't know he was murdered."

"Right. Ramona may be a black widow triple murderer, but she didn't do this one. I think Simonetti beat her to the punch."

"What about Wallace? She's a doctor. She could get Fentanyl."

"Wallace was in Chicago at a medical convention when the drug went missing. The security video of the hospital corridor around the time of Sam's death shows Wallace was never alone with him in his room. Ike was, on at least two occasions."

"Where is Ike now?"

I remembered not to shrug this time. "No one's seen him. The other blood at the parking lot was his, so I wounded him, but he escaped before the cops arrived."

"One other thing doesn't make sense."

"What's that?"

"Your investigation of the Cleveland fire uncovered Simonetti's involvement in several murders. Why would Simonetti hire you to investigate the fire in the first place?"

"He didn't."

"But you told me that Simonetti was your client."

"Oh, he was, but he didn't hire me to investigate the fire."

"What did he hire you to investigate?"

"That part is confidential."

TWENTY

Wallace wasn't dressed like a Hollywood version of Businesswoman of the Year. Quite the opposite. She wore old blue jeans, a faded Polo shirt, and sneakers. I would not have thought she owned an old pair of anything. She had put on a couple of much-needed pounds too. It made her look less harsh—matronly even. She wore little makeup, just lipstick and eyebrow pencil. She looked forty-one, but it was an honest forty-one.

She bounced Gloria on her knee. "That's a pretty girl. Can you say 'I love you, Aunt Lorraine'?" she cooed.

Gloria babbled and blew spit bubbles.

"You're taking to motherhood in a big way."

"What's not to like? I always wanted children, but Ike didn't warm to the idea. I can't figure out how he fooled me for ten years."

"You know that old saying—hindsight is 20/20."

Wallace set Gloria on a blanket. "With that famous hindsight, I realize that Ike would never have settled for one-third of Pop's estate—not if he could get it all. After Pop had his first heart attack, Ike and I discussed how much money was enough. Ike used to say 'You can never have too much money.' I thought he was kidding; now I know he meant every word."

"Ike didn't care much for his half-sisters either."

"No, but having them killed? Why would Frank Turbot do such a stupid thing? He was a successful family lawyer. When he hired that arsonist, he lost everything."

"*Was* is the key word, Lorraine; he *was* successful."

"What do you mean?"

"Turbot refinanced his house at the top of the real estate bubble. He put every penny into an internet stock that went belly up. When his income from the law firm collapsed, he couldn't make his mortgage payments."

Wallace stroked Gloria's hair. "The law firm appeared to be doing okay when I was there last September."

"The firm was trying for a turnaround last summer. Later, they cut expenses right and left. They fired a third of their partners and laid off half their employees before Halloween."

"What about Frank? He wasn't fired. He should have been okay."

"Not really. His firm was essentially broke. To make matters worse, Ike held the mortgage on Turbot's house. He could foreclose if Turbot refused. Turbot took Ike's money and contracted with Lenny Lucas."

"Lucas is the guy who knew the arsonist?"

"I told you about him when I confronted you in your office."

Wallace shook her head. "I was so shocked that I don't remember anything you said."

"I'm truly sorry about that. If I were you, I would be plenty pissed at me."

She waved it off. "You did what Ike hired you to do. If not for you, Frank and Ike would have gotten away with it."

"It's ironic that Ike's hiring me exposed his own crimes. And now he's vanished, Ramona's in a Mexican prison, and you're Gloria's new mom."

Wallace handed Gloria another rattle to replace the one she had dropped. "And I love that, don't I, pretty girl? Yes, I do. Aunt Lorraine loves you, loves you, loves you."

Wallace made a serious face. "Changing the subject, I read Pop's autopsy report. A Fentanyl injection precipitated his heart attack. Who did it?"

"At first I suspected Ramona. Then I suspected you, but it had to be Ike."

"That's hard to believe. Not his own father. Ramona, I would believe. She murdered three husbands in Mexico."

"But she had them cremated to destroy the evidence," I said. "Ramona had Sam buried, not cremated. And no one else had a motive."

Wallace shuddered.

"Lorraine, let's talk about less gruesome matters. There's a business decision you need to make. Can we talk a little private investigator business?"

"Business decision? Shouldn't Vicky Ramirez make those, now that Ike's gone?"

"Technically, Vicky Ramirez's law firm is my client as counsel for the executor of the estate. Vicky said that Sam's will named you as Ike's successor if Ike were unable to serve as executor. Since he's on the run, you've been promoted. Vicky told me to talk to you."

Wallace tapped her index finger on her bottom lip. "Okay, since Gloria is Pop's only remaining heir, and I'm her guardian."

"That's what we need to talk about."

"Gloria?"

"I received more DNA results yesterday. I know who Gloria's biological father is."

"Who is it?" Wallace asked.

"It's Ike."

"You're sure?"

"DNA doesn't lie," I answered.

"Well, that's a whole new ballgame, isn't it?"

"Yeah, and you need to look at the ramifications of that so you can make a business decision."

"What ramifications?"

"So far, Vicky and I are the only ones who know."

"The DNA lab knows."

I waved a hand. "They're bound by a confidentiality agreement."

"What difference does it make who knows? The truth always has a way of coming out. You, of all people, know that." Then Gloria cooed, and Wallace gazed at her with wide eyes. "So, this is Ike's daughter."

"That's the decision you have to make. Legally—until someone contests her parentage—she's Sam's daughter and heiress, not Ike's."

"Well, I have my own money; I don't need Pop's. Gloria can have it. Hell, she would eventually inherit it from me anyway. Gloria being Ike's daughter smacks of incest. I would hate to have the family name associated with that. I have decided to become a full-time, stay-at-home mom. At least until Gloria starts school."

"Congratulations. That'll be great for Gloria. If you want me to, I can prove that Sam is not Gloria's father without disclosing who her real father is—no incest implied."

"How?"

"With the DNA from Sam's autopsy."

"I forgot about Pop's DNA."

"You're her guardian regardless of who her father is." I raised both hands. "I'm not suggesting that you cut Gloria out of the will, but I have a duty to ensure that you know all your options. Only you can decide Gloria's fate."

"God, that was so long ago when I wanted to cut her out of the will."

"Anyway, if no interested party challenges Gloria's paternity, she inherits half of Sam's estate. Now that Ramona is in a Mexican prison, you and Ike are the sole remaining interested parties. As Gloria's guardian, you're in charge of her trust fund. You can make sure she's taken care of and draw a reasonable salary for that."

"What happens to Ike's half of Pop's estate?"

"If Ike killed his father and we can prove it, he can't profit from his crime. Ike could not inherit. Then Gloria inherits the whole shebang."

"Can you prove that Ike killed Pop?"

"Not yet. If we can't prove it, I don't know what happens. Vicky would be in court a long time sorting out Ike's half of Sam's estate. Remember, I have a personal stake in your decision."

"Personal?"

"Yeah, my success fee. If no one challenges Gloria's paternity, I don't get my $1,000,000 bonus, which I almost got killed several times to earn."

Wallace waved a hand dismissively. "As the new executor under Pop's will, I'll direct Vicky to pay your bonus anyway. I don't want Gloria labeled as a bastard. Deal?" She stuck out her hand.

I shook it. "Deal. Changing the subject, what are you going to do about your marriage to Ike?"

"If he stays hidden, Vicky says I can claim he abandoned the marriage and divorce him after twelve months."

She smoothed Gloria's hair. "Ike cleaned out our joint account last Friday while he was in Alaska. There was less than $100,000 in it. That won't last for long."

"Ike never went to Alaska," I said. "He got off the flight in Chicago and flew back to Port City under another name. He wanted an alibi for my murder. He even got a satellite phone to call me on, so I would think he was in the wilderness. He had already planned to run. Ike cleaned out his brokerage and bank accounts and transferred $60,000,000 to a bank in some Pacific island kingdom last week."

"*Hmm.* Let's get you some carrots, sweetheart." Wallace carried

Gloria into the kitchen. I pulled the high chair into position with my left hand. My right arm and shoulder were still in a sling.

Wallace began to feed Gloria. "How did you get Ike's DNA?"

"After our last meeting in Vicky's office, I took his coffee cup to my lab; his saliva was on the rim. He was the next logical man to check after Reynaldo." I paused. "And speaking of Reynaldo…"

Wallace said, "I can explain, Chuck. I knew Ike screwed around—Ramona wasn't the first time. I felt entitled."

"You don't have to explain to me, Lorraine. Reynaldo looks like a Latin movie star, and you're a red-blooded woman. Besides, you're the client now; you don't owe me an explanation."

"But you're also a friend; you deserve an explanation."

"How can you call me a friend when I accused you of murder?"

"Doing your job, remember?"

"You're a better person than I am, Lorraine."

"Don't be silly. You're making the world safe for democracy."

I sipped my morning coffee as I strolled to the office window. The sun had risen above the parking garage across Bayfront Boulevard and glared through my windows. I gazed at the roof where Tom Collins hid when he tried to ambush me.

I used my right hand to adjust the blinds enough to block the sun. It felt good to have the sling off. I could move my right arm pretty well, even though I had been practicing with my left hand at the shooting range. My left ribs had healed. The scar from the bullet that grazed me would fade soon enough. They always did.

Nancy had placed the previous day's snail mail on my desk. I thumbed through the stack and stopped when I saw the engraved envelope from Vicky's law firm. Vicky said she was mailing my bonus check. I had never seen a check for $1,000,000. I wondered if I would feel different when I held it in my hand. Yes, I decided I would feel different. I laid the envelope aside in anticipation while I opened the other mail.

There was a bill for the Silver Ghost repair—again—from my classic car mechanic. I tossed other junk mail into the recycle bin. I read a postcard of Notre Dame Cathedral from *Abuelita* and my great aunt Carolina, vacationing in Paris. I smiled at the thought of the two widows giving confession in Notre Dame. I could not imagine *Abuelita* having any sins to confess, but I knew she would come up with something in order to get the full Notre Dame experience.

I picked up the envelope from Vicky again. "Come to Papa, baby," I whispered. I savored every second. I wanted to remember that moment for the rest of my life.

I reached for my letter opener, listened to the blade rasp as it cut the paper. As I expected, the envelope held a transmittal letter. I listened to the engraved letterhead crinkle as I unfolded it to find the law firm's check. The check was printed on golden paper—somehow appropriate. I held the check to my nose and inhaled. I wanted to remember the smell of $1,000,000. It smelled like Vicky's perfume—probably transferred from her hand as she signed the check.

My eyes caressed every word of Vicky's transmittal letter. I kissed the check over the dollar sign. Then I folded it once and stuck it in my shirt pocket.

The bank opened at 9:00. For a check this size, I wouldn't trust an ATM even if it would accept a deposit that large. No, the inside teller was better. Besides, I wanted to see her face as I deposited a $1,000,000 check. I decided to check my email before heading to the bank. I deleted the first spam that made it past the filter.

Then the knob on my hall door clicked.

I cut my eyes to the right and saw the knob return to normal position. Someone had tried the door—quietly. I always enter my office through the adjoining conference room, so I leave both conference room doors unlocked when I'm in the office. Nancy knew that, and she always entered through the conference room. She also knocked before she entered my office.

Who had tried to enter directly from the hall? Whoever it was, he or she would try the conference room next.

Ike Simonetti was in the wind.

I slid my Glock from its holster as I crossed to the storeroom door in the back wall of my office. I opened it six inches, reached in, and flicked on the light. I quick-stepped around the desk as I pulled the slide back with my left hand. I stood against the wall behind the conference room door and transferred the Glock to my left hand.

I could be wrong about the hall door. If it was a false alarm, it did no harm to wait a minute for an intruder who never came.

I didn't have to wait long.

The conference room door opened and a left hand, holding a Smith & Wesson Model M&P R8 revolver, reached through the opening. The R8 is the only Smith & Wesson with M&P on the barrel; other models have the logo above the trigger. It's an expensive handgun a wealthy sportsman like Ike Simonetti would own. The R8 holds .357 Magnum bullets like the ones found at the site of my gunfight with Simonetti. Now I knew why Simonetti had shot me only once. The R8 holds eight rounds. He had run out of bullets. If he had used any Glock, like I did, I would be dead.

I couldn't see his face, but it had to be Simonetti. Simonetti was right-handed, but I had wounded his right arm with my shot, and he wouldn't have recovered yet.

I wasn't a hundred percent myself. That's why I held the Glock with my left hand.

The gunman opened the door wider and tiptoed across my office toward the storeroom. I stepped behind him and stuck the Glock behind his left ear. "Drop it, Ike."

He froze, then lifted both hands. His left hand went up to chest height; his right only to his waist. He spoke without turning around. "Congratulations. You fooled me with that open door. Is that your file room?"

"Drop the gun."

Simonetti raised his left hand to shoulder height, but he didn't drop the gun. "You wouldn't shoot me in the back."

"I'll shoot you in a heartbeat if I need to. If you cooperate, you may get out of this alive, but it's self-defense no matter where I shoot you. You're in my office. You're carrying the same revolver you used to shoot me, and I'm the sole witness. Do the math." I pressed the pistol harder behind his ear. "I'll count to three. One…"

He dropped the revolver onto the carpet.

I frisked him with my right hand. "Sit in this chair." I pulled him backwards to a chair in front of my desk.

I kept the Glock aimed as I moved around the desk to my office chair. "I thought you would be on a tropical beach, sipping a rum drink with an umbrella in it."

"That was Plan A."

"What happened?"

"You did."

I started to ask, but he waved me off. "I should have waited for you to get closer for that first shot. Yada, yada, yada, whatever. Plan A didn't work out. Now I've had three weeks to hole up while I healed."

"Are you okay now?"

"No, I am not okay now. You hit me in the shoulder, through-and-through."

"Did you go to a doctor?"

"Yeah, right. Like I would take a gunshot wound to a doctor. I'm not crazy. I won't be arrested."

"So where have you been?"

Simonetti gestured with his left hand. "A no-tell hotel near the harbor that takes cash and doesn't ask for ID."

"You look terrible."

"I have an excuse—I've been living on takeout delivered to my hotel room."

"How is the wound?"

"I've been better."

"What's your Plan B?"

Simonetti shook his head. "I have things to do before I split."

"Like what?"

"Like my unfinished business with you."

"Killing me now won't save you from an attempted murder charge. The cops have your DNA from the blood you lost at Jerry's Gym. You didn't need to risk coming here."

"I didn't come here to kill you. The gun was for protection. I wanted to talk with you before I leave."

"You're not leaving."

"You calling the cops?"

"Of course. Our business was finished and no one has hired me to find you, but since you dropped in my lap, I won't let you walk away."

"Hear me out first."

"Okay. I want to ask you a couple of things too."

"Such as?"

"First, how did you get in?" I asked.

"I took the back stairs from the parking lot. I made sure the hall was empty before I came to your office."

"Next question—I'm curious how Ramona got you to father Gloria."

He smirked. "The usual way."

"Yeah, but you were more discreet with your other affairs. You usually wait until you're out of town. If I were guessing, I would guess that she put the moves on you, not the other way around."

"How did you find out I was Gloria's father?"

"Same way you found out—a DNA test."

"I never gave you a DNA sample."

"You left your coffee cup at Vicky's office when we last met. Your DNA was on the cup. You were the logical guy to check after Reynaldo."

"I never intended to sleep with Ramona."

"Don't bullshit a bullshitter. Ramona is hot as a jalapeño sandwich. You have a history of womanizing."

He laughed. "Well…maybe it was in the back of my mind. Anyway, Lorraine attended a medical convention in Puerto Rico. I would have gone with her because I love to deep sea fish in San Juan, but Dad was in the hospital. Ramona and I spent all day with him and we were tired and depressed. She claimed she hadn't slept well the night before, and she was too tired to drive home."

"And you, being a gentleman…"

"I drove her home. When we got there, she wanted to cook me dinner to thank me. I protested, of course." He peeked down to his left where the revolver lay on the floor.

I had screwed up. I shouldn't have left Simonetti's gun on the floor. I couldn't see it from my angle, but Simonetti could. I debated whether to retrieve the revolver, but I didn't want to interrupt the conversation. My security system was recording his confession in High-Def video.

Simonetti continued. "She said she didn't get a chance to cook with Dad in the hospital. She told me I would be doing her a favor. She insisted."

"Of course she did. You couldn't tell a lady no, could you?"

"Of course not. It wouldn't be gentlemanly." He eyed the revolver again. "She fixed mango daiquiris while she cooked. You ever have one?" He didn't wait for an answer. "They kick like a mule." Simonetti managed a laugh, then grimaced with pain. He rubbed his right shoulder. "We had more daiquiris during dinner and Ramona told me how lonely she was in the big, empty house. And how she needed someone she could lean on."

"She wanted to lean on you," I repeated.

"That's what she called it." He contemplated the revolver again. "Then she said I was too drunk to drive home, and she insisted I spend the night in a guest room. Well, to make a long story short, she slept with me literally and figuratively in the guest suite—three times. And then two more times in the morning before we went back to the hospital."

"And now you have a daughter to show for it."

"I still find that hard to believe." He sighed. "That's my unfinished business."

"Okay, what about Gloria?"

"I haven't thought about anything else for three weeks. I came to tell you she's my daughter. Gloria deserves the best of everything, including parents." He wheeled the chair back a foot on its carpet rollers. I raised the Glock and he held his left hand up. "I'm crossing my legs, okay?"

"Okay."

Simonetti rolled the chair back a little more and crossed his left ankle over his right knee. "I have screwed up big time, Chuck, but I don't want to hurt Gloria."

"Lorraine is her guardian, legally and as godmother."

Simonetti gestured with his left hand. "Lorraine always wanted children. Will you look after them?"

"If they need it, I will, but so far Lorraine and Gloria are fine. Lorraine moved into your Dad's house. Gloria has the same nursery and nanny she's always had, and Lorraine is trustee of Gloria's portion of your dad's estate, so they have money. In fact, Lorraine's decided to be a stay-at-home mom until Gloria starts school."

"Good for her. No matter what happens to me, I don't want them to lack for anything."

"By the way, buying the mortgage on Turbot's house—that was a stroke of genius."

"You found that, huh?"

"I'm the World's Greatest Private Investigator."

"Once I bought his mortgage, I had that shyster by the balls."

"Did you know he paid Lucas only $50,000 to arrange the fire in Cleveland?"

"Chump change. Turbot needed the extra money to catch up on his mortgage. I knew I would get it all back plus a few hundred million for me."

"Another question. Where did you get the Fentanyl to inject your father?"

He waved a hand dismissively. "I had nothing to do with Dad's death." He ponderously crossed his legs the other way.

"We know a hospital janitor stole the Fentanyl. It had to be for you."

He stared at me.

"Everything's coming out into the open now anyway. Tell me, okay?"

He contemplated me for a while. Finally, he shrugged. "Yeah, everything has hit the fan now anyway. A $1,000 cash to this poor schlub was like a million to me." He stared at the revolver again. His eyes widened.

At that moment, I knew how this confrontation would end.

In police academy, they taught us about suicide by cop. A suspect aims his weapon at a cop, forcing the cop to shoot him in self-defense. In the movies, the cop shoots the suspect in the leg and doesn't kill the guy. In real life, you can't shoot a handgun that accurately. You're trained to aim for the center. A torso shot is usually fatal.

I considered how to change the outcome without getting myself killed. I knew I didn't have much time.

"What happened to the janitor?" I asked.

Simonetti shrugged. "You know, loose ends to tie up."

"Did the Santorinis handle that too?"

"Yeah, they have connections with the Cuban gangs here. They subcontracted the hit. He's sleeping with the fishes."

"How did you connect with the Santorini family in the first place?"

Simonetti shrugged, causing a wince. "Back in the day, Tom Collins used them to arrange accidents in Texas if a landowner wouldn't sign an oil lease."

"Accidents?"

"Yeah, you know, a slashed tractor tire, a busted windshield, a cut fence to let cows out of the pasture. Accidents on the farm."

"And the hypodermic needle to inject the Fentanyl? Where did you get that?"

"Any pharmacy has syringes. Diabetics use them to inject themselves with insulin, for God's sake." He shifted his weight and uncrossed his legs.

He took a deep breath and dropped to the floor between his chair and my desk. I couldn't see him, but the chair rolled back, slowed by the carpet, and banged against the wall.

I figured he would try for the revolver. He had killed at least four people and sent four others for me to kill. He would kill me if he could.

I dove to the floor on my right. All I could see was the back of my desk and Simonetti's Smith & Wesson lying on the carpet. I pointed the Glock midway between the revolver and the desk and waited for Simonetti's arm to appear from the other side of the desk.

And waited.

I had made another rookie mistake. I hadn't checked him for an ankle gun. If he had one, he might be creeping around the other side of my desk. I scooted back to watch both ends of my desk.

As I waited, I heard my office door open and close. I checked the other side of my desk to make sure it wasn't a ruse. Simonetti had escaped.

I bolted after him and glanced both ways down the hall. The rear fire door was closing as I ran toward it. I cracked the fire door and checked the hinge gap to make sure he wasn't lying in wait. I heard the downstairs door open and close. I took the steps three at a time and hit the door to the parking lot at virtually full speed.

Simonetti must have heard me slam the fire door open. Hell, the whole neighborhood must have heard it. He stood in the open door of yet another black SUV. He raised his left hand and pointed a gun at me. This time I didn't hesitate.

We fired simultaneously like we had in the gym parking lot. Simonetti's gun had a two-inch barrel—worthless beyond five or ten feet. My Glock 17 had a four-and-a-half-inch barrel. My shot hit him in the right shoulder, spun him to his right. He fell backwards and sat heavily on the driver's seat.

"Drop it," I shouted as I walked toward him, keeping my aim steady with a two-hand grip. "Don't do it, Ike."

He tried to raise the gun again. Call it suicide by private eye.

I squeezed off two more rounds. At thirty feet, the Glock was accurate—I should say 'dead on.' The first bullet caught him in the upper chest and knocked him across the seat. The second passed through air where his head had been an instant before and shattered the passenger side window. His gun fell to the pavement.

I approached the open SUV door, kept the Glock trained on him. I kicked his gun away and felt his pulse.

He opened one eye. Blood trickled from the corner of his mouth. "I told you I wouldn't be arrested."

Then he was gone.

TWENTY-ONE

U ncle Felix carried a fresh pitcher of sangria onto the balcony and refilled Terry's glass. Then he refilled Janet's and Snoop's. He raised an eyebrow at me.

"I'm good."

He refilled his own glass and set the pitcher on the table. "The *zarzuela* will be ready soon."

"*Zarzuela?*" Terry asked.

Felix grinned. "Think of it as Spanish seafood stew."

"You sure you don't want me to help you, Felix?" Janet asked.

"I cook the best *zarzuela* in Mexico, *señora*. This is my way to thank the *gringo* for letting me stay here while I handled this Ramona Gamez business. No, you and Terry sit there and inspire us with your beauty."

Terry smiled at me. "Is your whole family like this?"

"Like what?" I said.

"You know, romantic."

"Pretty much all of them on the Mexican side. The Texans are a little more subdued."

"I'm glad you take after the Mexican side."

"Oh, my dad is romantic too. After all, I have a sister and two brothers."

"I'll drink to that." And she did.

Felix leaned on the rail. "Nice view, *gringo*."

"Do you refer to Seeti Bay or to the ladies?"

He laughed. "Yes."

Snoop raised his glass. "I'll drink to my lovely wife."

My new condo was on the southeast corner and the balcony wrapped around both sides of the unit. We sat on the south balcony and watched the sunset develop. An ocean breeze carried the scent of salt water from the Atlantic. An unplanned flotilla of pleasure boats swung at anchor on Seeti Bay in a daily ritual of sunset watching.

Felix joined us at the table.

"So, Felix, did you finish examining Ramona's belongings?" Terry asked.

"*Si, chiquita*. I found evidence—emails and such. I have arranged to extradite Ramon, so I must return with him to Mexico."

"It's a shame you can't stay longer," Janet said. "I love your accent."

Felix favored Janet with his smoothest Latin smile. "I have squandered my vacation days fishing in Acapulco. These days in Port City have been business; they don't count as vacation. But they have come to an end."

Terry placed her hand on Felix's arm. "We'll miss you."

"I'll second that," said Snoop. "I can smell your *zarzuela*. I know you're a better cook than Chuck."

"Better looking too," Felix answered. "Changing the subject, how fares the daughter Gloria?"

"She and Lorraine are well," I answered. "Lorraine inherited Ike's assets as his widow. Gloria inherited Sam's estate as his daughter."

"What about Ike's assets in the Pacific?"

"Vicky is after them like a hound on a raccoon."

Terry and I took the *Gator Raider* out to celebrate.

This would be our last time on the old boat. I had used part of my bonus to buy my condo outright and part to order a bigger boat. I hadn't decided about the rest. All PI businesses fluctuate, so I needed a cash reserve, and there were income taxes, of course. I gave the balance to my CPA and told him to invest part of it short-term and set up a retirement plan with the rest. Thanks to Ike Simonetti, I was in a high enough tax bracket to worry about such things, at least for this year. Who knew what the vagaries of a PI practice would bring next year?

We dropped anchor in Seeti Bay about ten in the morning. I set up a table and deck chairs in the shade of the hard top on the rear deck. Terry brought cheeses, crackers, and fruit from the galley.

She set the table and tossed her bikini top on a deck chair, leaned back on a padded bench, and stretched out to embrace the sun. I sat beside her. She clinked her wine glass to mine. "It's five o'clock somewhere. You ever wonder what the poor people are doing right now?"

"I'll bet they're not admiring a good-looking, sexy sunbather."

She grinned. "Thanks."

"I was talking about me."

She punched me on the shoulder. She shimmied and her breasts did their magical dance. "Am I not also a sexy sunbather, mister?"

"Wow, yes. You make great boat candy."

"Boat candy?"

"Boat candy is a beautiful woman who makes the boat she's on look better. It's like arm candy except you decorate the boat instead of my arm."

"Thanks...I think."

"Oh, it's a compliment."

"Okay. But I have a question."

I raised an eyebrow. "The answer is yes."

Terry dimpled. "Not that question. I'll ask that one after we finish our wine. It's a different question...about the case."

"Fire away."

"What happens to Ike's escape money he transferred out of the country?"

"Ike squirreled the money away on a South Pacific island with nice beaches and no extradition treaty. Vicky told me she has to travel there to get it on behalf of his estate. She said it'll take weeks of paper pushing."

"Sounds like a nice place to take a business trip."

"It is." I set my wine glass down. "She invited me to go with her."

Terry leaned away from me. "Business or pleasure?"

"Business for her; pleasure for me. She leaves in three days."

There was an uncomfortable silence. "What did you tell her?"

I put my hand on her knee. "I told her I couldn't go, because I was involved with someone...someone I care a great deal about."

Terry sat on my lap. "Thank you."

"You're welcome. And you're welcome to stay right there."

Terry leaned her head on my shoulder and relaxed as we continued to sip our wine.

She downed the last of her wine and squirmed out of my lap. "It's not romantic to say it, but I'm getting sweaty here. I'm going to sit in the shade for a while."

"So, what happens to Ramon Gomez?" she asked as she refilled our wine glasses.

"Felix took him back to Mexico where he'll stand trial with Ramona for killing one or more husbands."

Terry raised her sunglasses with one hand. "Chuck, are you staring at my boobs from behind those sunglasses?"

"I'm a private eye; I'm looking for clues."

"Clues to what?"

"If I look long enough, I'll think of something."

She laughed and replaced her sunglasses. "What about Hopper and Turbot? How do you feel about them? Are they still missing?"

"The cops won't find their bodies. The mob used them for chum somewhere in the Gulf of Mexico."

"Why didn't the mob guys overdose them like they did Lucas?"

"Who's to say they didn't? An overdose is more plausible for Lucas. Turbot was an upstanding citizen, so he had to disappear. Either way, it's karma."

"Karma? Who's that?" she asked.

"Karma's not a 'who;' it's a 'what.' It's a Buddhist thing, like cause and effect. A person's actions, good and bad, come back to them later."

"You think the universe got even with them?"

"Yep." I sipped my wine.

"I like your style, McCrary." She raised her glass. "To us."

"To us."

We drank, the silence stirred by the lap of small waves against the hull.

A line of pelicans skimmed low across the bay, headed for a place only pelicans know.

After a while, Terry said, "I wish we could stay here forever and watch pelicans and listen to the silence."

"*Mmm.*"

"Remember that first time we went to the beach, when you asked me if we were a couple?"

"You said, 'A couple of what?'"

She put her hand on mine. "I'm sorry if I hurt you. I'll make it up to you, I promise."

"Now? Before lunch?" I winked, then realized she couldn't see it behind my sunglasses.

"After lunch too. But that wasn't all I planned to make up. That day at the beach, I said I wanted to see where our relationship was going."

"I remember."

She brushed her fingers across my lips. "I like where this relationship is going. If you still want to 'be a couple' as you put it, I'm in. I don't promise forever; it's too soon for that. But I promise that you and I can have an exclusive relationship until one of us says otherwise."

I raised my glass. "I'll drink to that."

And I did.

DOUBLE FAKE DOUBLE MURDER
CARLOS MCCRARY PI, BOOK 2

I walked into Rayburn's reception and locked the door quietly. I carried the sports bag I'd brought with me back to Rayburn's office.

Rayburn frowned up from his desk. "Didn't hear you come in. I'm Ted Rayburn." He stood and stuck out his right hand while his left hand snaked toward his desk drawer.

Gun! I thought. The bastard's recognized me.

I grabbed his right wrist, and pounded his nose with a hard right.

Rayburn managed to finish opening the desk drawer and grabbed a pistol with his left hand. I hacked his wrist with the edge of my hand and the gun clattered across the tile floor.

I punched him on the nose again, spattering the desk and my suit with blood. The blow knocked him over his chair. It rolled across the floor and slammed into the wall as Rayburn's forehead smacked the tile.

I kicked him in the ribs, and he skidded across the floor. I stomped his right hand and felt a couple of the metacarpals break. He wouldn't shoot anyone with that hand for weeks.

I leveled a Glock at him and picked up his pistol. I opened the other desk drawers. I found a .45 automatic in the top right drawer. "You got any more, Rayburn?" I dropped both guns in the sports bag.

"That's all. Who the hell are you?"

"If you don't know who I am, why'd you pull a gun on me?"

"I saw you in the bar taking my picture the other day. I knew this weren't no social call. Who are you?"

"That's not important. Assume the position."

I removed his cellphone and wallet and tossed them on the desk along with a key ring.

The file cabinet was locked.

I held up the key ring. "Which key?"

"The little one."

I opened the file cabinet and ransacked the drawers.

Rayburn moaned and held his bloody nose. "For crissakes, what the hell do you want?"

"You are no longer in the blackmail business."

"I'm not blackmailing anybody."

I strolled over and kicked him in the head, not hard. I didn't want to put him in the hospital, but I wanted his undivided attention. "Don't lie to me again. I know all about you."

I opened the file cabinet again and sorted through its contents.

Rayburn raised his hands. "That's private property. You don't have a search warrant. You can't do that."

"Just your luck. I'm not a cop, so I don't care about your rights."

The bottom drawer had more than a dozen folders with no names on them. Each folder contained notes and a stick drive.

"Is this all the data on your blackmail victims?"

"I'm not black—" He stopped and pressed his lips into a thin line.

I opened his laptop. "What's the password?"

Rayburn told me.

I clicked through the icons on the desktop and found his internet Cloud backup service. "Login ID for your Cloud backup?"

Rayburn dropped his head and gave me the login and password.

I went online and deleted all Rayburn's Cloud backups. I used the Account Setting to cancel the account. That would at least slow Rayburn down if he tried to go back into business.

Rayburn groaned and started to get up.

"Don't. I'll tell you when to move. Roll over on your stomach. Hands behind you." I took a plastic tie from my bag and fastened Rayburn's hands behind him. "Sit up."

When I reached for another plastic tie, Rayburn tried to kick me. I backlisted him. "Not smart, Rayburn. Play along and I'll let you live."

I fastened Rayburn's ankles together. "Where's the other cellphone?"

Rayburn glared at me.

I waved the cellphone bill at him. "You have two phones. I want them both."

"In the glove compartment of the van."

"I'll get it later." I switched the phone on. "What's the password?"

Rayburn told me and I listed it with the other passwords.

I shut down his computer and stuck it and the power cord in the bag.

"I found a pair of scissors in your file cabinet. You can use them to get out of those plastic ties. I'll put them in the top desk drawer." I wanted to slow Rayburn down, not starve him to death. Worst case, someone would cut him loose Monday morning if he didn't free himself before then.

I locked the office door behind me and retrieved Rayburn's other cellphone from his van. I flung his office and van keys far across the empty parking lot.

Ted Rayburn's whole life was open to me.

Available in Paperback and eBook from Your Favorite Bookstore or Online Retailer

ABOUT THE AUTHOR

Dallas Gorham's books combine murder, mystery, and general mayhem with a touch of humor—all done with a PG-13 rating. His Carlos McCrary, Private Investigator, Mystery Thriller Series can be read and enjoyed in any order.

Dallas writes in the mystery, thriller, and suspense genres. (Take your pick: His novels have all three elements) His stories will get your heart pounding and leave you wanting more. He writes to hit hard, have a good time, and leave as few grammar errors as possible (or is it "grammatical errors"? Hmm.)

In his previous life, Dallas worked as a shoe salesman, grocery store sacker, florist deliverer, auditor, management consultant, association executive, accountant, radio announcer, and a paid assassin for the Florida Board of Cosmetology. (He is lying about one of those jobs.) If you ask him about it, he will deny ever having worked as an auditor.

Dallas is a sixth-generation Texan and a proud Texas Longhorn, having earned a Bachelor of Business Administration at the University of Texas at Austin. He graduated in the top three-quarters of his class, maybe. He has also been known to lie about his class ranking.

Dallas, the writer, and his wife moved to Florida years ago to escape Dallas, the city, winters (Brrrr. Way too cold) and summers (Whew. Way too hot). Like his fictional hero, Chuck McCrary, he lives in Florida in a waterfront home where he and his wife watch the sunset over the lake most days. He is a member of Mystery Writers of America and the Florida Writers Association.

Dallas is married to his one-and-only wife who treats him far better than he deserves. They have two grown sons, of whom they are inordinately proud. They also have seven grandchildren who are the smartest, most handsome, and most beautiful grandchildren in the known universe. He and his wife spend waaaay too much money on their love of travel. They have visited all 50 states and over 90 foreign countries, the most recent of which was Indonesia, where their cruise ship stopped at Kuala Lumpur.

Dallas writes an occasional blog post at http://dallasgorham. com/blog that is sometimes funny, but not nearly as funny as he thinks. The website also has more information about his books. To get an email whenever the author releases a new title (and sometimes a free book), sign up for the VIP newsletter at http://dallasgorham.com/

If you have too much time on your hands, you can follow him at the following social media links:

www.DallasGorham.com

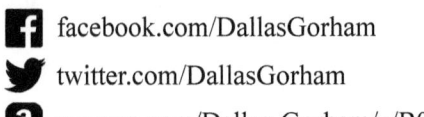

facebook.com/DallasGorham

twitter.com/DallasGorham

amazon.com/Dallas-Gorham/e/B00J4LISCS

www.ingramcontent.com/pod-product-compliance
Lightning Source LLC
Chambersburg PA
CBHW051334020726
47501CB00007B/2083